THE WILLING RESISTANCE

THE TRAVELING COMPANION
BOOK TWO

KIM BLACK

THE WILLING RESISTANCE

The Traveling Companion Series
Book Two

Kim Black

DEDICATION

*To the men and women who so selflessly
give more than their share.*

Thank you for your service.

ACKNOWLEDGMENTS

Thank you to Riley, my husband and forever love. You know what you did.

Thanks to my cohorts in the Lone Star Women of Letters, Donna, Kristine, Karen, and Cindy. Y'all help to make this look good.

Thanks to all the strong women in my life who have inspired me and others to keep our chins up and carry on.

Thanks to all the good men in the world, willing to fight and protect the women they love. Keep fighting. You are loved and appreciated more than you'll ever know.

Thank you to every single one of my readers. You inspire me every day.

June -3, 1945

My dearest Henri,

I was so pleased to hear of your release from hospital. I hope you keep to your doctor's Advice for an eXtra walk eAch afternoon. The weather in LoNdon has been pleasant.

Dahlia, Jack, and I made a brief stop in Paris for a gift for MoTher. We found a lovEly silK scarf Printed with aQua roses.

Please wrIte soon; I look forward to shAring that bottle of wine once you've fully recovered.

With love,

Penelope

FRIDAY, JUNE 15, 1945, HAUTE-PYRÉNÉES,
ALONG THE BORDER BETWEEN FRANCE AND
SPAIN

he train thumped along the rails as it climbed the
Pyrénées Mountains. The rhythm dragged me back to
my last train ride—rails screaming, smoke choking, the crunch of
metal tumbling down a hillside. The ride that ended my service in
the trenches marked the beginning of my career as a police
inspector. My gut tightened, panic rising. I forced a deep breath.
This is different. I'm safe now.

The rocking jarred the letter in my hands, Penny's letter.
Written as if from a lover. I knew better. Penny Tompkins was
clever and dangerous; any man seduced by her should fear for his
life.

I'd read her missive a hundred times, memorized it as I packed
my valise, recited it as I dressed my wound and buttoned my
brown tweed suit. Her block letters leapt from the page, too deliberate to be an accident. P-K-A-X-A-N-P-T-E-K-P-Q-I-A. I shuffled them forward, backward, into acronyms. *Penny Keeps An X-*

ray... Nonsense. I needed a cypher key. *Mon Dieu, what is she doing to me?*

Nearly a week after I first received the note, the answer glared at me from the top of the page: not June 3, but *June -3*. Of course. Shift the letters back three places. P becomes S, K becomes N, and so on.

SNDADRSWHNSTLD. Gibberish—until I mouthed it aloud: *SND ADRS WHN STLD.*

Send address when settled.

So simple. I am *l'enfant*—a child compared to her cleverness.

I forced myself to relax and take in the countryside. France was a patchwork of ruin and beauty. Villages had been reduced to ash. Meadows bloomed as if war had never touched them. But my thoughts returned to Penny. Why did she want my new address now? Our letters since the war had been polite, nothing more.

My hand pressed against the scar in my chest, the one left by Yann Kohler, the Nazi who nearly killed me. My last memory of that night was Penny's face... her dark hair, sharp blue eyes, and full pink lips. I'd imagined she kissed me, pleading for me to live. A foolish, romantic memory. She belonged to her superior officer, Jack Vogel.

"Sheer whimsy," I muttered. Yet, was I hoping?

I folded the note again and slipped it into my breast pocket.

The carriage around me was subdued. Men perused newspapers in French and Spanish, with headlines debating the Berlin Declaration and the division of Germany. I scoffed. The day Germany surrendered was the same day Kohler drove a six-inch knife into my chest.

A woman two rows ahead closed her book, *Joy Street*, and slid it into her handbag. She turned her gaze on me, lips coral-red beneath a wide-brimmed hat. She smiled knowingly, a hint of challenge. Was she bound for Spain? Portugal? Beyond?

The air pressure shifted, and my ears pricked. I yawned and glanced at my watch. We were nearing the Somport tunnel, a one-mile spiral through the mountain that dropped nearly two hundred feet into the valley, where Canfranc Station awaited. My refuge, the doctor's prescription for convalescence.

Two months of peace, he promised.

Or so I thought.

2

FRIDAY, JUNE 15, 1945, CANFRANC, SPAIN

*T*he electric train glided to a stop without the fog and fanfare of a steam engine. Passengers filed out of the car in quiet patience. The platform at Canfranc spanned the full length of the train—impressive in size if not in frills.

Behind me, the French train rested on standard-gauge rails sitting four feet, eight-and-a-half inches apart. Ahead, the narrow-gauge rails, only three feet apart, waited for the Spanish train to arrive. Different gauges meant the trains could not merely stop and resume the journey—everyone must disembark and check in. All the luggage went into a massive storage room to wait for delivery to a hotel room or onto the next train. The situation was unusual—singular, one might say. My mind engaged at once, calculating every repercussion that one difference made.

I let the crowd swirl past while I lingered, reminding myself I was off the train and convalescing. No hurry for the next two months. No danger or intrigue.

When the platform settled, I found the entrance to the station lobby. What the platform lacked in amenities, the station terminal displayed at every turn. Hand-carved cabinetry and trim framed every desk, from the general information counter to the *Bureau de Change*. From the doors of the French Embassy to the two post offices, both French and Spanish. The wood shone with fresh polish as the gleaming marble floors reflected the natural light from the wall of windows facing the mountainside.

Beyond the windows, a lush forest reached up to the blue peaks, interrupted only by granite terraced walls, underpinned with Roman arches, framing waterfalls and natural rock formations alike. I vowed to take a long walk tomorrow to explore the paradise.

Still marveling at the luxury of this resort, I considered myself fortunate—not only to find this place but to afford it as well. My superior officer had suggested it and assured me the bill would be paid.

"We want you back in full health, and this is the perfect place for you to recover," he'd said.

"Well, Canfranc lacks no amenity," I mumbled to no one, and my voice faded in the clamor of chattering guests and clicking footfalls over the marble floors. I scanned the great hall from one end to the other, passed the waiting room and café, my gaze landing on the concierge desk for the Hotel Morocco-Santiago.

The man at the desk wore a dark blue uniform with only slight embellishment of gold cording at the collar and cuffs. He was a narrow-shouldered man with grey-brown hair and pale grey eyes, accentuated by the full grey brow above. He spoke to a woman as I approached, and my attention turned toward her, though her back faced me.

Her form was petite but curvy, though the padded shoulders of her dress exaggerated an hourglass figure. I thought there was something familiar in her stance, but before I managed to move closer, I was halted by a group of Spanish travelers, clucking in wonder at the grandeur around them. By the time they'd passed, the woman was gone.

"May I assist you, sir?" the clerk asked in French.

"I am checking in. The name is Toussaint. Henri Toussaint."

"Yes, sir." The man held out his hand as a new business associate might. "Monsieur Angier said you would arrive today. Allow me to direct you to him. My name is Rocher, and I am at your service." He led me to a polished brass elevator at the back of the room, between the Embassy and the *Bureau de Change*. He pointed to the Bureau window. "If you wish to exchange currency, you may do so here at any time." He pressed the gleaming elevator call button. "This will take you up one floor to the Hotel front desk. Angier will show you to your room and have your luggage sent up immediately."

"Thank you, Monsieur." I tilted my forehead in a short bow. "You've been most helpful." I paused. "The woman you were speaking with just before I found you—what is her name?"

His brow rose a fraction of an inch, and his lip matched for a second. "Her name is Elize Belfort. She is the assistant to the hotel manager, Albert Lebeau. Would you like me to introduce you later?"

"Erhm," I coughed. "That isn't necessary; I didn't mean..." I waved off the request. "I thought she looked familiar, but I don't recognize the name. I must be mistaken. Madame Belfort?"

"Mademoiselle." He nodded to the elevator operator when the door opened. "See Monsieur Toussaint to Angier, then come back down quickly. Mademoiselle Belfort needs your help."

Rocher directed me inside and stepped back with a low bow.

"Merci," I said as the doors closed. The car rose more swiftly than I expected, considering the beamed ceilings downstairs were at least fourteen feet high. A bell chimed, and the doors opened upon another magnificent space.

Purple-red carpets spread in every direction, and the desk directly ahead was a glowing oak semicircle topped with white marble and embellished with every brass accouterment available.

"Monsieur Toussaint," Angier said without question. "Welcome to Canfranc." He wore a thick, ruddy mustache across his broad face. Though he was a few inches shorter than I, he was wider at the shoulders. He would have made quite the *gendarme* back in my little village.

"Yes." I offered a confident smile. "I plan to make a temporary home here. I must confess I'm quite impressed by the hotel already."

"We are glad to hear that." He shuffled a few papers and drew a heavy brass key from beneath the marble top. "The Morocco is the size of twenty average hotels. If you find yourself lost, you may ask for assistance from anyone dressed in a navy-blue uniform. Our complete staff is at your service."

Leaning over the counter, I signed my name in the register, noticing my room number—217. "And is there somewhere I may get a drink soon?"

Angier waited until I faced him. "We have a restaurant at this end." He stretched out his right arm. "A ballroom on the other side." He extended his left. "And a full bar with entertainment in the room behind me. The entrances are at either end." He snapped his fingers, and a spry youth appeared from behind me. Angier handed him the key and a slip of paper. "Show Monsieur to his room and then bring up his luggage right away."

"*Absolument.*" The boy bowed to Angier and then to me. "Follow me."

We strode at a clipped pace toward the ballroom first and then down a long hall. The young man stopped at the end of the hall. "Your room," he chirped. "You have the best view in the hotel."

Following him inside, it was clear he didn't exaggerate. The broad, arched windows wore blue velvet curtains that matched a sofa and chairs. On the wall behind the door was an arch flanked on either side with ornate cabinetry. The boy opened one cabinet to display a stocked bar and the other to a radio set. "We are in the mountains, but we receive a good station for news and music."

The archway led to the bedroom, also draped in blue velvets and damasks.

"This is a suite?" I hadn't expected so much room.

"Of course, Monsieur." He scanned the room for anything out of place. "I will bring up your things right away. Is there anything you need?"

"No, I should find this room quite comfortable." I moved to the large bedroom window as soon as the boy left. The sun had already dropped behind the mountain range, casting an early, pink shadow over the whole valley of Canfranc. I slid the window open and rested my arms on the sash. Drawing a deep breath of pine-tinged mountain air, I listened to the distant tumble of a waterfall and felt the tight tug of my scar. No pain, just a reminder.

I hooked a finger behind the knot of my burgundy silk tie and pulled until I could undo the top shirt button. After I unpacked my luggage and had settled in, I decided to spend the rest of the evening smoking and enjoying the beautiful night sky.

A soft scratch on the matchbox, a quiet crackle of flame as the tip of my cigarette ignited, and I was ready for some solitude.

Smoke rings shimmered out of reach with an extra puff,

creating vignettes here and there. I pondered the utter luxury of the hotel, convinced there had been a mistake in my reservation. How would I pay this bill? But it was taken care of, according to my commander. If he'd realized—if he'd glimpsed even a closet in the corner, he would move me to a more meager accommodation. And I would agree.

The first stars flickered above the ridge of the border mountains, and I reached for the glass of bourbon I'd been sipping for half an hour. I stubbed out the cigarette butt and sucked in the cool night. By this point, my jacket was on the bed beside my tie. I'd undone all my shirt buttons and rolled my sleeves to my elbow. My undershirt was the only thing covering the scar over my sternum, and the cool air soothed my itchy skin.

On the side of the mountain, a light caught my eye. Not a flickering of firelight, but a steady glow of an electric torch moved horizontally, swaying with the steps of someone on a moonlight walk. A guest, perhaps—more likely a groundskeeper or security guard, making one last round before locking everything up.

The light stopped bobbing. The person was probably enjoying the view of the resort from above—precisely what I intended to do in the morning. Suddenly, another light appeared and joined the first. Two people meeting in the starlight? A romantic rendezvous?

I studied the scene as a voyeur, imagining tender seductions in the dark when the lights began to dance feverishly around each other. A struggle?

I strained over the sash to see more clearly. My eyes didn't focus. Tired from the train ride and dulled by the bourbon, my vision blurred at the edges. Only the lights were clear.

But then one light came down hard upon the other. The second light dropped and flailed. The wild motion continued as the light plummeted. It dropped down the side of the wall and disappeared into the trees below.

My gaze jumped back to the first light. It stayed in place for several seconds before moving steadily back down the mountain along the stone walls. Longing for my field glasses, I followed the person with the torch, watching the light sway all the way to the footbridge that crossed the river running in front of the station.

That's when she stepped out. Elize Belfort met the man—now I determined that it was a man—under the light post at the hotel side of the bridge. The man extinguished his torch and handed it to the woman. She snapped her fingers, and another man appeared from beneath the narrow canopy at the door. She gestured to him with some instruction, and the three spoke for another minute.

Though too far away to hear distinct words, I recognized the urgency in the grunts and murmurs drifting upward. Belfort's assistant took the torch and headed down the walkway as she latched onto the other man's arm and directed him inside. Whatever I'd witnessed, it was over.

But what had I seen? An argument between two people. One torch had fallen. It didn't drop straight down—the torch hadn't simply fallen over the side; it waved wildly as it descended. Someone had fallen with it—been pushed?

Murdered?

I staggered back to the edge of my bed and sat. Two bourbons on an empty stomach affected me far more than I expected.

"Rest for a moment to clear your head," I whispered into the dark bedroom and closed my eyes.

3

SATURDAY, JUNE 16, 1945, CANFRANC, SPAIN

Sunlight cleaved through the heavy curtains and stung my eyes open. My muscles ached with the slightest movement. I'd slept all night as I'd landed—half dressed, with my feet hanging off the bed. My calves buzzed with renewed circulation, and my toes revived from a cold numbness.

I spent a full minute struggling to remember where I was, let alone what had happened last night. My eyes refused to focus for several seconds, pulsing with a dull pain behind them. My pocket watch had stopped at 3:42, but the powered clock on the bed table ticked steadily, reading 10:04.

Rushing through an abbreviated morning routine—I managed a quick bath, shave, and a frustrating attempt to slick my dark hair back to tame the waves that had formed overnight. I should have sat for a haircut before my journey, but time ran short. I'd deal with it later.

My light grey linen suit seemed the best option for the day, as the room was already warming from the open window. Pants, undershirt, shirt, trousers, socks, and black brogues. I opted to leave my suit jacket in the room and wear only my waistcoat. Finally, I reset my watch, knotted my violet silk tie, and flew out the door.

"Ah, *bonjour*, Monsieur." Angier's voice dripped with appropriate pleasantry. "I hope you slept well. What may I do for you this morning?"

"Thank you, but I need to speak to the hotel's head of security, please." The veins in my neck throbbed, and the scar on my chest tugged.

Angier's wide face paled a shade, and his upper lip disappeared completely beneath his mustache. "What has happened?" he asked. "Is there something I can do?" His shoulders crowded his ears.

I leaned over the desktop between us and whispered. "I believe I witnessed a murder last night."

Angier's posture relaxed. "A murder?" he asked, *sotto voce*.

"I intended to report it last night, but I fell asleep."

"Did this murder occur in your room?" His whiskers trembled at the corners.

"Of course not in my room," I huffed. He was mocking me, and I didn't have time for nonsense. "I witnessed it from my window."

"But you fell asleep. Are you sure you were awake when it happened? Perhaps a dream?"

I shifted my energy elsewhere. "Where may I find Mademoiselle Belfort? Or the manager, Monsieur Lebeau?"

Angier glanced at the small brass clock on his desk. "It's after ten; Mademoiselle Belfort will be in the ballroom, seeing to preparations for tonight's reception." He swept his arm toward the ballroom. "Would you like me to take you to her?"

"I will find her myself. Thank you." I raised my hand to stop him from following.

While I marched toward the ballroom doors, I recalled my first glimpse of the woman yesterday. Someone I recognized, but somehow different. I pushed the urge to reminisce from my mind. Lisette was dead; I'd seen her die. But this woman—even in the moonlight—reminded me of her.

I pulled the heavy door open and scanned the room. The unlit chandeliers cast prismatic sparkles around the room as the flood of sunlight danced through the crystals.

Once inside, I paused for a quick perusal, though no one even glanced in my direction. Hotel workers scurried around the perimeter of the expanse, shifting chairs and tables for optimum views of the dance floor and the scenery beyond the windows. In the center of the dance floor was Mademoiselle Belfort, her back to me, surrounded by staff members requesting her opinion on this linen or that and which hors d'oeuvres to serve with what cocktails.

Her perfectly coiffed hair shone a deep amber in the rays of the late morning sun. It was darker gold than Lisette's, and perhaps the woman was not quite as slim as my love had been, but everything else—my scar tightened.

My steps slowed as she sent her disciples away, two by two. Her voice. I knew it from the first note. Three years melted into a dull shadow as she turned to face me.

Her aqua eyes stared into mine. "*Allo*, Henri." She closed the space between us when I could no longer move.

My face contorted; I struggled to understand—to reconcile what I understood with what I faced. "Lisette?"

She placed her warm fingers over my lips and shifted her head a fraction of an inch.

"Elize Belfort."

"How?" My brain scrambled. "I was there when you died."

"You saw what you were meant to see." Her alto voice cut like glass.

My arms ached to draw her to me, to breathe the scent of her hair, caress her skin, and pull her lips to mine. But I was frozen as I had been in 1942—on the street corner, watching her disappear into a crater of smoke and ash. "But no one ..."

"It was war; it still is." She dropped to the slightest whisper. "I had to die to survive. You were a soldier. You must understand."

"How can I?" My words scraped my throat like sand. "You changed your name."

"Many things changed when Germany occupied France, Henri. You know this as well as anyone. My name was the least changed of all."

Her lack of emotion finally settled over me. She wasn't the woman I loved—not anymore. She had left her life—the one we shared—intentionally. I shivered as the last twelve hours rushed back.

"I must speak with you. I witnessed something last night. You may be in danger."

Elize pressed her coral lips together, erasing whatever smile she had left. "You shouldn't have come to Canfranc. It's not safe for someone like you. You see too much. Let me send you to Lisbon; you will love the architecture."

"I'm not leaving you." I wished the words back as her eyes flickered. "I'm not leaving Canfranc." I released a heavy breath. If I understood anything about her, it was not to push. "Have dinner with me tonight. We can talk. You can tell me about your adventures—"

"No."

"Then I can tell you about mine."

"No, Henri. No." Elize glanced over my shoulder and motioned for whoever entered the room. "I'm very busy. And you should leave." She walked to the other staff member without another word.

I strode back to my room, determined to find out what happened on the mountainside last night.

4

SATURDAY, JUNE 16, 1945, CANFRANC, SPAIN

The dining room hummed with the last of the morning guests and the first arrivals of luncheon. Like the ballroom, the great room glittered and glistened with sunbeams fracturing through chandelier crystals. The gold and white tableware gleamed over the dark blue linens.

I found a seat and ordered coffee and a pastry. Perhaps I should have requested an egg, but I was anxious to go outside and search. I finished my breakfast within minutes of arrival and stopped only briefly in my room to freshen up, gather my pencil and note pad, and check my watch against the hotel clock.

"*Bonjour,*" Angier said again.

"*Bonjour.*"

"May I direct you somewhere, Monsieur?"

"No, *merci*. I am simply off for a morning walk on the mountain."

"Should you like to make other arrangements for the day, you may see me or Rocher. Anyone in uniform can direct you, of course, but we have special instructions to take care of you."

Was the man threatening me? "Of course."

I took the elevator down to be greeted by Rocher. *"Bonjour!"* He took a step toward me.

Side-stepping the man, I returned the salute and strode to the doors facing the mountain. The sun glared down from high over-head, and I crossed the footbridge at a brisk pace and headed up the mountain path.

The granite stone path rose in one direction and then the other, terracing the steep slope, creating breaks for winter avalanches and bridges over summer waterfalls. Portions were shaded by lush forest and then suddenly opened to breathtaking vantage points overlooking the hotel.

Pausing to roll my sleeves to my elbows, I surveyed the area, surmising that this must have been the spot on the pathway where the incident had occurred. I traced my gaze to the windows of my room, deciding it was a little farther—to the other side of the clearing. I searched everywhere for evidence of a struggle, but the dark granite betrayed no secrets.

Looking over the edge told me little more than that a man falling from where I stood had only a minuscule chance of surviving. But then again, a man stabbed in the chest with a six-inch blade had about the same chances, and here I stood.

I was about to move on when a glint of red stopped me. I crouched, studying the curb. Blood—several drops darkened the granite. Red-brown spots speckled the purple-black stone. But I found a pattern in the spots. Experience told me they were cast-off spatter from a blow. This was indeed where it happened.

I pulled my notebook from my vest pocket and began my notes, making sketches and detailing how many spots were visible, guessing how many more weren't. I noted unique details on trees for landmarking purposes and peered over the edge again, working out how far the victim may have fallen. From where I stood, I deduced probably a fifty- to sixty-foot clear drop. More than enough to be deadly.

Retracing my path down the mountain, I found an area near where the body may have landed and left the trail to conduct my search.

Shrubs and saplings covered the black soil, but after scouring the area for half an hour, I found nothing out of place. I intended to give up when I discovered a few saplings with bent and broken trunks and branches just below me, as though something heavy had fallen on them.

I weighed the toll the search would take on my brogues and let my heels slide sideways down the steep mountain face. Another fifteen feet down, I discovered a recently made clearing.

The soil was as black as night, and any broken branches had been tossed to the side. Again, I made notes and sketches of the area, standing back from the space where I supposed the body had landed. I made a small circuit of the scene, crouching when necessary. The overgrowth crowded, and I had to squeeze under a low branch to see the sunlight reflecting red tones in the back soil. As carefully as I was able, I pressed a scrap of note paper into the soil, and it absorbed a smudge of crimson mud.

Backing warily to the footpath, I noticed a shard of glass at the base of a shrub. One edge was rounded and beveled, the other sides sharp from a break. A smear of red caught the sun. Blood. Dried, but fresh last night. I picked it up by the corner edges and wrapped it loosely in my handkerchief. I couldn't be sure, but I suspected it was a piece of torch lens. Another half hour of searching turned up nothing.

By the time I arrived back at the hotel, my shoes were in a terrible state, and my clothes needed laundering. I wasn't blind to the odd glares I received from other guests and staff.

Rocher's eyes went wide as I approached. "Good afternoon," he said, almost as a question.

"Good afternoon." I smoothed my palms over my vest. "Who might I speak with about hotel security? Is there a gendarme or police inspector here?"

Rocher's gaze went wider still. "Perhaps you should tell me what happened, and I can direct you."

My gaze shifted, and my tone dropped. "I believe I witnessed a murder."

Rocher gasped, clutching his hair as if it might turn grey on the spot. "Here? In the hotel?"

"Actually, no, but on the mountainside. I was at my window last night."

Rocher's shoulders relaxed, and he donned his ever-pleasant smile. "Oh. That wouldn't fall under the hotel's jurisdiction, I'm sure."

"But I assume you can direct me to the person I should speak to?"

"I—erhm." Rocher swallowed hard. "Ah, yes. You should speak to Mademoiselle Belfort." He extended his arm somewhere behind me.

I was afraid of that.

"Henri, you look a sight. What has happened to you?" Her voice rang honey-sweet.

"It isn't what happened to me," I started.

She took my arm as though she still owned it and led me away to the elevator. "Let's go upstairs to your room. You'll have a bath, and I'll take your clothes to be cleaned and your shoes to be shined." She gave me no time to respond. "Once you've freshened up, we can sit down and talk."

"We're losing time. Someone must be notified." We were almost to my room.

"Yes, but we must hear the whole story to know exactly *who* to notify." She gestured to my door and waited while I unlocked it.

"Lis—Elize, please, I may have already waited too long. I should have called the gendarmerie last night."

"If you've waited this long, I think another hour will not hurt." She waggled her finger like a mother hurrying a child. "Now undress and leave me your clothes. I'll take them down to be cleaned while you bathe."

Her pacification annoyed me, but she would have it no other way. I removed my vest and put the bloody torch lens, handkerchief, and notepad into the bedside table drawer. I dropped onto the chair, unlaced my shoes, and pulled off my socks.

Elize worked the squeaking handles to start the bathwater.

"Nice and warm—no one else is bathing at this time of day." Her voice was too sweet for the occasion.

I glared in protest as she shooed me into the washroom. "Don't worry at all. I'll have the shoes sent up before you're out of your bath. The suit will take longer, but I'm sure you brought another." Her tone was patronizing. "I have a few things to do, but when you're ready, come and find me in the dining room, and we can talk about your concerns." Without another word, she closed the door behind me.

The small oval mirror began to fog as the claw-foot tub filled. I shrugged out of my sleeves, tugged my undershirt over my head, unbuckled my belt, and stepped out of my trousers and pants. I held the neat pile of clothes out the door and felt Elize's soft hands take them. A second later, I heard my door close, and I slipped into the tub.

The hot water soothed my aching muscles. The hike up the mountain had proven more strenuous than I expected. It had been the first such outing since leaving the hospital.

Amazed at how much black soil had penetrated my socks, I scrubbed around my toes and ankles up to my knees. I thought about how different Elize was from my beloved Lisette.

Lisette had been quiet but not meek. She was tender, always looking after my needs, and considerate of my feelings and expectations. Elize was not loud, but she made her voice heard. She had her own agenda and made her own rules. She was quite self-sufficient, as she'd have to be in her position.

I rocked my head back on the curve of the tub's rim. Memories of my last day with Lisette flooded my mind. We'd packed her up, preparing for the raids we'd been told were coming. There was a truck leaving town, and she was to be on it. My company was saying goodbye to our loved ones before we moved out.

How many times had we told each other *I love you*? How many kisses would be enough? She was on the truck, headed out of town. I saw her. But then I saw her again, an hour later, on the street. She waved to me as our truck drove out. And then the bomb. And then nothing.

I pressed my hand over the ring that hung on the chain around my neck. Pressed it against my scar, warm against my skin.

"We found this," my commander had said as he handed me the ring. It had belonged to my mother.

This morning, I thought I'd been given a second chance. She was alive. But my Lisette was gone—replaced by Elize, cool and calculating. The woman who'd covered up a murder.

5

SATURDAY, JUNE 16, 1945, CANFRANC, SPAIN

The waitstaff hovered relentlessly, bringing us soups, fish, potatoes, asparagus, and breads of every kind. Sharing a table with the manager's assistant came with advantages, but left us little time to talk.

"I'm sure of it—someone has been killed. I have evidence. I'm not raving mad."

She tutted through a sip of sherry. "Of course, you're not mad. But I think your inspector's mind is working hard when you should be resting."

I closed my eyes and drew a deep breath to temper my patience. "Just tell me who the man was you spoke to last night at the footbridge."

"He was another assistant to Monsieur Lebeau. One of the night managers." She dabbed her lip with a napkin as another server attempted to refill our glasses.

"No more for me," I said, holding my hand over my

glass. *"Merci."* I turned my gaze back to Elize. "The one who gave you the torch?"

"Oh, no, he was a guest here." She gazed out the window with a dull expression.

"I'm telling you; he pushed someone off the stone wall. Murdered him."

She held up a palm. "Please, you're going to worry others over a simple misunderstanding. There was no murder—no death at all."

"I went up there this morning. I saw blood and broken branches; I have the evidence."

She reached across the table. "Give me what you have. Part of my job is to take care of things like this."

The handkerchief with the bloody lens weighed heavily in my pocket. "I'd feel better if I kept it."

"You don't trust me?" Her chin quivered as her lashes blinked at invisible tears.

"No more than you trust me, apparently." I straightened my spine. "The last time we spoke, you told me you loved me and would wait for me to come home."

"That was war."

"And then you purposely made me believe you were dead."

She leaned across the small table and reached for my hand. "And what if I told you I was sorry?"

"Apologies come with actions. Changes."

"And I have changed." Elize pursed her lips enough to shift my gaze to them.

Perfect lips. Pink and full. She had, indeed, changed. Everything she did now was precise and calculated. Perhaps it had always been so. "No."

Elize tilted her head slightly and flicked her lashes. "No, what?"

"No, everything." My temper flashed. "I won't give you my evidence. And I don't accept your explanation of how you faked your death. You couldn't have known about the air strikes or whether you'd be safe from them."

She waved away my refusal as if I were no more than a pestering midge. "You were supposed to see me hit by a bus. Does that make it better? The fact that a mortar struck between us that day saved us a little time, that's all. And I was quite fortunate to escape without a serious injury."

"Escape the bomb or escape me?"

Her mouth twitched. "Would you hate me if I said both?"

I scoffed automatically. "*Ah, je comprends.*" The heat rising in my cheeks gave my tongue pause. At that moment, I did hate her, but before I responded, another staff member approached and whispered into her ear.

She nodded and pasted on a farcical smile. "I have matters to attend to." She pushed out her chair, and I forced myself to stand, feigning respect.

"Perhaps we can talk again soon?" I could pretend as easily as she could.

"I will be busy with the reception tonight. And I still believe you should journey farther south." Elize leaned to my side, put a hand on my lapel, and kissed me on my cheek. The warmth of her hand on my chest and her lips on my face brought back a host of sweet memories. She snapped her fingers again, and the table was cleared before she reached the door.

My brain ached. I had loved her with all my heart. When she died, when I believed she had died, my entire being had shattered. I thought I'd never love again. Then came Penny Tompkins— beautiful, ruthless, efficient. England's perfect assassin. But even she never unnerved me as Elize did now.

And of course, she was quite enmeshed with Jack Vogel. The only reason she had cast an eye on me was because I was investigating her for murder.

As I returned to my room, I pondered Penny and her mesmerizing ruthlessness. She was a beauty despite her gaunt frame. She looked and played the part of a damsel in distress perfectly. England couldn't have found a more perfect assassin for their Special Operations Executive. I had no idea how many men she had seduced and murdered. With her beguiling smile and flashing eyes, I guessed it might be a dozen or more. Her only limit was time.

A quiet laugh escaped my lips as I unlocked my room and walked through the door. At first, nothing was amiss. My mind still lingered on the fascinating brunette. But as I slipped my jacket over the hanger in the closet, I saw that the bedroom curtains were crumpled on one side. I straightened them, unsure whether I had mussed them before I left. But then I discovered the bar cabinet in the parlor was unlatched, with one door standing slightly ajar.

I flung the whole cabinet open, looking for a sign of an intruder. The bottles were all in place, and the glasses were as I'd left them. Perhaps the latch was just fussy.

A knock at the door startled me, and I had to draw a deep breath before I answered. A young woman in a navy dress, white organdy apron, and cap curtsied. She pulled a mahogany cart alongside her.

"*Excusez-moi*, Monsieur. I have fresh linens and glasses for your bar. I apologize, but I ran out when I was here before—when I straightened your bed."

I stepped out of her way, and she pushed the cart inside.

"I will only be a minute," she said.

"Take your time," I answered. A fool. I was jumping at ghosts—but ghosts were all I had left. Had it been so long since I was last on holiday that I forgot about housekeeping?

She took the used bar glass and replaced it with a fresh one. She pulled a neat stack of white towels from the bottom of the cart and disappeared into the bathroom for a few seconds.

"Is there anything else I can do for you?" she asked. "I can refill your bourbon bottle if you like."

"Let's wait until tomorrow for that." I paused, and she started for the door. "What can you tell me about the reception tonight?"

The young woman paused. "*Oui*, Monsieur. It begins at eight o'clock, as it does every night. There will be a band and singers. Drinks and dancing—some good food too."

"And for whom is the reception held?"

"Our most important guests. Did Miss Belfort not invite you?"

"We were interrupted before she had the chance."

She nodded. "Mademoiselle is very busy." She pursed her lips slightly and let her lashes rise and fall a few times. "Is there anything else?" Her voice slowed suggestively.

Her eyes focused on my lips, and I got the distinct impression of being in her crosshairs, not unlike when I'd been alone with Penny. "Erhm, not that I can think of," I sputtered.

Her shoulders dropped half an inch, and she resumed her place at the cart. "Then I suppose I will see you tomorrow."

As I closed the door behind her, I wondered about what she *did* here at the hotel.

6

SATURDAY, JUNE 16, 1945, CANFRANC, SPAIN

The grey-haired attaché at the French Embassy informed me my concerns belonged to the local police and civil guard. He reminded me—firmly—that I had no jurisdiction here and directed me to the Canfranc Guard office a few blocks away.

At the Guard office, another grey-haired man bristled at my Spanish and doubted every word I spoke. The clatter of type-writer keys and the shuffle of papers echoed behind the counter. I extracted the handkerchief from my breast pocket and unfolded it to discover a small flat rock instead of the bloodied torch lens. When I opened my notebook, I found the pages of notes I'd taken on the mountainside ripped out at the seams. Elize, or one of her minions, had stolen all my evidence. I left the Guard office no better than a fool.

I passed a few quaint shops and eateries on my way back to the train station, but apart from the aromas of sweet baked goods, I barely noticed them. Self-pity and betrayal welled inside my chest, leaving me to replay the last few hours in my mind.

As I returned to the grandeur of the hotel, I took a moment to appreciate its architecture, with a blue slate mansard roof holding rows of arched dormer windows and a prominent central dome featuring Art Deco pinnacles. I released a heavy sigh. Such a place as this was an *objet d'art*, no matter the circumstances.

Determined to enjoy my surroundings, I was also set on finding the killer from the previous night. Elize lied about so many things, but perhaps she told the truth about the killer being a guest. I wondered about the other residents at the hotel. Were they here long-term or only for a brief layover between trains? People-watching was in order.

Finding a bench in the center of the train platform, I began my surveillance of the comers and goers. A train arrived, and I scanned the face of every man who passed, certain I would be able to identify him if I came across him again. The longer I looked, the less sure I became.

Then a man stepped into view, and the hair on the back of my neck prickled straight. He stood stooped slightly, wearing a charcoal suit and navy silk tie. Nothing special about him, but the way he carried himself was suspicious—as though he were hiding.

He squatted down beside the next bench, appearing to tie his shoe, with his back toward me. His hand inched away from his side, and he picked up something small resembling a cigarette from beside the front bench leg. As he stood, he peeled the paper open, nodded, and slid it into his breast pocket. A clandestine message!

The man—at that point, I didn't believe him to be the murderer—hurried away, and I didn't follow. Instead, I made a note in my book and continued my surveillance.

Another train arrived with squealing wheels and a huffing whistle, this time from the Spanish side of the platform. As travelers disembarked, a woman stepped off with a small bag, slightly larger than a briefcase. She set it at her feet and perused the platform, obviously looking for someone. She wore a cornflower blue suit with a darker blue hat pulled low over her eyes. Her hair was dark, and her figure slim. For a moment, I imagined it might be Penny, but a second look told me she was too short, and she was coming from the wrong direction.

Within a few seconds, a young man in a forest green tweed approached her and set his bag next to hers. They spoke for a moment, he motioned toward the station, and they picked up their bags and walked in opposite directions. But as the man passed in front of me, he was carrying her bag. I glanced over my shoulder at the woman, and what did I see? *Mais oui*, she had his bag. A switch.

My heart pounded now as I took my notes. This place was filled with spycraft. But as I contemplated my surroundings, I wondered whose side these people were on. Spain and Portugal were neutral, although the war was all but over. With both Mussolini and Hitler dead, all that was left was paperwork.

That wasn't quite true, as the Allies were rounding up players for war trials and punishment. These days were surely the last chance for escape for the Nazis. Once they reached Spain, they might disappear in Lisbon or move on to South America or wherever. Money would buy whatever fake documentation was necessary for a new identity, free from prosecution. But did they have the money at hand?

In all my self-righteous indignation, I pored over my notes and added to them with detailed fervor. But then a stark realization crashed around my ears. I had no one to whom I could take this information. Elize was most assuredly aware of this situation. The local guard seemed to want to do as little as possible. Neutral.

I could only think of one person to direct me to the proper channels. Penny.

I hopped to my feet and pointed myself toward the telegraph office. But what would my message say?

Short, but not too obvious. I needed a code that wouldn't garner attention from anyone but her. We didn't share a cipher, so that was out. I took a form from the telegraph window and found an empty counter space to work it out. I couldn't use the word spy or anything like it. What had Penny called her department? Mother, yes. I would keep it in the family.

I jotted down a few ideas in my notebook, and once I'd found the proper wording, I filled out the form.

RECUPERATING IN CANFRANC. MET YOUR COUSINS HERE. NOT SURE WHICH SIDE OF FAMILY. PLEASE ADVISE.

Surely, she'd understand and send me a letter to help identify the Allies from the Axis agents. Something with details.

I paid, and the telegraph machine clicked and snapped, like nervous fingers drumming the truth into code. I prayed she would be in London to receive it. I glanced at my watch. Five-thirty-five. But that meant four-thirty-five in London. She might not receive it until tomorrow. Even then, a letter would take several more days to reach me.

I resolved to continue my surveillance and add to my notes until she responded with instructions. Perhaps by then, her missive would be mere confirmation of what I suspected. But to form my opinions, I first must study and even interact.

It was time to dress for dinner—and to keep my eyes open.

7

MONDAY, MARCH 2, 1942, BOULOGNE-BILLANCOURT, FRANCE

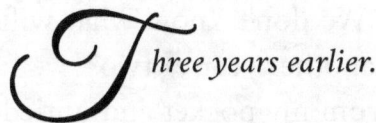*hree years earlier.*

BOULOGNE-BILLANCOURT HELD its breath as German troops thundered through its narrow streets.

Inside a cramped flat above the bakery, Lisette and I shared a meager feast in her flat before I left. If I'd been caught, I'd have been executed without a hearing. My friends and I had volunteered for the Vichy French Army and had been sent to southeast France as a show of compromise. The Germans didn't know we had been stockpiling arms for the Resistance, using our resources to undermine them whenever possible.

Allied air raids made every task more complicated, every neighbor suspicious, every journey perilous.

"I don't want you to go back." Lisette clutched at my hands as she spoke. "Please stay here."

"They'll kill me if they find me." I paused for a split second. "And you."

"Then why did you come at all?"

"I can't tell you. You'd be in danger, and they would force you to talk. No." Her thin fingers dug into my wrist, pale against my sun-burned skin. "When the war is over, we'll marry. Can you wait for that? It won't be long now. The Americans are—"

"Of course, the Americans. Because our own troops have been turned into…" She stopped short, her words dripping with disdain. "*Je suis désolée*. I'm sorry. I shouldn't have said that."

"No, you are right. But we are doing the best we can. And the Resistance is strong. You must believe that."

"But nothing is certain, Henri." Lisette pulled her hand away and straightened herself in her chair. "We don't know what will happen tomorrow. How can I consider another year or two?"

I pulled my knotted handkerchief from my pocket and untied it, spreading it open on the table between us. "This is certain." The ring glimmered in the dim light. I slipped it onto her finger. "Marry me, Lisette." I dropped to my knee beside her and gathered her into my arms. "Just say you will marry me when this is all over."

Her tears dampened my neck, and her back shuddered in my embrace. "I will," she sobbed.

Pulling us both to our feet, I motioned around the room. "Then pack a small case. I have a friend who will take you someplace safe. We must go now."

Lisette knit her brows. "What do you mean now? I can't leave my home."

"My friend will take you to his farm in the country. It will be much safer than here. Take only what you must. But you must go with him today. He will leave Boulogne in an hour." I glanced at my watch. "Less than that. We must hurry."

"And you are coming too?"

"No, I must go back to my base. But you are not to worry for me. I will be fine."

We raced around her place, gathering only the barest of necessities. Her clothing, a packet of letters and photographs, and a few things from her medicine cabinet. So much had already been taken from her; it was not hard to abandon the rest.

I took her to my Resistance contact a few blocks away and put her things in the back of his small cargo truck.

"When this war is over, I'll be back for you." I held her for a few minutes more and kissed her forehead. "Wait for me."

Lisette buried her face in my shoulder. "I'll wait for you for as long as I must." She climbed inside the truck and pressed her fingers to the window. She stared, with tears in her eyes, as they drove away.

When the truck was out of sight, I brushed back the mist in my own eyes and hurried to my rendezvous with the other men from my company. They had delivered our bundle of guns and munitions to their Resistance contacts, and we were ready to go. All we lacked was our driver.

Ten minutes late, he arrived with steam pouring from his radiator. We waited impatiently as the engine cooled enough to refill it with water.

While we sat beside our truck, a band of Nazi soldiers rounded the corner at the head of the street. They began inspecting vehicles and interrogating bystanders. Our time was running out.

The driver filled the radiator with water, and we piled into the truck, but when we backed into the road, something at the end of the block stopped my heart. Lisette.

She stood, staring in our direction, with her fingers to her lips, blowing a kiss.

The noise of the bustling street quieted as the faint sound of air raid sirens rose like wolves howling, drowned out by the whine of falling shells. Before any of us could move, the pavement in front of us exploded into a great cloud of fire and ash.

The truck we were in was thrown on its side, and shrapnel perforated the sides, cracked the windows, and ripped through my uniform. A hundred hornets stung my arms, legs, and back. Nothing was broken, though. Keep going.

"Everyone in one piece?" the Commander asked.

We all answered in the positive, hopping out of the vehicle to push it upright.

"Lisette," I whispered, looking to where she'd stood only a moment ago. There was nothing but a fiery crater. Once we got the vehicle upright and started, I glanced at the Commander. "I have to see—"

"No time, soldier. We have to leave here."

"But—"

"If she survived that, it would be a miracle. But I'll use my connections to find her. I give you my word."

The word lodged in my chest—*miracle.*

8

SATURDAY, JUNE 16, 1945, CANFRANC, SPAIN

My heart thumped with anticipation, or maybe it was strain from walking around the village. The scar over my chest pulled tight, and hunger growled just below that.

I rubbed at the tiny shaving nick on my chin as I strode down the hall to the ballroom. Ahead of me, dozens of couples funneled through the double doorway, garbed in their finest evening wear, the likes of which I hadn't seen since before the war began. I dressed for the black-tie affair and felt conspicuously single as I entered the grand hall.

"Good evening, Monsieur Toussaint," Rocher said with a nod.

"Good evening." I offered a slight bow and took a coupe of champagne from a tray when offered.

The band on the stage played a snappy "Don't Sit Under the Apple Tree" as a slim blonde alto in a green beaded gown sang along.

I found a small table in the corner, and a server brought over a platter of hors d'oeuvres for me to select from. I chose a few and ate slowly while I searched the room for Elize. The singer crooned through two more Andrews Sisters songs, then took a break while the band played "Song of India." During the last score, Elize entered the room with two assistants—one at each elbow. Our eyes locked after a few seconds, and she waved her shadows away.

She floated to my table wearing a peach chiffon dress with a sequined leopard slinking over one shoulder. Her platinum hair was pulled tight behind one ear, and pinned with a black jeweled comb.

"I thought you were leaving." Her tone cut through the music.

"I don't know why you'd think that. I told you I wasn't going anywhere." I stood and gestured to the chair opposite mine.

She shook her head. "If I sit with you, all the guests will expect me to make an appearance at their tables."

Sliding the chair out for her, I insisted with a sweep of my hand. "You stole the evidence I had. Evidence of a murder. Picked it right from my pocket. I think you owe it to me, don't you?"

Elize pulled a deep breath and relented. "I don't know what you expect. I must protect my investment in this hotel. Listen, I've given you as much explanation as I'm going to." She waved to a server with a tray of champagne and took a glass. "You have your life now, and I have mine."

"And our lives were supposed to be together." I sat and leaned close. Her perfume—orange blossom and jasmine—pulled me closer still. "It's the war that separated us. And that's over now for us."

"It's not over." She spoke with a razor's edge in her tone, then softened with a nonchalant flick of her wrist. "There's still money to be made."

Her words sliced my heart open. My Lisette would never have spoken so, but the woman she'd become tossed them about like grenades. I steeled myself to respond. "And criminals to reveal."

She tipped her glass to pour her drink down her throat quickly and stood again. "I can't make you leave, Henri, but I wish you would. There is nothing for you here." She turned and strode away from my table toward the band leader.

Her slim hips swayed to the rhythm of "These Foolish Things" while she chatted with a couple on the dance floor and then a server on the way to the bandstand.

"Foolish indeed," I muttered, pushing away my empty glass. I stared across the dimly lit room, barely seeing anything but the past I once had and the future that might have been.

A reflected light caught my eye, and I turned to see a woman in cream silk with a large diamond ring taking something from her bosom and slipping it into the breast pocket of her dance partner. I wasn't positive, but she resembled the woman who arrived on the train with me. He responded with a quick nod, and they walked away from each other. My lungs tightened.

The woman found another man and finished the dance with him, whispering nonstop in his ear as her bejeweled fingers inched into his jacket pockets, retrieving a small object that she concealed in her curled fist. As the song finished, she bobbed her chin and begged away, then out the door.

I followed.

"*Excusez-moi, mademoiselle,*" I called to her back while I pulled my handkerchief from my inner breast pocket. "Did you drop this?"

The woman stopped without turning to me. Her chin swiveled over her shoulder, and she blinked twice at the white linen square I held in her direction. She showed no recognition of me. *"No, merci."* Without another word, she swished through a door and slammed it shut.

I turned back toward the ballroom and listened. The band began a new song, and a woman's voice crackled and dipped into "La Mer."

Two men left the ballroom and strode swiftly to the elevator. One barked to the lift attendant, and the doors slid closed before I got there. I lunged for the stairwell and began my descent downward. Curiosity had me in her grasp, but before I'd bounced down the second flight, the pain in my chest slowed me to a near crawl.

I leaned onto the first-floor lobby door and swung into the room, clutching the polished brass handle and gasping for a full breath. Rocher raced to my side on sight.

"Monsieur, what has happened?" he asked, bracing under my arm with his. "Come and sit. Are you hurt?"

"No, I'm fine. I merely rushed when I should have—." I caught a glimpse of the men hurrying out the front doors. "Rocher, do you know who those men are?"

As he settled me onto a bench, he turned his chin to where I pointed, but the door closed, and the men were gone. "I'm sorry, Monsieur, I did not see."

Still panting, I placed my hand over my heart. "It's fine, Rocher." I waved away his fussing. "I'm fine now. I need to catch my breath."

"Oui, Monsieur." He stood at attention. "You will call me if you need anything?"

"Of course."

A brass bell dinged, and a porter danced through the lobby with a chirp in his voice. "The last train into the station will arrive in twenty minutes. Anyone wishing to meet their party on the platform should make their way there now."

I stood and crossed my arms, testing out my breath and my pain level. Sure I hadn't torn anything, I was less certain about my stamina. I needed to see the train arrive.

Rocher clicked to attention again, and I shook my head at him. I ambled to the back hotel doors that led to the train platform. The pain dulled as I filled my lungs with cool night air. The short walk between the buildings reinvigorated my investigation.

A few people stood in groups and chattered to themselves while I positioned myself near the bench where I'd seen the man retrieve the cigarette message earlier. I'd already witnessed two apparent spy interactions, as well as whatever was happening in the ballroom.

Once I'd made myself comfortable against the wall, the two men stepped into my peripheral vision, and my focus centered on them. Still in dinner jackets, but now wearing hats, one wore a full, dark red beard and the other a narrow mustache. They smoked and stared at the tracks as though the rails might transform into black adders and slither onto the platform.

They mumbled to each other, moving their lips only enough to bob their cigarettes. The taller man tugged at the brim of his hat, obscuring the upper half of his face completely. Grey swirls of smoke escaped his brim and coiled up to the high ceiling, swaying to the rhythm of the oncoming train. A moment later, the whole room filled with the music of the engine.

Within ten minutes, the platform bustled with tired travelers herding into the hotel for the night. A dozen men with a valise tucked under one arm and a woman draped over the other tromped toward the double doors. A few families with children hurried past. A young woman helping an elderly woman down from the train caught my eye. For a split second, I thought it was Penny and Dahlia Lundt, and my heart skipped.

But, of course, it wasn't, and I soon realized whatever might be afoot around me, I'd have to investigate on my own.

I spun a full circle when I realized I had lost sight of the men. I froze when I picked them out again, but now they had a man between them. Someone from the train—stumbling, bumping one man, then the other, his head bouncing until his hat flipped off his bald head and rolled a few yards away.

"Grab it," the taller man said, wedging their new friend against a wall.

The shorter one took a few steps back and scooped up the homburg, crushing it back down over the bobbing dome and returning to his place alongside the others.

The bald man was unconscious, or very nearly so, and these two men were strong-arming him into the hotel. I kept as close as possible without being obvious. I was the last person to leave the platform as a band of porters and rail workers hustled to the luggage cars.

I glanced back over my shoulder to see the conductor rushing toward me. "You cannot be in here, Monsieur. You must go now."

While I continued out to find the men with their captive, the man's words piqued my curiosity. Why would they clear the platform for a routine luggage transfer? Perhaps Rocher would know.

The night was thick and black, the stars merely a ceiling between the walls of mountain ranges. In the doorway ahead, the three men were silhouettes in the golden light of the lobby until the doors closed between us.

I rushed through the doors, hoping to catch them, but the pain returned to my chest and halted me just inside. They disappeared into the crowds shifting between the café, the hotel check-in, and the embassy. As I searched the faces and hats, I realized that I didn't have a clear description of the men individually. If they'd separated, I wouldn't be able to identify them well enough to be sure. I was the worst kind of witness.

After several minutes of scanning the room, I gave up and made my way to the queue at the telegraph window. Perhaps Penny had answered my missive.

"Any messages for Henri Toussaint?" I asked.

The young woman smoothed the sides of her auburn hair and smiled. "I will see, Monsieur." She turned to a shelf out of my view and shook her head. "Nothing today. If you do receive anything, I can bring it up to your room if you like?" Her eyes flashed with something… wicked?

I chuckled, considering every connotation of her offer. She couldn't have been older than twenty-five years, and I had difficulty comprehending why she might flirt with me. But unless I was suffering from delusions, that was precisely what she was doing.

"I'll just check back in the morning," I said.

She tucked a fingernail between her lips for a second and batted her lashes. "It would be my pleasure, I assure you."

Definitely flirting.

I nodded and took a step back from the window, slowly enough to hear her address the next person in line more professionally. "Yes, Madam?"

The whole evening was a waste. Nothing from Elize, nothing from Penny, and nothing for my investigation. I dragged myself back to the elevator door and waited for a moment. When the brass doors slid open, my two friends stood inside, without their half-conscious companion. But this time, instead of racing away, they reached out their arms, took hold of mine, and yanked me inside with them.

"Wait!" But before I managed to fight back, everything went black.

9

SUNDAY, JUNE 17, 1945, CANFRANC, SPAIN

*M*y jaw slammed against my shoulder, and a sting in my cheek roused me to full consciousness. My fist went up instinctively, but caught nothing but air.

"Ah, he's awake," a voice whined with a Spanish accent from a stocky man pacing in front of me.

I squinted for a better examination of my situation, only to realize the full fury of a headache. I didn't recognize the whining man or his bearded partner for several seconds, but decided they must be the men I'd been following. They had me slumped in an armchair in a small hotel room with sparse décor and a small, round-top window at my side. The sun glared through the panes, screaming that I'd been out for several hours.

"Yes. I couldn't wait any longer." The taller of the pair eyed me like I was a fillet mignon. "Who do you report to?" His voice was low and even, with a German tempo.

What was he asking? Did he want my military affiliation? I

decided to play dumb. "I don't know what you are asking. I'm a tourist on holiday."

"You have a rather nasty scar for someone who is just on holiday." The German waved his cigarette toward my chest.

That's when I realized my shirt was unbuttoned to my waist. Without thinking, I grabbed for the ring on my chain.

"Don't worry; we didn't take anything, Inspector Toussaint." The whining man stopped pacing and crouched down in front of me until our eyes were level. "We know who you are. We just want to know why you're here in Canfranc."

My fingers closed around the ring for a second, then went to work on the shirt buttons. "I'm telling you the truth. I was injured on my last case in France, and I'm here to recover. The doctor wanted me in the cool, fresh air of the mountains."

The German stared without blinking, though his jaw flexed and released several times. His muscles were visible even through his thick auburn beard. "And why here? You have mountains in France."

He asked the question I'd asked myself continually since I'd been released from hospital. Why did my commander suggest the *Haute Pyrénées*? Why send me out of the country for my recuperation? Why Canfranc specifically? I didn't have the answer, but I didn't want to suggest otherwise.

"Madame Belfort is an old friend of mine. I thought I might surprise her."

Whiner shook his head. "Belfort doesn't have any old friends."

"Perhaps friends is too strong a word," I said. After all, we were so much more than friends. We were more…

"So you're working for Belfort?" Redbeard asked. His face was stone, offering no clues to his position on that possibility.

"No. I'm not *working* for her." I pulled my vest around to

straighten it. "I told you. We're old friends." I picked up my tie from the arm of the chair and rested it across my knee.

Redbeard flicked his wrist in my face. "You were following us last night. Why? It is not a common tourist activity—following people you don't know."

"I am not sure why, exactly." I shrugged and rubbed my temples. "I'm a police inspector, and perhaps I thought you were acting suspicious. You were carrying a man off the platform between you."

"Just helping a friend who'd had too much to drink on the train." Whiner's voice remained steady, but his eyes shifted to Redbeard for reassurance. "An *old friend.*"

Though his actions told me that was not, in fact, what they were doing, I didn't have proof to the contrary. There was room for more questions, so long as I went with it. After all, I wasn't tied up or held at gunpoint—yet.

"Well, that explains it." I inched forward in my seat. "I'm sure you can appreciate how I, as an inspector, might be curious about the matter. You're intelligent men. You see how it might appear to a stranger."

Redbeard placed his hand on my shoulder and put a little weight behind it. "Let me give you a little advice. You are here to recuperate. You should rest. Don't allow your curiosity to jeopardize your health. If you stick your French nose into other people's business, you may find yourself recovering from yet another injury. Do you understand, Inspector?" His fingernails dug deep through my shirt into my flesh.

"I do, indeed, understand." His hand released me, and I stood. "May I introduce myself? Henri Toussaint." I offered my hand.

The men stared with sneering faces. Whiner handed me my

suit jacket, and Redbeard opened the door. He sighed as I paused on the threshold. *"We're* not friends, Toussaint."

With an understanding nod, I exited the room. "See you around."

Redbeard cut a sharp eye at me. "No, you won't." He slammed the door between us.

The empty corridor stretched in both directions without numbers on the rooms. To my right stood an open door, and I proceeded in that direction.

Peering in, I found two women dressed in maids' uniforms sorting papers on a table in the middle of the small space. I smiled and began to ask for directions, but another door slammed in my face.

A ding caught my attention, and I found the elevator just around the corner. Two more women got off the carriage and gave me long, hard stares. My tuxedo would have looked stale in the best conditions, and I was decidedly not in the best condition.

I stepped into the carriage and rode down a floor, slipping past Angier's desk, where he directed a bellman toward the opposite hall with a guest's luggage. A few seconds later, I was safely back in my room. My bed appeared freshly made, and everything stood in place in the bar cabinet and in the washroom.

As I passed the mirror over the lavatory, I examined my state of ill condition. My hair had been slicked back the previous evening, but was now no more than a pile of dark waves reaching in every direction. My jaw, now needing a shave, throbbed red—scraped from the right hook wake-up call I received from my new friends.

Turning on the shower tap, I peeled myself from the tuxedo and frowned at my pitiable body. Scars formed constellations over my chest, arms, and legs. My bloodshot eyes stared angrily at the old man I'd become in just a few short years. War was hell, as they say.

After a quick shower, I opted to shape my stubble into a beard in progress rather than give it a full shave, working the edges of my fuller mustache into the thick whiskers at either side of my chin. I was on holiday, after all. Nobody in Canfranc would care so much what I looked like.

With that in mind, I raked through my hair to push it in one general direction, giving my pomade the day off. I donned my brown tweed trousers and slipped my casual green twill waistcoat over my ivory shirt. My green and navy foulard tie finished my ensemble.

Planning to investigate the hotel, the train station, and the mountainside, I pulled on my boots and loaded my pockets with my essentials—a good knife, my pocketwatch, cigarettes, lighter, and my wallet.

I picked up the room phone and waited for the operator. "What may I do for you, Monsieur Toussaint?"

"I'd like to have my tuxedo pressed for this evening, if I may."

"Someone will be up to retrieve your suit momentarily."

My watch read a few seconds after eight. Perfect. I had time for breakfast and a trip to the telegraph office before I started my investigation.

One of Angier's boys gathered my clothes and wished me a good morning. I spent no more than ten minutes getting coffee and a triangle of toast with marmalade. I scanned the room for Elize, but with no luck.

The telegraph office had nothing for me; the same for the post office and Rocher. I'd hoped for word from Penny, but it seemed I was on my own in this little adventure abroad.

In the lobby, a dozen bellmen pushed their carts to the back door, forming a gleaming brass samba line.

"What's this?" I asked Rocher.

"A train is arriving in a few minutes. The first of the week." He waved proudly at his employees. "It's quite a sight to behold."

"I'd hate to miss the show." And I followed the last young man through the exit doors, across the narrow yard, and onto the platform.

The youths waited patiently in rows as the train pulled into the station. As the travelers disembarked from the cars, the bellmen rushed to gather luggage, freight, and scheduled hotel supplies.

The crowds of travelers, mostly groups and families, came off first, followed by businessmen in suits with valises. I studied faces and attitudes, noting who appeared nervous, suspicious, and such. An inspector is always curious.

The final traveler to step from the train caught my attention and held me captive for several seconds. Swallowing hard, I examined the woman's face and demeanor. For a moment, I thought she was Hedy Lamarr—the most beautiful woman I'd ever seen in moving pictures.

She wore a red traveling skirt suit with a broad-brimmed red hat over her glossy brunette hair. Her lips formed a victory-red pursed smile, and her darkly made-up eyes flashed around the space as though she was searching for cameras or a spotlight.

As the crowds around me grew smaller, I found myself staring —mesmerized by her confident stride in my direction. *She walked directly toward me.* It wasn't until she was within arm's reach that I regained my composure and began to breathe again.

It wasn't Hedy Lamarr. The woman folding me into her tight embrace was Penny Tompkins. Not the frail, half-starved waif I'd investigated last month for the murder of a Nazi officer. *This* Penny Tompkins had regained her healthy curves and complexion back in London.

"It's wonderful to see you again, Henri." Her voice was a low purr behind my ear. "I almost didn't recognize you." Her soft finger traced over my whiskered jaw.

"I—I didn't expect you to come." I offered her my elbow. "You surprised me."

She pressed an unexpected kiss on my cheek. "I do love surprising people." She glanced around us. "But you were waiting for me here. So perhaps not so much of a surprise."

"Let me see you inside." I scrambled to piece together a coherent sentence. "Why did you come?"

She stopped and faced me, tapping her finger on my jaw again. "Your message. You asked me to come. And it looks like I arrived just in time. Someone here has been bothering my beloved inspector. I can't have that. I'd never forgive myself, especially after nearly getting you killed the first time we met."

The warmth of her hands gripping my arm sent an electric charge through my body. She'd been confident before, but her attitude, her appearance, her figure—this was something else. And I was no more than clay in her hands, waiting to be molded into whatever she wanted.

"You're here to help with my investigation?" I whispered.

She stopped again and stared into my soul. Her steely blue-grey eyes bore deep, and I immediately recognized the scared young woman buried behind her confident façade.

"Penny?"

Her thick black lashes blinked away any fear or doubt, and she squeezed my arm. "Something like that."

10

"My room is the last door on your right at the far end of the hall." I tipped the bellman as he left, and I peered into Penny's room.

While still elegant, her accommodations were less than half the size of my room. Similar blue damask curtains hung to the side of a much smaller window, overlooking the tin roof of the train platform and a less grand view of the mountainside beyond.

"Perhaps we might meet in the café downstairs." Penny unpinned her hat and placed it carefully atop the bureau opposite the bed. "I'll brush out my hair and unpack a bit first, if you don't mind."

"That would be perfect. Shall I order you something to eat?" I took a half step back into the hall, making sure to maintain an air of propriety.

Penny angled her chin and narrowed her gaze at mine. "How do you know what I want?" Her voice was a smoky whisper tickling my ear.

My brain raced for the proper response. "I can guess." Stupid. I stammered, "I—erhm—I'll order something that perhaps will be new to both of us. And we can have a bit of an adventure."

Her red lips curved up in a broad smile, and she leaned closer. "Mmm, you know I do love a good adventure." Her perfume. The sparkle in her eye. The hint of danger. It all consumed me.

"*Eh bien.*" I couldn't conjure another syllable.

Penny leaned against her doorframe, and her eyes studied me from head to toe and back. "You look quite different out of uniform."

"I'm on holiday, you know."

"Yes, *en convalescence.*"

"*Comme tu dis, mon amour,*" I replied without thinking.

Her smile grew wider still. "My love?"

"I apologize." I took another step back, but she reached out and caught my hand in hers.

"No need. I like it." She glanced in either direction down the hall and then set her gaze on my lips. "I will be in the café in ten minutes. Order us an adventure."

"WHERE WILL you take me after this?" Penny asked, dabbing the corner of her mouth with her napkin. She had changed into an ensemble more suitable for walking. She wore a lightweight cream blouse with a ruffle at the neckline, topped by brown breeches, similar to the jodhpurs my school friends wore on fox hunts. Shiny cordovan boots and a matching shoulder satchel completed her look. "To the side of the mountain? Back to the platform? To the room where you spent last night?"

"I thought the mountain first." I gestured toward the front doors, which led out to the mountain path. "Where it all started."

"But that isn't where it started, is it?"

My mind stalled. "It is." I'd told her everything that had happened since I'd arrived in Canfranc, and her question made me rethink my tale.

She again took my hand in hers. "Let me see your room. I want to see exactly what you witnessed that first night—from your window."

"My window?"

"You were in your room, were you not?"

"*Oui*. Yes." I marveled at the effect she had on me. How did she not seduce me before, *cette femme*? Where was my stoic investigator façade? I had to reclaim it. I drew a deep breath. "I can show you."

"Good." She stood and waited for my elbow to be offered.

On the way to my room, I reminded myself that this was part of an investigation. That she was here to help solve a murder. She was not, in fact, seducing me.

Was she?

No. I shouldn't be so fanciful. She was a spy. She was trained to see things that others missed. To notice details. To kill. Don't forget, Henri, she is a trained killer.

I managed to rein in my emotions long enough to give her a quick tour of my room, downplaying how much larger my suite was than hers.

"This is luxurious, Henri." Her fingertips skimmed over the bedspread and velvet chair upholstery. "How does an inspector afford this kind of holiday?"

Since the moment I met her six weeks prior, I had been in awe of her gift to ask the questions no one else asked. This particular question was one I'd asked myself as soon as I arrived at the hotel. And again, when I entered this room. I'd have felt more than grateful for the quarters she'd been assigned. Even that was a luxury compared to my sparse *maison* in France.

"My superiors arranged everything," I explained, though I wished someone would explain it to me.

"I see." She stepped to the window with the view of the mountain face and reached back, motioning for me to join her. "Tell me what you saw," she said once I was close enough to breathe in her perfume again.

Her attention leaped back and forth while I explained. One moment, she studied my face, and the next, she focused on the mountain. From her shoulder bag, she pulled a small pair of opera glasses. "Not as powerful as I'd like, but they will do."

I gestured to the place where I believed the struggle occurred and then to where the torch fell. Her breath quickened when I spoke of searching through the shrubbery and finding the blood-stained lens. Her chin dipped half an inch, and she returned the glasses to her pouch.

Electricity sparked from her fingers and eyes when she turned and finally spoke. "Henri, take me."

Dropping my gaze from her eyes to her lips, I searched for words but found no more than a breathless, "Penny?"

"Take me to the mountain trail. I want to see it for myself."

11

SUNDAY, JUNE 17, 1945, CANFRANC, SPAIN

"The view is quite remarkable from here." Penny knelt near the edge of the path and looked both out toward the hotel and down to where the unknown victim had fallen.

We'd hiked the path slowly, observing where branches might have bent, or stones might have been knocked loose. I explained to her everything I witnessed on the night of my arrival, leaving out no detail.

"*Mais oui*; the view encompasses everything in the valley. The murdered man must have enjoyed his descent." I offered Penny my hand to help her back to her feet.

She took it and returned a quirked grin. "That's not what I implied. I simply meant that perhaps someone else witnessed the fall."

"If so, I've not been informed." I didn't release her hand. "But then, who am I that anyone should tell me anything?"

Penny sighed and snaked her arm around mine. "It's true that you have no jurisdiction here. But several people here do know you are an inspector."

"They do. But that fact hasn't seemed to ingratiate me with anyone."

She turned to face me. "Tell me more about this hotel manager. Madame Belfort, was it?" She paused as I considered my response. It occurred to me that perhaps I had indeed omitted a detail or two. Her tone turned impatient. "You said that she may have *managed* the situation?"

"Erhm, yes. Rather." I fumbled. "I spoke to her the next morning." I wasn't sure how much to say. "She told me not to worry— that she had everything in hand."

Penny gripped my arm and added a pronounced squeeze. "We shall have to push her for an explanation. Perhaps she ordered the murder. You spoke with her afterward, yes?"

"I did."

"And you explained what you saw?"

"I did." I coughed.

"And you explained who you are?"

I coughed again. "It's…"

"You didn't tell her who you are?"

"There was no need. We were already acquainted." I prepared for her to release my arm and scold me. Instead, she snugged me closer.

"Ooh, I see." She glanced around as if to assure our privacy. "Tell me all about that."

I looked around as well, as much to stall as anything else. I worked my mouth for a moment without sound, and she put her free hand along my jaw.

"Relax. You can tell me."

Her touch calmed me and sent my senses reeling. I might tell her anything, perhaps, but first, I had to remember what it was I wanted to say. Once I regained my presence of mind, I began. "A few years ago—when the war was just beginning—I met her. But her name was Lisette Deneau. We fell in love and were to be married. But on the day my regiment shipped out, she was killed when her village was shelled. I was there when it happened."

"But you can't believe everything you see, eh?" Her expression revealed no surprise or alarm. "And her name now? Belfort?"

"Elize Belfort." I released a tight breath. "No ring on her finger. She didn't say whether she married after me. She told me almost nothing of her past after that day. Both Lisette and Elize are variants of Elizabeth, so that was easy enough. Belfort may be nothing more than a label name she saw on a tin of kippers."

Penny laughed. "You seem quite jaded when you speak of the woman you almost married."

"When she changed her name, she changed the rest of her as well, I'd say." My tone was colder than I intended. Colder than I expected.

"But she is still the same woman inside. And if she once loved you, she would still have a soft place in her heart."

I answered before she asked. "If she ever did. That's what I question now. Not only did she tell me to leave the hotel—Spain, in fact—but she also took the meager evidence I did have that a murder even occurred. The bloody torch lens. She picked it from my pocket."

A smile hinted at the corners of Penny's full lips. "I see. She got close enough to pick your pocket? I see you have a soft place for her as well."

I didn't answer. Her ability to see through me and my situation was infuriating and intriguing. What couldn't this woman do?

"You must introduce me to her tonight." Penny tugged my elbow to lead me back down the mountainside.

"I don't think that's a good idea." But it didn't matter what I said.

"There is a reception every night?" She leaned her head on my shoulder as we walked.

"Yes."

"Good. When we're back at the hotel, I'll dress, and you can take me when you're ready."

That phrase again. Was this some subtle seduction, or just a common turn of phrase for her? I expected it to be the latter, though part of me wished for the former.

We took a quick tour of the hotel lobby, café, tiny embassy, post office, and other amenities. We walked back to the platform where one train departed, and another arrived. I was about to tell her about the dubious exchanges I'd seen when she dropped her handkerchief next to a bench and retrieved it with a scrap of paper.

"You knew about this dead drop? That *is* what you call it?" I asked.

"Of course. This one is the most obvious for the platform, but I feel like I should probably check out a few more." She glanced down at the now unfolded page and smiled. She folded it as it had been and returned it to its place.

"What did it say?" I enquired. "Why did you put it back?"

She turned her eyes up to meet my gaze. "Not everything secret is sinister. Some secrets are meant to keep the good guys safe. It was not for me."

"And you're not going to tell me what it says?" I folded my arms over my chest.

"You are in such a rush to know everything." Penny's tone was almost maternal and oddly calming. "I will tell you soon."

"When?" My curiosity piqued.

"I'll need to decipher the message. It was, of course, written in code."

She could read, memorize, and decipher without having the note in hand? Of course, she could.

I considered what might impress her. "And will you want to stay and learn who picks it up?"

She patted my arm as if I were a pitiable fool. "Dead drops not only convey messages, but they also keep the identities of the senders and receivers protected. If I don't know who dropped or picked up the note, I cannot be made to reveal that information." She paused with a gleam in her eye. "And neither can you."

SHE STUDIED every inch of the hotel as I escorted her back to her room. "Pick me up at eight?" Her question was half command and half tease, and I was entirely under her spell.

"I'll be here." I glanced at my watch. "In an hour."

She nodded and kissed my cheek, leaving a warm sensation in my whiskers. I pondered that sensation all the way to my room.

I brushed out my dinner suit and let it steam while I showered off the mountain trail. The hot water melted the knots in my shoulders, and I wondered what Penny might be doing in her room. Deciphering the coded note? Selecting her dress? Brushing her hair? Applying that luscious Victory Red lipstick?

I pushed all of that aside for the moment and chastised my musings. I was a police inspector and a witness to a murder. I needed to concentrate on the task at hand. Penny wanted to meet Elize, and my mind only conjured catastrophic outcomes.

But why? I toweled off and reminded myself that neither woman was in love with me, nor was I in love with either of them. Penny was in Spain to help me, and Elize wanted me to leave. I was not in love with Elize—not anymore. And I was certainly not in love with Penny—not yet.

I dressed for dinner as I had the night before. Fresh white shirt, black trousers, and black socks. I opened my valet box and pulled out my cuff links and the chain with Lisette's ring. The ring dangled as I held it out, ready to place it around my neck. I shook my head and set it back into the cedar case. I tucked in my shirt, inserted the cuff links, and began working my shirt buttons closed toward my throat. But I stopped again. In the last three years, I'd worn it around my neck every single day.

What would it feel like to be free of it? Free of it? Did I loathe it now? Had it become an anchor?

I picked it up again and dropped the chain over my head. I would think about it later. For the moment, I'd go on as usual. I tucked it into my collar and finished with the buttons. My black bow tie was next, followed by my watch, my shoes, and finally, my jacket. I tucked a grey silk square into my breast pocket and checked the time. Five to eight. I swept a quick gaze over the room and shifted a few things for a neater appearance. Why?

At the door, I reviewed myself in the wall mirror over a small console. I pushed a strand of hair over my brow and pressed it back into place with the palm of my hand. I decided I should have shaved, but there was no time.

Every thought I'd ever had about Penny Tompkins jumbled in my head as I strode to the other end of the hall to her door. The moment I'd met her merely six weeks ago, I'd assumed she was guilty of murdering a Nazi on a train from Amsterdam that stopped in my jurisdiction. But that supposition was promptly dispelled with her testimony and my discovery that she worked for the British government in a secret department of warfare. For most, learning she was a spy and assassin would have been the nail in her coffin, but for me, it was all but proof of her innocence.

Getting to know her and experiencing her attempts to seduce me only cemented her standing. She was adept at everything she did. I was convinced that if she had assassinated the German officer, no one would have ever discovered the thing. The man's body would have surely disappeared, or perhaps his death ruled an apparent suicide. No murder, and positively not at her nimble hands.

Before I realized it, I stood at her door, which opened. I couldn't remember if I had knocked.

Penny stood in a silver silk gown that puddled at her feet. The neckline was cowled in a daring drape that fell between jeweled straps at each shoulder. A blue-black pearl hung from each earlobe, and a matching pearl ring glinted from her right index finger. Her hair fell in loose curls except for a portion pinned back behind her left ear, baring her throat.

For a second, I was frozen, mesmerized by the flutter of her skin as it revealed a pulse point.

"Are we going?" Penny asked. Her posh English accent shook me free of my reveries.

"You look lovely," my only response.

She stepped into the hall and handed me her key.

I locked her door and handed it back. She dropped it into a silver beaded clamshell clutch and looped her arm through mine.

"I'm anxious to meet Elize."

And without another second ticking by, my thoughts focused sharply back on the business at hand. I was going to solve a murder, and Penny was going to help.

12

SUNDAY, JUNE 17, 1945, CANFRANC, SPAIN

We sat in a dark corner of the ballroom, with our backs to the wall, watching every person who entered or left. Sipping on the same coupe of champagne for an hour, we enjoyed several hors d'oeuvres and light conversation, making up stories for each couple that sat or danced around us.

At least, I was making up stories. For all I knew, Penny was telling me the truth. I laughed at the thought.

"What?" she whispered.

"I was just thinking about what you might already know about everyone in the room." I tapped a finger on the foot of my champagne glass. "I am playing games while you are mobilizing armies."

She dismissed my words with a flick of her long, narrow fingers. "The war is over."

I chuffed. "I doubt that very much. Not for you."

She drained the last of her drink. "Let's dance." She took my hand.

I led her out to the dance floor, and we waltzed to Irving

Berlin's "Always." Penny's gaze roamed the room with a wary eye. I tried to do the same but had a terrible time wandering from her face, with its beautiful determination and fierce efficiency.

"Turn me," she whispered.

I obeyed, shifting my hand from the small of her back to the center and turning her lithe body into a controlled twirl.

She nestled back into my arms and rested her forehead lightly against my jaw. "That's her, isn't it?"

Beside us, Elize entered the ballroom. One of her attendants hurried to her side with one question or another. She answered and then dismissed them with a slice of her chin.

"Yes."

"Dance me in her direction and introduce us."

I twitched my head a quarter of an inch. "She doesn't want to see me, and she surely doesn't want to talk to me."

"If you don't want to do it the easy way," Penny said, taking the lead and moving us too quickly toward Elize. She stepped on my foot as we approached and feigned a tumble into the other woman.

Elize and Penny gasped as they collided, though both maintained their footing.

"I'm so sorry, my dress is too long," Penny alternated apologies and excuses until I intervened.

"It was my fault." I obliged. "My big feet never could make it through a whole waltz."

Elize shot Penny and me a look of frustration and surprise. "It's fine. Are you hurt?"

Penny shook her head. "No. Thanks to the champagne. I might tumble off the roof and wouldn't feel it. They serve the good stuff here." She intentionally pretended to be slightly intoxicated, hiccupping once for effect.

Hedy Lamarr had nothing on Penny.

I scooped her up by the waist and held her against my side. "Penelope Tompkins, this is Elize Belfort. She's the hotel manager's assistant."

"The who?" Penny faked another hiccup.

I offered Elize a sheepish grin. "The one serving the good stuff." I shot a glare at Penny and then softened my expression toward Elize. "And this is my friend, Penny Tompkins. She just arrived this morning from London."

Penny reached out for Elize's hand, and they squeezed their palms together without a shake. "How do you do, Miz Belfort?"

"I'm quite well, thank you." Elize shot me another look. "I see why you had to stay another day, Henri, but I hope now that she's arrived, you'll travel on to Lisbon, as I suggested."

Penny continued with her tipsy routine. "Henri, are you taking me to Portugal? Is that my surprise?"

"No," I said to both of them. "We're staying here until some things are settled."

A cold shot fired from Elize's eyes. "I can settle everything in my hotel—without your assistance."

I expected Penny to react, though I couldn't guess how she might do it. Would she suggest we all work together? Would she imply Elize was up to something, and we were aware of it?

Penny rocked back on her heel as if she was falling into my arms. "Oops." She turned soppy eyes up at mine. "That champagne really is the good stuff." She pulled my arm around her shoulder. Should we have another?" But before I could answer, she cupped her hand around her mouth and whispered loudly, "Why don't we have a drink in your room?"

Elize's lips pursed into a tight *o*, and she patted my arm. "You should take her somewhere more private before she embarrasses herself or you."

Penny's eyes went wide. "That's what I said."

What was this? No clever ruse to learn more about Elize. Nothing clever about any of this. I took Penny's elbow. "I'll escort you back to your room."

"Buh-bye, Elsie," Penny said with the slightest hint of a slur.

"Goodnight," Elize said through a cough. "Think about what I said, Henri."

In the hall, Penny's demeanor barely changed. "Take me to your room. You can make us a drink."

"What are you doing?" My voice was a low growl, and I turned us toward her room.

She twirled as if we were still dancing and dragged me toward mine. "We need to go to your room for a drink." Her tone was soft but intense. "You have to trust me."

I stopped, wrapping my arm around her waist to keep her from walking farther. "Penny?"

She came to an abrupt halt and let her gaze float slowly up to my face—a contented curl on her lips. "If you take me to your room, I'll tell you what the note said." It was almost a prayer.

And without another word from me, we walked to my suite.

She giggled once I had the door locked behind us. "You're easy."

"I'm not easy, and I'm not stupid." I was feeling both. "And I'm not in the mood for games." I crossed my arms as she backed up half a step and swept her hair off her shoulders. My breath caught. I forced myself to refocus. "What was in the note?"

She dipped her chin in a sober nod and took a steady step in my direction. "No more games. Why don't you make us a drink?" She gestured to my bar cabinet. "I'll take a moment to freshen up, and then we can talk about the note and other things."

I motioned toward the washroom and nodded. "We need to make a plan."

She raised and lowered her lashes as if the movement was a code unto itself, then disappeared behind the door to my bedroom.

I flipped on the radio to Glenn Miller's "In the Mood" and opened the bar cabinet to peruse my options. Settling on a Lillet Rouge, I opened the bottle, inhaled the dry, oaky liquid, and poured two glasses. Before picking them up, I shrugged off my jacket and draped it on the back of the chair by the radio. The song ended, and static crackled through the speaker, so I leaned down to fine-tune the receiver. Soon, Hoagy Carmichael's "Stardust" crooned across the airwaves.

Penny cleared her throat from behind me, and when I turned, I almost swallowed my tongue. She stood mere inches from me, clad only in a black silk slip and stockings. She held our drinks, offering one to me, though I could barely feel the glass in my hand.

My heart pounded in my ears momentarily before the blood left my brain. "Oh, mon Dieu!"

She took a step closer, and the warmth of her body licked at mine like a flame. We sipped our Lillets, and she took my glass from me and set them back on the bar. "Are you surprised?" she asked.

Her hands reached for my tie, pulling it off in one quick move. My hands moved automatically to her waist. The thin silk of her chemise allowed my fingers too much. I argued with myself whether to pull her closer or push her away.

She worked through my shirt buttons in seconds and slipped

her hands around my neck, constantly moving closer until there was no space between us. Her lips moved to my ear. "Do you like this?"

I couldn't speak or move or breathe. No, breathing was all I was doing. For three years, I hadn't held a woman in my arms. I hadn't even been tempted. How could I? But as she swayed to the music, her lush fabric against my scarred chest, I struggled to control myself.

And then something clicked in my brain. We hadn't been in my suite for ten minutes, and I was entirely under her control—body, mind, and soul. She was so good at this. Too good at this.

She slid one hand into the hair at the nape of my neck and one over the scar on my chest. The scar from where I'd been stabbed— because of her. She tiptoed to press her lips to mine. Soft, deep kisses pulled me into her full embrace. I was in the throes of a battle between heaven and hell. My body begged to know her better, but my mind insisted I already knew more than enough.

When my lips left hers, panting and longing for more, I drew a deep breath and asked, "Are you here to kill me?"

13

*B*efore Penny could answer, a soft knock at the door interrupted. Our heads swiveled simultaneously, and I gestured for her to hide in the bedroom, if for no other reason than she was half-naked.

I leaned against the door and murmured, "Yes?" through the wood.

"Henri, it is Elize. May I speak with you for a moment?"

Pulling my shirt back over my arms, I began rebuttoning from the bottom up, opening the door as I did.

Elize stepped inside and glanced around. "Are you alone?"

"What do you want, Lis— Elize?"

"I wanted to apologize to you for my behavior toward your friend." Her gaze still roamed my room, stopping at the bedroom door. "I was rude."

"Then perhaps you should apologize to her." I tucked her ring into my shirt as I buttoned, but not before her eyes flashed upon it on the chain around my neck.

"I thought she might be here with you." Elize crossed her arms. "Is she?"

My thoughts screamed, but I resolved to stay collected. Penny's perfume lingered in the room, stirring both panic and lust within me. I struggled to remain calm. "I'm getting ready for bed."

"I can see that. But you didn't answer my question." She let her arms slip to her sides and stepped toward me, shifting her focus to my eyes. She moved like a lioness on the hunt, and I was her prey.

"Don't you think—" I began, raising my hands. I wanted to stop her from reaching me. I wasn't sure I could resist whatever she would ask, but my common sense reminded me that Penny was just on the other side of the door, for better or worse.

And then Penny was standing next to me. She looped her hands around my arm, and I was tempted to look to see if she had put her dress back on.

"I see," Elize said, taking a half-step backward, her hunt resolved. She waved a graceful hand between Penny and me. "I came to apologize for my rudeness earlier."

"Apology accepted," Penny replied without a trace of emotion. "Was there anything else you needed?"

Penny motioned toward the door, cold as ice, directing Elize out without another word.

It played like a scene from a movie, and I was completely detached from the action, though I was relieved Penny wore her dress again—mostly relieved.

Elize followed Penny to the threshold and glanced back at me. "I still urge you to leave Spain." She turned to face Penny. "I assume you're leaving his room, too?"

"In a moment." Penny picked up her clutch from the bar, along with her glass, and took one last slow sip of her whiskey. She walked to me with a pronounced sway in her hips and slipped her arms around my neck. Her whiskey-flavored lips seared against mine, and I sensed a little scratch at the back of my shirt collar. "Goodnight, sweet prince," she said as she followed Elize out the door, closing it carefully behind her.

"Blazes," I muttered. "That's the line from Hamlet after he's dead. The woman's killed me." I shook out my collar, expecting to see a venomous scorpion or the like, and a scrap of paper fluttered to my feet.

Downstairs bar - 10 minutes was scrawled in Penny's hand.

Perhaps she hasn't killed me. Yet.

REDRESSED, I hurried downstairs, checking the corridors to be sure I wasn't seen or followed by Elize or by my two brutal friends in hats.

I found Penny sitting at the bar, but she stood as I approached. She picked up two highballs and gestured to a small booth in the corner, lit only by a single candle. "Over there."

We slid around the blue velvet-upholstered seat to look out on the room. "What is all of this?" I whispered.

Penny's face glowed in the candlelight, framed with her dark waves of hair. "I want you to look around this room and tell me what you see."

I sighed. "There are two men at this end of the bar and a woman at the other. Two couples at a table in the center of the room, and another couple on the opposite wall."

She cocked her chin and blinked. Not in the seductive slow blink from before—not with the coy chin tilt. No. This time, she gazed at me with utter disappointment. "That's all you see?"

I drew a deep breath and resigned myself to another study. I was an inspector, after all. "The barman is chatting with the woman but watching the men." A flash of recognition struck me. "I believe the woman arrived on the same train as me. She's definitely a spy. For who is still to be determined."

I watched the barman's hands fiddle with something below the bar top. "Now he's making a drink, no—he's polishing a glass. His eyes are on the mirror; he's scanning the room, looking at all of us, but coming back to the two men."

From the corner of my eye, I glimpsed Penny's smile. "And now?"

"He's placing the polished glass in front of the men. One nods and finishes his drink. Wait… the other man is picking up the cocktail napkin from under the first man's drink and tucked it into his breast pocket. Now he's leaving." My whisper became breathier. "Now the woman is joining the man with the napkin." I released a low gasp. "She's taking the napkin from him, putting it in her purse. Telling the barman good night. She's leaving."

"What do you think just happened?" Penny asked.

Her hand rested on my forearm, which held my glass a few inches off the table. "If I were guessing…" but something caught my eye. "The couple from the other side of the room is getting up to follow her. They're leaving—following her out." My heart pounded as I thought of the danger the woman might face at the hands of the couple.

"Hold." Penny's fingers squeezed around my arm. "Keep watching."

Once the couple walked out, I noticed something else. "The barman is still staring at the man. The man is pulling another napkin from his pocket and handing it to the barman. There is something written on it."

Another smile from Penny.

"Now he's coming out from behind the bar, checking on the two couples. Now he's going back to the bar. Making two drinks." Surely, she was aware the woman was in trouble; I needed to say something, to do something.

"She will be fine." Penny's voice was no more than a breath—a sigh. "Drink."

"But," I started, then stalled, frustrated. I tipped my glass back and finished the burn down my throat.

The barman loaded two drinks onto a tray and walked out toward us. "Two more?" It was directed at Penny, who nodded.

"*Merci.*"

He set the tray on the table and took our freshly emptied glasses. He then placed a napkin in front of me, and then my drink. In front of Penny, he placed the napkin with the note and then her glass on top. I held my breath until he turned away.

The barman stopped suddenly and twisted to face us again. "Oh, Pen?"

"Yes?" she answered.

"I heard your man was coming down to help. Is that so?"

Penny nodded. "I expect."

"Hmm." The barman frowned. "Just tell him to stay out of our way. I don't want a repeat of Paris."

Penny shrugged. "I'll warn him, but you know *Jack*."

"That's why I mention it."

My thoughts tumbled. Once the man was back behind the bar, I turned to face Penny. "What's happening in this place?"

"You know very well what's happening. That's why you wanted me to come down here." Her hand moved from my arm to my shoulder. "You needed my help." She pressed the napkin into my hand.

Last train Tuesday.

"Who—or what—is on the last train on Tuesday?" I asked. "Or is this another code?"

Penny's soft hand inched up to the back of my neck, slipping beneath my shirt collar. "You ask the right questions, *mon chèr*. That's what we're going to find out."

Her warm fingers softened the tension in my neck, though my thoughts were divided between the intrigues around us and her sparkling grey eyes. No. I had to be the inspector—not give in to her seduction every time she touched me. "So the woman just now—she was a bluff—to draw out the couple."

Penny flashed a smile.

"But what was all of that back in my room? You... you came out in your... your underpinnings."

Penny's lips spread in a wide grin. "Don't you know?"

"I do not."

"I needed to see if you were under surveillance. And it turns out you were. I was almost certain of that, but I wanted to know who was responsible. I was not altogether surprised that it was your friend Elize." She took another sip of her drink, and when she set it back on the table, she clinked the glass against mine, sharing the corner of the clean napkin.

"You think she's watching me inside my room?" The idea seemed nonsensical, but Penny had a point. The timing of Elize's appearance was uncanny. "What does that mean?"

"I can think of a few things." Penny inched closer to me. "First, that she's afraid of you. She wants you to leave—to be out of her way."

Jasmine, whiskey, and the scent of her skin clung to her silk dress, filled my nostrils and pulled my attention to her mouth. "And second?" The words came out in a rasp.

"She still cares for you." Penny moved her body until she was pressed against my side. "Her place is filled with spies—good and bad, doing all sorts of things—good and bad. She doesn't want you to be hurt. She put you in that room to make sure you are safe. Under her watchful eye."

My body burned, and my heart pounded so loudly that I was certain Penny heard it. "And what if she hadn't been watching us? What if she hadn't interrupted us?"

She leaned toward me until our lips were mere inches apart. "Then I suppose we'd be having this conversation tomorrow morning... in your bed."

Our lips pressed together for a long, hot kiss before my presence of mind returned. I pulled back for a breath. "But what about Jack? The barman said he'd be joining you soon."

She shifted so my arm was around her, and her hands grabbed my jacket lapels. "You're going to have to trust me. Jack won't be a problem."

"What happened in Paris?" I asked, though Paris was the last thing on my mind.

14

MIDNIGHT, MONDAY, JUNE 18, 1945, CANFRANC, SPAIN

A tall, gold-enameled grandfather clock in the lobby tolled a deep chime, marking the passing of another day in Spain. We scanned the corridors in either direction as I accompanied Penny back to her room.

"Come inside for a moment. I want to show you something." She tugged my arm. "I promise I'll behave."

It wasn't that I wanted her to behave; I needed her to. I needed time to sort everything out. She hadn't been with me for a whole day yet, and part of me was terrified of her. The other part wanted to hold her and never let her go. That was the part that followed her into her small room.

"Don't turn on the light," she instructed as she led me to her window. "What do you see?"

Unlike my view of the mountain face with terraced walkways, her room faced the opposite side of the valley and overlooked the train platform, utility buildings, and a less dramatic mountain beyond them. I wasn't sure what to focus on, except for a few dim lights and movement, and I suddenly realized.

"Men. Moving luggage or gear or something from the train platform to the far building." I searched for more.

"What else?"

"It's not luggage—the luggage is going to the first building. Steamer trunks and such," I said. Penny's hand was on my shoulder, and she placed her small pair of field glasses into my hand, grazing my fingertips with hers. Through the glasses, I concentrated on the carts entering the unnamed building. "Crates of every shape. Some under tarpaulins. Some marked—I can't read anything from this distance."

Penny's perfume, mixed with the faint scent of whiskey, swirled around my eyes and clouded my vision. The warmth of her body pulled my attention from the window.

"What else do you see?" Her voice broke into my thoughts like glass cracking from too much heat.

"I can't— *Mon Dieu*, how can I see anything?" I turned, wrapping my arms around her waist. "All I can see is you. All I can smell, all I can touch… all I can taste." I covered her lips with mine.

She pulled away. "You must stay sharp. You can't be distracted. Not by anyone. Not even me."

"But," I began.

Penny stepped forward again, pressing herself against my body. "If you lose focus, even for a second, very bad things can happen."

When her whisper faded, another sound took its place. The quick click and snap of a switchblade opening beside my ear made me jump away from the woman.

"What are you doing?"

"I'm training you. You can't relax for even a second. I could have killed you, and you'd have barely felt it—until it was too late." Penny put the knife down and smiled. "*I probably* wouldn't do that, but plenty of people here want you gone."

My arms stretched out, partly in surrender and partly in desire. "But how?"

"Go back to the window and tell me what you see." She stepped behind me and wrapped her arms gently around my torso. "Don't think about me other than to remember that I have a blade on me."

"And that should be how I regard everyone?" I raised the glasses back to my eyes.

"Exactly."

"Why are they moving these crates at midnight?"

"You again, asking the right questions." Penny's tone carried an unseen smile.

"What else, besides the knife, do you have on your person?" I imagined she probably had her little Browning pistol and probably some poison—either in a syringe or sachet if my memory served. Maybe both.

"All good questions you need to answer soon." She chuffed into the darkness. "But not tonight." She took my arm and led me to her door. "I'll meet you tomorrow morning, and we can have breakfast and take a quiet walk around Canfranc."

I stopped in her open doorway. "Should I kiss you *bonne nuit*?"

She put her finger to my lips. "You have learned enough for tonight. Tomorrow will be long and probably difficult. Save your energy, Henri."

∼

STRETCHED ACROSS MY BED, I stared at the ceiling as long as I could stand. My eyes refused to close. Her lips, her body, her scent, her voice. They all mingled with the sights out the window. And what was out *my* window?

Moonlight shimmered between the velvet drapes, luring me back to my feet. *Just a peek.* I pulled myself up with the crackling in my stiff joints and a slight groan escaping my throat. "Just a peek," I muttered aloud.

The view was swathed in blue darkness, as heavy as any draperies. The mountain blocked the sky except for the narrow strip of stars overhead. The sconce lights on the hotel's façade offered a meager glow in the darkness—not enough to reflect on the river's surface. A light over the nearest bridge cast a little shine, but only enough to see the water rushing beneath.

No one wandered. No one tarried. No one came or went. Canfranc lay silent on this side of the hotel.

But I understood the other side had secrets. Secrets that wouldn't be revealed by my waiting until morning.

I dressed quickly in my darkest clothes and made my way down the corridor to the stairs, avoiding the attention of the lift operator or any bellman who might be awake. I slipped out the back door and headed toward the platform building, keeping to the shadows for concealment.

Beyond the platform, men continued to enter and leave the unmarked building. They shifted their crates on hand trolleys without conversation. I inched closer, watching every man's serious expression. No words. These men had their instructions, and they followed them without protest or question.

All I needed was a glimpse at what they were moving. What freight would be such a secret? The war was over, but I wasn't naïve enough to think all the smuggling and black-market deals were over. If I could only see—with just a little proof to take back to Penny—she would be proud, and we'd know our next step.

My greatest fear was that Elize was somehow managing this operation. My brain hadn't allowed me to dwell on that suspicion too long, but it was there. After all, a border train station between Occupied France and neutral Spain would be the ideal location to sneak Nazi officers away to escape prosecution. Not to mention anything they might like to take with them.

My thoughts raced back to my friends in the Resistance. Their stories of intercepted gold, heirlooms, and artwork being stolen from Jewish families and sent to neutral countries to be picked up later. I thanked the good Lord that my friends could stop what they were doing. But who would stop these fiends?

I'd finally crept up to the side of the storeroom and found a pair of double doors with a gap between. Peering through the gap, I discovered my two friends with hats sorting through the labels on the crates, directing them to be placed on one side or the other.

"These will go out tomorrow." Redbeard waved to the crates behind him. "Madrid." He pointed to one crate, then another. "That stack goes on to Lisbon in two days."

A man wheeled another trolley in with a few small boxes. "These are heavy."

"Let me see," the stout man said. "Yes, these go to Madrid. To the office as payment—it may be the last of it."

My hand gripped the door handle. I had to stop whatever this was. The door started to open, then slammed shut again as my breath rushed from my lungs. I landed on my face.

"Have you learned nothing? You'll get us both killed." Penny whisper-screamed as she landed atop my back. "You can't rush them like this. You have no weapons and no idea of what you're walking into."

"What are you doing here? You told me to wait until morning."

She stood and helped me to my feet, dragging me into a wooded area for protection. "Yes," she hissed. "Until I could come down here and see what they were doing." She wore a dark, long-sleeved jumper and dark trousers.

The two men stepped out of the doorway and looked around. Redbeard tossed a cigarette to the ground. "Maybe just the wind, but we need to be sure. Find a few guys to help search the area. If you find anyone, bring them to me."

Penny took my hand and led me back toward the train platform through the trees, around the hotel, and to the front doors. While we walked, she picked pine needles and dirt from my shirt. "They are on alert now. We can't move against them, and they will be even more rushed to move all this safely away."

"I made it worse." I hoped that saying the words would garner sympathy or at least an acknowledgment of my intentions. It did not.

"You did." Penny nodded toward the bridge. "Let's move over there. We can appear as lovers in the dark."

"And make plans for tomorrow?" I slipped my hand to her lower back.

She rested her head on my shoulder as we stood at the bridge railing. "Jack is arriving tomorrow."

"You said he wouldn't be a problem."

"I may have exaggerated." She glanced over my shoulder. "Take my face in your hands and kiss me. Quickly."

I followed her instructions, listening for footfalls behind us. She took my face in her hands as well. We stood in the dim lamplight and kissed for several seconds as whoever was watching walked away.

"So Jack will be a problem?" I whispered, gulping to catch my breath.

"Not if we keep our relationship professional." Penny slid her hands from my cheeks to my chest.

"And this is how you'll do that?" I took her hands in mine. "Professional?"

"Well," Penny hemmed a bit. "I'm not supposed to be working down here. Not for Mother. Not for… You know."

"You came to Spain for fun?" My thoughts sputtered. "Are you mad?"

"No. And no. I have a job to finish." She squeezed my hands. "I'm just not authorized to finish it."

"What do you mean, you're not authorized?"

"It was passed off to Jack." Her gaze dropped from mine.

A thousand worst-case scenarios paraded through my brain in a flash of lightning and fear. "Jack is coming down to kill me?"

"What?" Penny laughed. "Nobody is going to kill you. I came to help you. This place is packed with spies of every kind and a few assassins. You need me. And I need you."

"But why is Jack allowed to finish your assignment? Are you in trouble?"

Penny drew a deep breath. "You might say so." She swallowed hard and looked into my eyes, her own pooling with tears. "The war is over, yes, but there is still so much to do. Our department can really only act in wartime. So, it's in the process of converting to a peacetime office. Men are staying active, and women have the choice to be secretaries—tending to tea trolleys and such—or return to civilian life. Finding husbands and building families."

"I thought that's what you wanted." I eased my palm against her cheek, and she leaned into it.

"It is. I mean, I do want that someday. But not yet." She chewed her bottom lip. "There's too much undone. I can wrap up some things. Make a few more pay for what they've done, you know?"

I nodded. "Like the guys in there. You can stall their shipments. Ensure that none of them escape safely to South America or elsewhere. That's the idea, right?"

"You understand?" Again, she leaned into my chest. "And you'll help me?"

It was my turn to drag her inside. "Let's have a few hours' rest. We'll need to be sharp if we're going to stop the train to Lisbon."

"Lisbon?" she asked as I walked her to the stairwell.

"The shipment on Tuesday is going to Lisbon. That's what I overheard."

Penny took my hand and dropped her room key into it. "I'm impressed."

I unlocked her door and checked her room before allowing her to enter. "I didn't mean to make things worse."

"Maybe you didn't." She kissed my cheek and patted my chest. "Try to sleep."

"You should, too." I kissed her forehead. "*Bonne nuit.*"

Her door lock clicked, and I stared down the hall toward my room. "I'll stare at the ceiling as long as I must," I chanted quietly under my breath. "I will not go out until morning."

15

MONDAY, JUNE 18, 1945, CANFRANC, SPAIN

A jackhammer pounded at my temples for the fleeting seconds between sleep and waking, ending only when my eyes finally focused on the blaze of sunlight slashing across my ceiling. Then the thrum of the hammer transformed into a rap at my door.

I shrugged into my mulberry silk dressing gown and cinched the belt at my waist as I opened the door to the hallway.

"Good morning," Penny chirped. Her gaze roamed my body from my head to my bare feet. "You're not dressed yet."

"You told me to rest."

"Yes, but now it's time to work. We have a lot to do." Her index finger traced the lapel of my robe, lingering slowly at my scar. "This is quite lavish for a police inspector. Lovely."

Her touch sent my thoughts ajar. "Thank you; it was a gift." Yesterday—in this very spot—I held this woman in my arms in a glorious state of undress, and today my words fumbled like a schoolboy. Ridiculous.

"You'll need to put on something a bit more… rugged than this. We'll be walking through the village today. Investigating."

Penny wore a brown tweed skirt, a simple blouse, a red cardigan, and smart brown ankle boots with sturdy soles. This ensemble might look matronly on another woman, but it gave Penny an air of subdued intelligence. And concealed her curves beneath the pleats.

"Am I not a man? A professional investigator, no less. Yet I need to be told what to wear," I muttered, protesting under my breath as I pulled on my walking boots and straightened the crease of my brown trousers. I tugged my necktie to length and tucked it into my waistcoat. "I'm French. If nothing else, I know how to dress."

"Don't dawdle, Henri." Penny's tone was sharp. "*Dépêchez-vous*." She wanted me to hurry.

I squinted into the small oval mirror over the washbasin. "I'll be out shortly." I decided my whiskers would take another day's growth without making me look like a raving Berserker.

I stepped into the sitting room where Penny stood beside the radio cabinet. "Darling, you look wonderful. Let's see if we can find a tea shop or café that sells pastry, all right?"

She called me *darling*.

PENNY FINISHED her breakfast tart and brushed pastry flakes from her skirt while I tipped my cup for the last drip of coffee. My eyes strained from studying the faces and details of the people passing by.

"Are you looking for someone specifically?" she asked through an exhale.

I dabbed my lips with my napkin. "Not specifically, no. Are you?"

"Let's just see what we might." She stood before I could hop to my feet and help her with her chair. "Shall we head that direction?"

"Allow me." I pushed her chair under the table and offered her my arm. I whispered, "Is there anything I should be looking for? Tells?"

She stopped and pulled me aside, letting others walk past. "I want you to be prepared and cautious and attentive to everything and everyone around us, but I don't want you to anticipate or expect anything. We need to be fluid. Whatever we expect, it will surely be something else. Our job is to react to whatever *does* happen. Simply be ready for that."

My thoughts shifted from the soft, sultry way she said *fluid* to the idea that I was wholly unprepared to react to the myriad unspoken possibilities. That revelation compelled me to follow Penny's lead.

I held open a door at a housewares shop and followed her inside. The stout shopkeeper stood at attention at the sight of Penny. I wondered, at first, if he recognized her, but soon determined the man to be as awestruck by her poise and form as I was.

"*¿Puedo servirle, por favor?*" He quick-stepped toward Penny.

"*Gracias. Tú...?*" She stalled a moment. "Do you buy jewelry? Consign, perhaps?" She held out her hand and pointed to the simple gold ring on one finger.

He shook his head and studied her ring. "*Es un anillo bonito.*" He bent for a closer examination. "*Sólo fuera muy especial. Pero, lamentablemente, no. I have too many in my case.*" He gestured to the glass display cabinet behind him, filled with gold and silver of every shape and style.

"I see." Penny glanced at me and dropped her shoulders as if she were disappointed.

"We can look around. Maybe you'll see something you like," I said.

The clerk nodded. "*Si, por favor.*" He eyed me for a split second and then returned his focus to Penny, his hand sweeping around the shop. "Or maybe you have something else to sell?"

Penny's brow rose. "What kinds of things do you buy?" She crossed her arms in such a way as to lift and emphasize her breasts. I was well aware of how effective this tactic might be.

The man's brow rose to match. "If you have artwork—paintings or small sculptures, even fine rugs—I have a gentleman who is always looking for such things."

Penny and I exchanged a glance. Were we making headway? I cleared my throat. "How does that work? Do you give us his name, or do we bring our things back to you, and you manage the transaction?"

"I take care of everything for you." He rubbed his double chin with his knuckles. "*Mi asociado...* he prefers to stay in the shadows."

Penny nodded and slipped her hand in the crook of my elbow. "We'll look around, and perhaps we'll be back later—if we think of something your friend might find interesting."

We perused a cabinet loaded with porcelain figurines, crystal baskets, and bells of different shapes and compositions. The next shelf contained tiny bisque dolls wearing Spanish costumes of red and gold. Penny leaned close to my ear and, smiling, pointed toward one of the more colorful ensembles.

"I'm going to try something," she whispered. She whirled around to the shopkeeper. "Do you know Elize Bellmont?" Penny shook her head. "That's not it, is it, Darling? Belfort. Do you know Elize Belfort?"

"At the hotel?" the man replied. His face reddened with disdain. "I have heard of the woman, but do not trade with her."

"Oh?" I raised my brow.

"No, she is a symp... I do not know the word. She does business with people I do not."

"I see," Penny said. "That is good to know."

The man's face returned to its natural tanned complexion. "If you want a particular item, I can ask my associates. If you are looking for travel arrangements, perhaps you should try another place."

Penny shot me a *your-turn* glance, and I obliged. "Nothing in particular at the moment, but perhaps we will return soon."

"And maybe then I can serve you better," the man said.

We visited a few other similar shops around the village, using the same questions and getting almost the same answers.

It seemed Elize was either loved or hated by those who knew her—and everyone knew her to some degree. All the shops maintained a surplus of jewelry; we attempted to sell both Penny's ring and the one that hung around my neck, with no interest.

At the last shop, Penny suddenly took a new tack. "Artwork?" She offered a soft exclamation. "You wouldn't have anything by Schiele?"

The owner, a thin, blond man with a reddish-blond caterpillar of a mustache, curled his finger around his chin. "Not here in the shop. Not today. Are you looking for a landscape, still life, a portrait, or something else?" He crossed his arms, leaned against a display case, and lowered his voice. "Something more risqué?"

I cleared my throat, protesting his ungentlemanly suggestion, but Penny squeezed my arm as if this was expected.

"I would be happy with anything by him."

"I have similar…"

"Sorry, but I'm only interested in Schiele." Penny pushed out her bottom lip.

The man's gaze focused on her lips—she was so good at manipulation—and then he offered an upturned palm.

"If you give me your name and where I might reach you, I can hunt for a Schiele. I have very good connections."

Penny scratched out her information on a scrap of paper from her handbag and gave it to the man. "I hope you can find what I want."

My jaw fell slack. She mesmerized me and everyone else to whom she spoke. "Penelope, *Chère.*" I placed my hand on her lower back. "We should probably go back."

"Of course." She sighed. "I shan't get my hopes up. He doesn't see the value in your ring."

It was his turn to clear his throat. "Perhaps I should look again." The man held out his hand again.

Penny loosened my tie and collar and extracted the ring from beneath my shirt. The gold band held a round-cut diamond flanked on either side with smaller twin rubies.

He pulled a loupe from his breast pocket and studied the gems while Penny tethered him with a tight grip on the chain.

"It is exquisite, isn't it?" he murmured. His gaze met hers. "I can offer you a fair price for it."

Without regard to me, Penny proceeded to negotiate a deal with the broker, handing me the cash as we left the shop.

We walked another thirty steps down the walk before she spoke. "Are you angry that I agreed to such a low price?"

I stammered, trying to catch up to her plan. "It was my mother's. But that was actually quite more than I expected it to bring."

"Then why are you angry?" She sucked her lips into a tight, thin line. "Oh, you're sentimental. Of course you are. That's why you kept it on the chain." She glanced over my shoulder. "Would you like me to buy it back?"

"No."

"I'm sure he'd give it back to me." Her eyes flashed with that... *je ne sais quoi*. She smoothed her hand over my lapel.

"I'm quite sure he would." I placed my hand over hers. "No. I don't need the ring anymore."

"You are angry because I didn't ask you?"

"I'm not angry." I took a step back. "I merely—I didn't expect him to buy it. No one else wanted it. I was surprised."

She slipped her hand into the crook of my arm. "Henri, when we walked into the shop, you had two things that he wanted. And now you only have one."

"And what about the painting? Why that particular artist? Isn't his work a bit crude, both literally and figuratively speaking?"

Penny dabbed at the corner of her mouth. Nothing was there, so I assumed it was a ploy to draw my attention to her mouth. Everything seemed a ploy with her. She clutched my arm tighter. "His portrait work is undoubtedly crude. Not ethereal like the impressionists or crisp like the masters. Nonetheless, he is the artist I need." She glanced down at her wristwatch. "Best we go back to the hotel."

"Do we have a train to catch?" I asked. Her pace quickened, and I took longer strides to keep up.

"We have a friend to welcome to Spain."

I stared at the side of her head, noticing the determined grin she affixed to her mouth. "You don't tell me anything."

16

MONDAY, JUNE 18, 1945, CANFRANC, SPAIN

The townsfolk of Canfranc bustled through the streets, conducting their business without looking up, and Penny strode down the street with the same determination. But my eyes scanned the block. She'd insisted I pay attention, and now I couldn't help but do so.

A scarf caught in my peripheral vision, turning my head more than I liked, and I slowed my pace. Gold and olive paisleys covered the crimson background of the scarf. I recognized the fabric. I'd seen it my whole life—a signature pattern of one of the shops in my childhood village. The woman wearing it used it to cover her hair, pulled more loosely around the face, to shield her identity.

"We need to keep going," Penny insisted.

"You go ahead. I want to check on something."

"Is it important? Should I stay with you?" Her hand tugged at my arm.

"It's probably nothing at all, *ma chère*." I pointed my chin toward the small stone chapel across the street. "I will catch up with you before you arrive at the train station."

"Be safe," she said. She skipped ahead of me, and I waited as she crossed the next intersection, keeping half my attention on the woman in the red patterned scarf climbing the church's steps.

As the woman reached the top step, one of the gothic arched doors swung open, and a priest greeted her and welcomed her inside.

I hesitated, wondering if this was the right thing to do. Shaking off my doubts, I strode across the road and took the steps two at a time. No one greeted me. I pulled the heavy door open with a noticeable creak. The inside was lit only with candles, perhaps a thousand candles, down the walls and in the chandeliers above. However, the dark mahogany walls and floors absorbed the light, reflecting only a somber glow into the room.

My eyes struggled to adjust to the change, and when my focus returned, I found I was alone. No priest, no woman, no one but the plaster saints mounted to ornately carved columns. The crackled white faces stared down with disapproving sternness from all sides. Acting out of deep-seated guilt, I crossed myself, dropped a few coins into the designated box, and picked up a narrow taper. I lit a candle and whispered a prayer as the flame grew and melded with the amber glow of the room.

I sat at the end of the back pew and pondered what to do next. Hurry to catch up with Penny? Probably. Wander the chapel until I found the woman? What would that accomplish? She was likely a cleaning woman or such. The scarf may have been a gift from a friend or a souvenir. Perhaps I'd been imagining the design. Wanting it to be more.

A click of a latch drew my attention to a confessional door opening at the side of the room, closer to the altar. The woman stepped out, and her scarf shone red in the dim light. She took a few more steps and knelt before the altar, crossing herself. I moved swiftly down the center aisle with silent strides until I stood behind her. When she turned and recognized me, her gasp echoed off the icons surrounding us.

"What are you doing here?" Elize asked.

I gestured toward the nearest pew and waited for her to sit. "I followed you inside."

"You've been following me?" Her fingers tugged at the ends of her scarf.

"No. I only just saw you on the street." I placed my hand on her shoulder and felt her trembling. She was suddenly the Lisette I had known years before. "What are you doing here?"

She jerked almost imperceptibly toward the confessional cabinet. "Taking care of some things. You know."

What I remembered was that Lisette was never a religious woman. She'd even made fun of my dependence upon my faith several times. Had her life changed so much when she became Elize? Or was she manipulating me—using my religious practices to avoid answering my question? I swallowed hard. This woman I had loved so fiercely was a stranger, and I had become cynical about everyone.

"Do you have so much to confess?" I asked, hoping my voice sounded light and teasing.

"Don't we all?" She shook her head. "Of course, not you, Henri. You pride yourself on your dignity and justice." She reached out and touched a finger to the lapel of my waistcoat.

"Perhaps pride, then," I whispered.

Her palm slid up to my cheek. "No." She blinked slowly, and a sadness came over her mouth. "You are not innocent—God knows how much you have seen. Too much to be innocent. But you are pure of heart. Somehow, in the midst of all of this, you kept that. Don't let that go, Henri. Never let that go."

"If you're in trouble, whatever it may be, I can help you."

"This is not for you to help." She glanced up as the priest left his side of the confessional and went back to the street doors. "I have to go. You must go, too. You've stayed too long already." She stood, pushing down on my shoulder. "Stay a moment longer. Say your prayers, whatever you must do. Don't move from here until I've gone. Do you understand?"

"I can help."

"By doing what I say, you are helping." She hurried down the aisle toward the doors, leaving without genuflecting.

I turned back toward the altar and murmured a prayer for her safety. I didn't know exactly what she was doing, but I was certain it was dangerous. I left the chapel with a bow and a blessing; the priest had disappeared like a whisper.

Scanning the street in both directions, I found no trace of Elize. I suspected she'd returned to the hotel, but I had no way to know. My pace quickened as I made my way back, and my neck swiveled to scan the road, the shops, and the faces of everyone around me. Light-headedness overcame me, and I realized I needed to keep my focus straight. I was a goose on the street, probably drawing attention to myself. This wouldn't do at all.

When I reached the last crossroads before my destination, with the majestic hotel looming, I stopped for a deep, woodsy breath of mountain air. I needed clarity. I was a knotted rope being pulled and yanked between two women. One drew me closer while the other let me slip away. But I was still a man, a soldier, and a police inspector at that. I needed to stand up and be strong, not jerked to and fro.

My next step was solid. I crossed the road with purpose and

determination. I would not convalesce as a man in a wheelchair, pushed around by a pretty nurse. I summoned Penny for a reason, and I would master this situation with or without her.

As the elevator door opened to my floor, Penny greeted me with her warmest smile.

"There you are, Darling." She tapped on her wristwatch and traded places with me. "Now go freshen up quickly and meet me on the platform. The train will arrive in just a few minutes."

Before I could utter a word, the elevator doors closed again, and she was gone.

"That woman," I muttered. I flared my nostrils as I inhaled every particle of oxygen in the hallway. "Don't stomp. Keep calm. Keep the anger, but use it to clear your mind." The words came out in near-silent huffs.

In my room, I pulled off my waistcoat and unbuttoned my shirt to check my wound and freshen up. I removed the empty chain from my neck and dropped it into my valet box. *She sold Lisette's ring without even asking me first.*

My anger swelled for a moment, then settled as I felt free from the past. Lisette was no more, but the woman wasn't dead—she lied to me to become someone else. As Lisette, she was sweet and adoring. As Elize, she was just as manipulative as Penny. Perhaps more so.

Reminding myself that I'd offered the ring for sale at three shops before Penny had sold it, I rebuttoned my shirt and shrugged into my jacket. Penny wasn't going to push me around anymore, nor would Elize.

Take a breath, man.

I glanced out my bedroom window to the mountainside where the murder had happened. The rumble of the arriving train vibrated the windowpane.

Down the hall, down the elevator, and across the walk to the train platform, I strode one determined step at a time. I nearly sprinted the last dozen steps, arriving just in time to see Jack Vogel—Penny's spy partner—stepping off the train and into Penny's embrace. I froze in place as he covered her mouth with his. My gut turned to stone, and I turned back toward the hotel. I needed a shot of whiskey to clear my mind. Maybe two. Maybe seven.

"Wait!" Penny's voice rose above the clamor of the platform. "Inspector Toussaint, we're over here."

I set my face to pleasant and turned to her without a word.

"Inspector Henri Toussaint, you remember my partner, Jack Vogel?" She shifted back to Jack, clutching his arm. "Jack, Henri is recuperating down here."

Jack pumped my hand with a vise grip. "What a coincidence that you should be here at the same time as Penny and me."

"Isn't it, though?" I answered. "Your woman is quite the coincidence coordinator, isn't she?"

Penny shot me a two-second glare and then softened her expression. "Why don't we all go to the hotel bar for a drink before dinner?"

"Just what I had in mind," I muttered.

Jack put on a grin that didn't reach his eyes. "Very good. I'll go ahead and check in while you two order the drinks. I'll catch up when I'm done."

Penny looped her arm through mine and kissed Jack's cheek. "Don't be long, darling."

Now, she was calling him *darling*. A growl swelled in my throat. "Penny, *ma chère*, why don't I leave you two to catch up? You don't need a third wheel complicating things, do you?"

Her hand gripped my arm tightly. "Nonsense, I need you with us."

Jack chuckled, striding ahead and into the hotel. I stopped, and Penny whipped around to face me, still clutching my arm.

"What is this about?" I asked in a low rumble. "What kind of trouble are you in? The truth this time?"

She stared after Jack and then focused her gaze on mine. "I tried—I will explain to you later. Everything."

"I don't think I can wait."

"There's no time right now. I need you to trust me. We'll go in and have drinks, and you'll see how Jack is."

"He seemed fine." I pulled her closer. "But I can't play any more games with you. I'm not your toy."

"I know that." Penny released a sigh. "I promise to tell you everything. I should have already, but I was afraid it would put you in more danger."

"More than all this?" I swallowed hard. "I've witnessed a murder, had my evidence stolen, been beaten and held by thugs—what more do you think will happen?"

Her left arm tightened around mine, and her right palm slid to my cheek. "You have put up with so much from me. Too much. You deserve much more than an explanation."

I swatted her hand from my face. "Don't. No more manipulation. I'll have drinks with you. Then you must explain everything."

17

MONDAY, JUNE 18, 1945, CANFRANC, SPAIN

We sat at the corner booth in the candlelight of the bar, as we had the night before.

"I have to make this quick—before Jack joins us. You deserve to know more." Penny's voice crackled with an anxiety I hadn't before perceived in her.

"Just about anything you tell me will be more than I know now." I tried to focus on her gaze, but her eyes were trained on the doors. "And when he comes back, what am I supposed to do? Just wait while you two make love over drinks?"

Her eyes shifted and fixed on mine. "You may, but you must trust that it isn't real." She glanced down at the table. "Jack is furious with me."

"So furious he can't keep his hands off you?" I wasn't being fair, but I didn't care.

Penny shook her head. "I tried to explain before. I lost my post in London. I've been shuffling papers for the last few weeks. I found this place in some of the documents. As you guessed, it seems to be a smuggling point—helping Nazi officers and soldiers with money escape justice. Some sell property stolen from the exterminated Jewish families to buy tickets, silence, and whatever else they need. They use this place to buy and sell priceless artwork and jewels."

"And so you came down here to investigate?" I punctuated my question with a sigh.

Her eyes shifted down and back to mine. "Actually." She licked her lips. "I sent you here to investigate."

A heavy veil lifted from my eyes, my mind, and my heart. "Of course," I muttered. She had been the one to make my reservations here. She'd been the one to pay for everything. I'm sure my superiors were given no choice in the matter. I pressed my palms into the table, ready to leave.

"Wait."

"You knew my—you knew Elize was here and who she was to me. You've just been using me this whole time."

Penny put her hand over mine. "I was. Yes."

"I can't…"

"Please." Her voice quivered. "Jack is going to send me back. I'll be fired and possibly jailed. Maybe worse."

"He won't. He loves you."

"I can assure you he doesn't. Maybe he thought he did." She swallowed hard. "Maybe he did before. I don't know. But that's over now."

"He came here for you." I slipped my hand from beneath hers. "Like you came for me." My words carried a cruelty I only partially intended.

Her eyes pooled with unshed tears. "I deserve that." She sniffed. "He knows why I'm here, but—"

"But he wants to be the one to wrap up the case?" It was all I could think to say.

"No," she replied. "He—the department, rather—doesn't think it's worth bothering with now. More pressing things on the agenda. He'll escort me back. He would never have allowed me to come here if he'd known. That's why I sent you ahead."

"You arranged for me to come ahead, knowing I would call you when I realized what was happening here?" I shook my head and scowled. "You probably set up the murder as well?"

"I didn't; I swear to you." Her eyes shot to the door, where Jack stood, scanning the room. "Please don't say anything," she murmured. "Just listen."

Another sigh escaped my lips as Jack approached the bar and ordered our drinks. "I'll listen. But you can't expect me to believe anything you say," I whispered.

"That's fair enough. But if I can—" She cut herself short as Jack slid into the seat next to her.

"You're looking well, Toussaint," Jack said with an insincere heartiness. "The mountain air must be helping with your recovery."

"Clean air, healthy exercise, and good food." I nodded and leaned my body half an inch toward Penny. "And, of course, devastatingly beautiful companionship."

Jack glared at the woman between us and waved a finger toward the room. "All the women here seem quite attractive. I'd imagine you have your choice."

"Yes, well, my choice is clear." This wasn't Penny's plan, but I no longer cared.

Her gaze shot away from me and toward the barman.

Jack's spine straightened, and his chest puffed forward. "You might remember that Miss Tompkins is spoken for."

Penny coughed.

I matched Jack's attitude. "I prefer women who speak for themselves."

Jack set his glass down harder than necessary.

She held up her palms toward both of us. "Stop this. We're all friends here. Let's enjoy our drinks, and then we can discuss who's who after dinner." She glanced down at her watch. "Tonight's reception starts in another hour or so. We only have a few minutes to catch up before we must go upstairs and dress."

"I don't think—" Jack grimaced and shook his head.

Penny stroked his arm. "The evening reception is quite the tradition at this hotel. You can't miss it."

The man humphed and stared at the barman making our drinks. "What's taking him so bloody long?"

I started to slide to the edge of the booth. "I'll see if I can hurry him."

Jack pushed to stand up on his side. "I'll do it myself." He all but stomped to the bar, leaving Penny and me alone.

"I didn't realize he was so angry," I said.

Penny leaned toward my ear. "I think your improvisation may have set him off," she said, *sotto voce*.

"You should be appreciated. He didn't treat you like this when we were in France."

"I still had a job then. And he was defending me to you." She coughed as Jack faced us with our drinks balanced between his fingers. "Now the tables have turned."

He returned to his place on the other side of Penny. "You like whiskey, right?"

"*Merci*," I said, raising my highball toward Penny. "*To Mademoiselle*."

"To Penny," Jack answered.

"To us all." She tipped her glass back and drained it in two swallows.

Jack's eyes widened at her empty glass. "Well, chap, I hate to cut your holiday short, but I'll be taking your playmate back to London with me tomorrow."

I kept my expression stolid. "Actually, Miss Tompkins is assisting me with an investigation." I lowered my volume. "The holiday is our cover, but this is work. I'm sure you understand."

Jack's upper lip sneered to one side. "Don't you have that the wrong way 'round?" He scoffed. "I know she wrangled you into helping her with one of her wild ideas."

Without looking at Penny, I planted my elbow on the table and leaned toward the other man. "Listen to me. I witnessed a murder; she is here to help me solve it. Who better to help me with my investigation?"

Jack squinted and sniffed in his oh-so-British arrogance. "Perhaps someone who works for you and not me."

At this, Penny took my drink and tossed it back like a chaser. "I do not work for you."

Jack huffed. "After this little adventure, you may not work for anyone."

"That's fine with me." She handed back my glass with an apologetic glance.

This wasn't going to anyone's plan. I considered apologizing. "Pardon, but—"

Jack held out his hands, palms down, as if he were pressing the tension into the floor. "Penny, you know you cannot simply walk away from your job. It's not the sort of thing that allows for it."

Penny turned her rage directly to Jack. "I see. They can walk away from me, but I cannot leave them?" She leaned another inch toward his face. "Are you here to kill me?"

"What?" he sputtered. "No. Of course not."

She eased her body backward in my direction. "I'll return to London when I've helped my friend resolve his investigation."

Jack gasped and slid from the booth, tossing "I'll see you at the reception," over his shoulder.

Penny's tension melted away as she leaned back against my chest. "I didn't realize he was so angry with me." She sat upright again and offered a tight-lipped smile. "I'm sorry about your drink. You can have mine at dinner." She gestured for me to slide out of the booth. "Thank you for defending me to him."

I didn't move other than to put my hands on her shoulder. "I meant what I said. All of it. I will help you do whatever you intend to do here. But I need your help in solving this murder on the mountain. I'll help you, and you help me. And then you can return to London, and you'll never have to see me again."

Her eyes softened in my cold gaze. "That might be the worst thing I can think of right now." Her hands slid to my cheeks, and she leaned in for a soft, slow kiss.

My body warmed as though *I'd* just tossed back two whiskeys.

"We should go up to our rooms to dress for tonight." She shifted to stand.

"Wait." I slipped my arms around her waist. "You asked Jack if he was here to kill you."

"Yes."

"Could he be here to kill me?"

She smiled and kissed the bridge of my nose. "No, *mon amour*. I wouldn't let him have the pleasure."

18

MONDAY, JUNE 18, 1945, CANFRANC, SPAIN

*a*fter escorting Penny to her room, I stalked the rest of the hallway to mine, with a chorus of warning voices screaming in my ears. *She's dangerous. She's an assassin. She's using you. She'll be the death of you.* Then the other side. *She's protecting you. She values you. She wants you. She's beautiful.*

"It doesn't matter what she looks like if she gets me killed," I muttered once I'd closed the door, locking it behind me.

I tussled out of my clothes and freshened myself quickly, wetting my hair and scrubbing the day off as if it were mud from the French trenches. I was ready to be free of the whole thing. I toweled off, splashed on a handful of cologne, pulled on my pants, and laid out my trousers on the bed.

"This is ridiculous. She's an assassin—it's what she does." I checked over my white dress shirt. No stains. No severe wrinkles. "Well, that may be, but she hasn't killed anyone here... yet."

I raked my damp hair into place. "Not yet. But what is it they say? No time like the present?" I dry-sponged the lapels of my dinner jacket.

Socks, trousers, shoes, shirt, belt, cufflinks, and watch. No need for the chain; nothing hanging from my neck anymore. "She's not going to kill you, man. And she won't let Jack kill you, either." The words hung hollow in the air of my suite.

Standing in front of my mirror, I made one last argument with myself. "*Mon Dieu*, are you not French? Are you not a man? A detective? A decorated soldier? Why would you hide behind a woman? Why do you doubt yourself with *this* woman?" I inhaled down to my core and left the voices behind.

At Penny's door, I didn't have a chance to knock. "There you are, darling." She pulled me into her room. "Just one last thing."

She wore a brilliant green figure-skimming satin gown with narrow straps and a choker of pearls. A black wrap draped from elbow to elbow, dusting her derriere, not that I noticed. She plucked a white rose from the bouquet on her dresser, pinching the stem short.

"You look lovely," I whispered as she stepped toward me. A cloud of jasmine and roses floated around us. "And you smell heavenly."

She tugged my lapel and poked the stem of the rose through the narrow buttonhole. "Now it's perfect." She grabbed my elbow and walked me to her door. "Are you ready?"

I locked her door from the outside, and she dropped her key into the black silk reticule at her wrist. She snugged my arm against her body as we approached the reception hall.

Jack stood at the door, staring at his pocket watch. "I have a table for us near the chanteuse."

"You would," Penny murmured as we crossed the room to the

woman at the microphone. "And blonde—just your type," under her breath.

I pulled Penny's chair out for her and moved my chair half an inch closer to hers than Jack's.

"I'll find the alcohol," Jack chirped and left us.

Leaning to Penny's ear, I whispered, "No killing tonight, right?"

She sighed. "I told you—he isn't here to kill you. And hopefully not me, either."

"I'm not asking about him. I'm asking about you."

Penny scoffed. "Why would you even ask such a thing?"

"You're forgetting; I've seen your work. I've witnessed you garrote a man while reciting the Lord's Prayer." The memory was hazy but still lingered, and I mentally crossed myself.

"I'm not garroting anyone tonight, my love. I promise." She patted my hand.

The singer began "The Nearness of You" after a trumpet trill faded. Jack eyed the curvy blonde while he distributed champagne to Penny and whiskey to me.

I took the highball in my hand and shifted it out of reach of Penny. Dancers filled the floor, and the room pulsed with every tss-tss across the snare drum.

Jack reached out for Penny's hand. "Shall we?"

She stood and offered a quick glance of apology to me.

"Have fun," I said, flicking my fingers toward the dance floor. I scanned the room for Elize, and my gaze finally landed on her, instructing her wait staff. She wore an amber strapless gown, with a narrow edge of dark brown fur at the straight neckline. I downed a full, fiery gulp of Scotland's finest and swayed my way across the room toward her.

Her eyes squinted at my approach. "I told you to leave."

"*Oui*, you did, but unfortunately, I'm disappointing everyone today." Without asking, I slipped my hand around her back and took her right hand in my left. "You see? I cannot help it."

She released a slow sigh, and the taut muscles in her lower back relaxed against my palm. "Henri, you are going to get us both killed."

"For some reason, I think you can take care of yourself." I rested my stubbled chin against her forehead.

"I can take care of myself better if I'm not having to guard over you and your friend." She leaned her head away from mine. She moved her hand to my jaw. "You haven't shaved since you've arrived. It's scratchy."

"You don't like it?"

She shook her head but smiled. She raised a finger to indicate Penny on the other side of the room. "Does she like it?" Before I could answer, she tilted her face toward my ear. "And who is her friend?"

"*Her* friend, indeed." I must have smirked.

"Not yours?"

"No. Not mine."

Elize sighed. "I am sorry for that—*they* appear quite affection-ate, eh?"

I shrugged. "You should know better than anyone that things are not always as they appear." I didn't apologize for the jab.

"That I do." She shifted toward them, undermining my lead. "Let's see if they're up to a switch, shall we?"

"Perhaps you only want to dance with men closer in height to you?"

She laughed. "Perhaps." She pressed her lips into a flat, tight line.

As we moved around the floor, we gained a few steps, and once we were within reach, I tapped Jack's shoulder. "Switch?"

His mouth quirked to one side, then opened into a broad grin at the sight of Elize. "Certainly." He offered Penny to me and took Elize into his arms in one swift turn.

Penny's gaze landed on my lips for a moment; then she rested her forehead on my jaw. "Have a pleasant visit with Mademoiselle Belfort?"

"I'm sure it was just as glorious as yours with Jack." I held her closer than I should have and then loosened my grip. "Sorry about the scruff. Elize said it was itchy against her face. I'll shave tomorrow."

"Don't you dare." Penny pressed her smooth skin against my stubble. "I like rough things."

I scoffed. "Of course you do."

She worked her left hand from my shoulder to the back of my neck. "The ability to grow a beard and shave it off is a great asset in my line of work. It completely changes one's appearance. Perhaps I'm jealous, but I loved your mustache the moment I met you in France."

"My mustache, but not me?"

"Well, Monsieur Inspector, you *were* trying to put me in prison."

The song faded into "The Very Thought of You," and I felt her smile rise against my cheek.

"You know, we still use the guillotine."

Her breath chuffed on my neck. "I don't think anyone would say what I'd done—had I been the killer—was premeditated. Maybe a crime of passion, no?"

I allowed my right hand to press into her back just a little bit deeper. "You are a woman of passion, I've discovered."

As we turned, we simultaneously realized that Jack and Elize were no longer dancing together. Jack had a raven-haired woman in his arms, and Elize danced with an older, portly gentleman. Another thing that caught my eye was the ring on Elize's left middle finger—the engagement ring I'd given her so many years ago.

"*Ma chère*," I began, trying a hand at nonchalance. "Do you mind if we switch again? I have something else I need to ask her."

"Of course," Penny answered almost before I finished my question.

We danced our way to Elize and her partner, and I tapped the man's shoulder, as was customary. He offered a stiff from-the-waist bow to Elize, and we made the exchange.

"You *really are* going to be the death of me, Henri," Elize whispered.

"The ring."

Her fingers tightened on my shoulder. "I always liked this ring."

"Then you might have kept it when I gave it to you the first time." My words seeped through gritted teeth.

"I couldn't." She drew a deep breath. "Someday, you'll understand."

A commotion stirred in the middle of the dance floor, and we turned to see what had happened. Penny stood with her hands over her face, huffing and stifling a series of moans and whines. Her dance partner sprawled on the floor, his face bright red. He clutched his left arm but couldn't speak.

We rushed to his side and knelt to see what could be done.

"Someone, please help him," Penny sobbed. Jack hurried to her and draped his jacket over her shoulders.

Elize studied the man and pulled his mouth open to expose a

purple, swollen tongue. I clasped my hands together and began beating a steady rhythm on his sternum, as I'd witnessed field medics do a dozen times. I stopped and checked for a pulse. Nothing.

Elize had called out for a doctor, and her assistants scrambled away in three directions. Her face showed more worry than had ever crossed her beautiful visage.

I pounded upon him again for another long minute, hoping to give him a second chance. But nothing. The color ebbed from his face; his eyes peered at the ceiling and beyond. He was gone.

With a snap of her fingers, Elize had his body removed from the room. She instructed her staff to bring out another round of champagne and asked the musicians to play something snappy. She followed the body out and disappeared.

Dance partners resumed positions and chattered as "Let's Face the Music and Dance" wound out from the band.

Jack and I escorted Penny back to our table from either side. She trembled but dropped Jack's coat from her shoulders and handed it to him.

"I'll be fine." Her voice remained steady.

I glanced toward the door to the hallway. "Who was that man?"

Jack turned a palm that direction. "He was an SS officer—I heard several people saying it while you were... working on him." Jack reached for Penny's hand.

She shifted away from him toward me. "I think I'd like to go back to my room." She took a beat. "Jack, you should stay here and see what more you can discover."

"I don't take orders from you." His tone carried no emotion.

"Fine," she responded. "Do what you want. I only thought you might *want* to look into it." Penny drew a breath. "We were dancing one minute; the next, he was clutching his arm and dropping to the floor."

"Probably a heart attack," Jack and I both said.

Jack continued. "Right age, right size, right situation for it. He'd probably spent the last several years overindulging in everything. It couldn't have happened to a more deserving man."

A tiny scoff escaped Penny's lips. "I just wish it hadn't happened in my arms."

I held up her wrap for her but decided against it. "This won't do you any good." I slipped my jacket off and snugged it over her shoulders. "Let's go out for a breath of fresh air."

She bobbed her chin and took my arm, casting a weak glance at Jack. "I'll see you in the morning."

As we maneuvered through the crowd toward the doors on the balcony, my mind whirred. Obviously, a heart attack, right? Just because he was a Nazi—just because he died in the arms of a Nazi killer—literally. That didn't mean she murdered the man. Did it? *It couldn't have happened to a more deserving man.* Isn't that what Jack said?

The door closed behind us, and the cool night air wrapped us together. Penny leaned against my body, her fingers inching around my waist. I breathed her perfume. Tightened my arms around her. Pulled her bosom to my chest. I held the moment in my mind, considering it almost perfect. Almost.

"*Chère?*"

"Yes, love."

I tangled my fingers through her long, dark hair. "You promised me, not an hour ago, that you wouldn't murder anyone tonight."

She leaned back and slipped her hands to either side of my

jaw. "No, darling. I promised not to garrote anyone tonight." She punctuated her statement with a long, deep kiss.

Pushing Penny to arm's length, I glared. "Penelope Tompkins, you cannot run wild, assassinating people at will."

She pushed out an exasperated sigh. "I'm not running wild. He was an SS Officer about to be smuggled to Argentina or somewhere. He was about to escape justice, headed off to live out the rest of his life on the wealth of the same people he murdered."

"We could have brought him to the authorities. He would have answered for his crimes."

"In this place?" She gestured toward the reception hall. "No. He wouldn't have answered for anything. He'd be handed another glass of champagne—by *your* mademoiselle."

I crossed my arms over my chest. "Killing him wasn't your call to make."

She swallowed hard and shook her head. "Three months ago—in these identical circumstances—it would have not only been my call but my duty to kill that man."

I sniffed. "I understand wartime directives, Penny. I fought as a soldier long before I was sent to be an inspector. You're not the only one pulled from fieldwork."

"Yes. You saw blood, death, and destruction. You witnessed people and homes and whole towns slaughtered and razed. Me, too." She drew a shuddering breath. "Have you ever seen a woman who'd been raped to death with a swastika carved into her breast?"

"No."

"That was the work of Yann Kohler, *your* would-be killer."

Squeezing my eyes closed against the sight I imagined, I shook my head. "But this man…"

"This man?" She swallowed hard. "Have you ever witnessed a

child being ripped from her mother's arms and then hacked to pieces in front of her family? No questioning. No reason at all other than to try out a new sword? For the mere amusement of that man?" Her arm stretched to a point. "*That* man."

Her words painted an image in my brain I didn't want to see. I didn't want to imagine such a thing. A child, dead at the hands of a devil. "That man," I repeated. It was no longer a question. The woman's fire suddenly burned in my chest.

"He made a point to tell the baby's family that it was no great loss. That a Jew was less than human. That he'd done the world a favor." She licked her lips and sniffled. "I did him a favor by killing him with a pinprick under his arm. It was so much kinder than he deserved."

Gathering her back into my arms, I struggled to calm the tremors that shot through both our bodies. I fought the bile churning upward from my stomach. I swallowed cool air, swallowed my righteous indignation, swallowed my past. "We won't let them leave here."

Penny nuzzled into my neck. "I can't do it alone, and Jack won't help."

I cupped her face in my hands, raising her tear-glittered eyes to match my gaze, and I resolved myself. "I will do whatever you ask me to do."

19

TUESDAY, JUNE 19, 1945, CANFRANC, SPAIN

*B*efore the sun broke over the mountains, I paced my suite, trying to walk out the knot that formed in the pit of my stomach. On one hand, I was beholden to Penny—perhaps not beholden. That word wasn't quite precise. I needed to help her. To keep her secrets and cover her vulnerabilities. I needed to protect her, though I believed she was capable of protecting herself—maybe better than I could.

On the other hand, I pondered my relationship with Elize. She wanted me gone. She'd have been happy to have never seen me again. How could she have walked away so easily? Allowed me to think she was dead. Allowed my heart to break so thoroughly that I might have never healed.

The choice shouldn't be a choice at all. So why was I still pacing? I wrung my hands and forced myself to still my feet and look out the window. Pink fingers of sunrise shot up from the jagged fringe of granite peaks. My eyes wandered down to the middle of the mountain opposite the hotel, where the first murder happened.

Murder.

Perhaps that was the root of my restlessness.

Penny had murdered a man in a room full of witnesses. No one had even suspected it—besides me. But her explanation was valid. A man who could kill a child, a babe, in front of her family as he'd done—he could kill anyone. He had killed. Probably more people than I could count. I'd read about the mass executions—by gas chambers or firing squads. By starvation.

Less than human. My blood boiled. My fists clenched. My nails dug into my palms. I would have murdered the man if I'd been in Penny's shoes... if I had seen what she'd seen.

Deep breath.

I shook off the tension and decided to dress. Penny would be around soon, and I didn't want to make her wait on me.

After a quick splash on my face, I put on my grey worsted tweed suit. The lightweight single-breasted jacket mimicked one worn by Cary Grant in *The Philadelphia Story*, my favorite movie.

By the time I was ready to walk out the door, sunlight poured through the windows, saturating everything in the room with a white-yellow gleam. When I opened my hotel room door, I found Elize and Penny waiting in the hall. They both wore cotton day dresses. Elize's was blue, and Penny's was a red rose print. Elize's hand was poised mid-air to rap.

"*Bonjour, mademoiselles,*" I said automatically.

Elize didn't wait to be invited inside, and Penny followed her, only half a step behind.

"We must talk." Elize's tone warned me of a storm coming. "It's important."

Penny dropped into the chair beside my radio. "I suppose it's too early for a drink."

A long sigh escaped my lips before I could halt it. "What is it? You both seem upset."

"Do you know what she did last night?" Elize's arm extended toward Penny.

"I, uhm…" I wasn't sure of the best response.

"She murdered a German SS Officer in the middle of my reception." Her voice scraped high and thin as she kept her volume down.

"You cannot prove that," Penny said.

The reply was so short and curt that I almost smiled. "Murder? That sounds a bit of a reach." I directed Elize to the other armchair. "Perhaps we should all calm ourselves and discuss this rationally."

Elize shot icy daggers at me. "You know she's an assassin, Henri. She murdered the man." She did not sit down.

"I'm not admitting to anything. But even if I did kill the man, he deserved it." Penny crossed her legs and examined her fingernails as if we were chatting about the weather.

I held up my hand, wanting to keep peace between the women, though my hopes were sinking fast.

"It doesn't matter whether he deserved it," Elize began. "Everyone *knows* he deserved it. But I needed him alive."

My face went flat. Had she said she needed the man *alive*?

Penny uncrossed her legs and leaned forward in her seat. "What?"

Elize stalked into the bathroom and turned on the water in the basin, then came back into the room and switched on the radio, tuning it to a music station as the static cleared. She glanced up at the wall and turned her back to whatever she detected there.

I assumed that was the location of a peephole or camera or whatever she used to spy on my suite.

She lowered her voice. "I was supposed to send him safely to Lisbon tomorrow. Today, rather. He was supposed to be on a train this afternoon."

"He still can be," Penny replied.

I couldn't help but chuff, and I put my hand up to stifle my "cough."

Elize scowled. "If you'd have assassinated him in his room, maybe. But you did it in the middle of my ballroom. Everyone in the hotel knows he's dead."

"That's true," I said, letting my gaze fall on Penny.

She stood and faced Elize, leaving only inches between their faces. "You were going to let him escape—to South America or the like. He'd have never faced justice for his crimes."

"You are neither his judge nor his jury," Elize answered.

"And you're no better than him," Penny muttered. Her arm swung back, and I caught it before she could slap Elize.

I pulled Penny back a step. "Please," I said. "I need you both to calm down."

At this, both women turned on me. "Don't tell me to calm down," they said with one voice.

I stepped back with my arms raised in surrender, deciding that if there was going to be slapping—or any violence at all—I didn't wish to be involved.

Crossing her arms at her waist, Elize huffed. "I'm aware the man deserved to die. But I needed to send him to Lisbon. The fact that he died in my hotel will throw suspicion upon me."

Penny shrugged. "Well, I couldn't allow him to leave this place."

"He was an assignment for you, then?" Elize asked.

"I won't confess to killing him. As far as I'm concerned, he died of a heart attack." Penny matched Elize's stance.

Finally, Elize turned to face me and adjusted her expression to one of piteousness. "Your friend here has put a death mark on me."

I shook my head. "Now you're exaggerating. Penny isn't here to kill you."

"I give you my word," Penny said.

I shot her a warning glance about making promises.

Elize drew a short breath. "I'm not worried about her killing me." She turned to stare out the window. "As you may have discovered, there are plenty of people running around this place with guns and knives." She paused to tilt her head toward Penny. "And various other weapons."

My thoughts cranked through the little scenarios I'd witnessed in the scant days I'd spent in Spain so far. I'd only had a mild suspicion of Elize's involvement until now. "You're working for the Nazis?" My stomach churned at the words.

"Not only the Germans. There is money to be made in both directions." Elize swallowed hard. "But only if you can deliver what you promise." She walked back and made a weak attempt at reaching out for me before dropping into the empty chair. "And now I can't."

My heart lurched. I loved this woman... once. I sank to one knee in front of her—as I had so many years ago. "We can help. If we all work together." I stared at the ring on her finger—the ring I had given her—and I thought about the shop where I'd sold it. "You have a network already in place. We can use that."

"No!" She leaned away from me. "No, you don't understand. I won't be safe as long as you're here in Canfranc. I've asked you to leave. Over and over, I've asked you. You seem to think that, because we had something before, I won't have you removed from the hotel. But if you push me, if you give me no choice, I will. Now, please, you have to leave this place. Both of you. And your friend."

I raised my gaze to Penny, who offered me an almost imperceptible shake of her head. I let mine rise and fall the same way. We agreed in silence.

"We aren't going anywhere, Elize." I reached out for her hand, but she pulled it from my loose grasp.

"Then you'll be here to see me die." She stood and marched to the door. "Goodbye, Henri." And she left.

I pulled myself upright while Penny turned off the sink tap and the radio. She slipped her arms around my waist.

"Perhaps she'll come around." Penny's tone lacked sincerity.

"She won't." I drew a deep breath of Penny's perfume. This time, I resisted the lustful thoughts that usually accompanied her nearness. Instead, my mind filled with a contented peace, knowing I was doing the right thing. My heart didn't race. My ears didn't pound. I only held her close and breathed in her confidence and strength.

20

*A*rm in arm, Penny and I strode swiftly down the hall to Jack's room, catching him as he opened the door to leave. Penny shooed him back into the room, where she hurried to lock the door and run the tap in his bathroom.

"What's all this, then?" Jack back-stepped at our barrage.

Penny wasted no time. "Your room is almost certainly under surveillance, and we need to talk."

Jack's brow dropped low over his eyes. "Under surveillance by whom?"

I directed him to a chair while Penny searched the walls and furnishings for holes or other spying mechanisms.

Jack protested, and I waited until Penny pointed to where I should stand to block our conversation from any possible intrusion.

Penny stood at another angle. "We don't have time to go over everything. Elize wants us out of the hotel, and there are operations happening today that we must disrupt."

"Operations?" Jack looked stupefied. "Listen here, if Miss Belfort doesn't want us in the hotel, we should leave. None of this is sanctioned, in any case."

Anger flared in Penny's face, so I held up my hand in a plea for rational conversation. "I understand that you don't want Miss Tompkins in deeper trouble than she finds herself already. But let me assure you that I will be conducting my investigation regardless of your participation or lack thereof."

Jack shook his head. "You say murder, but you can't even prove that anyone died. Even if it happened at all, it was more likely an accident than a murder—someone having a misstep on the mountain path and simply falling."

Penny chewed on her lip and leaned close to Jack's face. "It's much more than that."

Jack matched her lean until their faces were only inches apart. "If you're suggesting I don't know that the Nazi's heart attack last night was by your design, then you forget who trained you."

Penny straightened her spine.

"But I don't have to report that to authorities. Not if you come back to London with me tonight." Jack crossed his arms over his puffed-out, self-pleased chest.

I shot a wary glance at Penny, asking silently for her to hold, and focused on Jack. "You don't have to stay. Go back to London. We won't think less of you. We won't consider you a coward."

"I'm no coward," he said.

"We know. That's what I said." I forced my voice to remain placating despite my insincerity.

"I'll have you know, I've been on dozens of very deadly, very complex missions all over the occupied territories. I've been in harm's way literally every day for the last five years. I have the scars to prove it." He tugged at his tie as though preparing to show me his scars.

"He does," Penny added with a matching flatness.

"Certainly, he does. I wouldn't question. Not for a moment." I shrugged one shoulder. "What I'm saying is that he does not have to participate in our venture, mademoiselle. I wouldn't want him to be in trouble with his superiors."

Jack furrowed his brow and crushed his chin to match. "It's not as though I don't have the authority to take action in the field. I'm not a dog."

"No, of course, you are no dog." I shrugged with the other shoulder. "But orders are orders."

"See here, man." He stood. "If there is something putting England at risk, I'm obliged to act. King and country and all that."

"Precisely," Penny chirped.

Jack planted his fisted hands on his hips. "But there's got to be a plan. We can't run into the line of fire unprepared."

It worked. I only had to keep my smug grin under control until we had him completely committed. "Right, I thought you'd be in for it. And Penny said you were the best troubleshooter in the world."

"He is." Penny nodded and took a step toward Jack.

I held up a finger. "But even with that," I said. I exhaled through my nose and worked my lips to one side. "Perhaps we shouldn't exploit Jack like this. No. If he feels it's best to go back to London, he should go."

"But I can't go back with you, Jack." Penny dropped her gaze to her hands. "Not yet. I've given my word to Henri. I'm the reason for some of his scars, and I have to make it up to him." She played on his sense of honor. "And when we've done with this investiga-

tion—assuming we survive—I'll come back and face the conse-
quences."

Jack shook his head. "A few more days won't make a difference, Pen." He offered his hand to me. "I'm in. But you'll have to
tell me everything. Our plan must be airtight."

I shook his hand, and Penny threw her arms over his neck,
whirling him around so she could wink at me. "I was sure you'd
understand. I knew you wanted justice as much as we did. One
last mission—isn't that what we always say?" she asked.

"One last mission," Jack echoed.

"One last mission," I murmured, letting my fears creep closer.

21

TUESDAY, JUNE 19, 1945, CANFRANC, SPAIN

We spent the morning planning how Jack and I might sneak back into the train storage building, and in particular, what we might find. My gut screamed that the smuggling operation and the murder were connected. Everyone in Canfranc seemed to have motive, means, and opportunity to commit murder, to escape justice, seek revenge, act on passion... any number of reasons.

Elize had all but admitted to smuggling Nazis out of the country. Though Spain was considered neutral, the country's proximity to Occupied and Vichy France made it a questionable refuge for escaping offenders. Even the short trip to Lisbon added another border between them and justice. From there, a Nazi might go anywhere.

Our jaunt around the town provided plenty of evidence of stolen Jewish family treasures and artwork being smuggled as well. We needed to be prepared for anything. Whatever it was, it was shipping out today.

Two trains were arriving soon. One shortly before noon, and one after. The first one shipping out was going back to France, so we assumed that was not our target. The latter one was headed to Lisbon, Portugal, and whispers around the hotel suggested it would be the perfect transport for anyone shipping out from the port city on their way to Argentina.

Freighters were certainly the means of transport. Plane passage was challenging to secure. Not only because of the shortage of passenger planes available, but also because the paperwork for tickets and such was more difficult to forge. A passenger would be easier to hide on a freighter.

Jack and I walked the perimeter of the hotel, then the train platform, and then the entire surrounding grounds, looking for any clues or vulnerable ways inside. What we found instead were extra guards on the storage facility, their jackets bulging to indicate concealed weapons.

"This may be bigger than just an SS officer," Jack suggested.

"As I suspect," I answered. "But Penny's actions last night, whether anyone believes it was murder or natural causes, may simply have them worried."

"That blasted woman." Jack huffed as we returned to the hotel lobby. "We'll all be killed. At the very least, I'll be discharged from service."

"As she was?"

He harrumphed. "She wasn't discharged. Her service was changed, that's all."

"And you are worried they will *change* your service?" I scanned the room. People bustled from every part of the lobby, anticipating the arrival of the first train.

"Well," Jack cleared his throat in the poshest, most British way. "They wouldn't station a man behind a tea trolley, would they?"

"Why not?" I asked as we paused beside a column and pulled out our cigarettes.

"It would be an insult." Jack tapped one smoke and discreetly replaced his pack in the inner breast pocket of his jacket. His fingers lingered on his shoulder holster for an extra second.

"But it isn't an insult to Penny? To any woman?" I stared at the pack in my hand and returned it to my pocket without taking a cigarette. I would save it for later.

"Bah, women are supposed to want a cottage and family and such. Servicing the tea trolley is just the short step down, a transition to that life while the home office debriefs her—assesses her liability." Jack lit his cig and gestured to me. "You aren't having one?"

"Not now." I flicked a finger toward the elevator. "Here she is."

Penny strode toward us as though she'd just won a prize. Her eyes dazzled, and she sucked on her bottom lip. I was jealous.

"Are you boys ready? The party is about to begin." She waved a cloud of Jack's smoke from between us and linked her hands over both our elbows. "Let's go." She dragged us toward the doors leading to the train platform.

This wasn't part of our plan. Was it something she'd concocted with Jack? The confusion in his expression said no.

"I thought we were going for lunch first," Jack said. "What has changed?"

"It's a surprise." Her voice was a morning bell, ringing with utter joy.

Jack obviously didn't care for surprises, and neither did I. "No. What is this? We never veer from our plans unless we have good reason," he said.

Penny pulled us to the edge of the walkway between the build-ings. "We're not veering at all. This is more of an addendum. And barely that." She pushed us next to each other and took the posi-tion of a mother scolding her children. "We've got a friend arriving on this train."

"What?" Jack and I asked in one voice.

She held up a finger before we said another word. "Don't worry. We are merely watching. When you see who it is, pretend you don't recognize—well, at least don't interact. All we are doing is confirming the arrival. After that, we'll go into the café and enjoy lunch, as planned."

Jack shook his head. "Is this another SS officer? Where are you getting information about this, and why do you have it and not me?"

I held up a placating hand. "Let's trust the lady, shall we?"

"She's going to get us all killed," Jack muttered.

"Pish posh." Penny shooed the statement away like a fly. "There are three of us. I doubt we'll *all be* killed."

Somehow, I didn't find that reassuring. I *was* the new recruit, after all.

Penny led us through the doors to the platform. Judging by the grip of her fingers on my upper arm, I wasn't sure if she was drag-ging us or being dragged.

We took our places just inside and out of the way of the people coming and going. The train from France approached with a rumble we felt through our shoes and up our legs. As it slowed to a stop inside the building, the rails screeched, and puffing white steam filled the room, dissipating as it reached the perimeter.

After a few seconds, travelers poured from the carriage doors like salt, spreading out and filling the room. I scanned faces, though I recognized no one. I'd assumed that Penny was directing that information to Jack, anyway.

Once most of the passengers disembarked, a few of the porters scrambled toward the door of the middle car. Two flanked the opening while one stepped up inside.

Penny tipped her forehead toward the car. "Good," she whispered.

The two porters on the platform reached up toward a pair of small, matching valises. One of the men took both bags, and the other reached out to the passenger exiting the carriage.

My eyes focused on the woman. Petite, with a soft roundness to her face and shoulders. Her wispy silver hair formed a braided crown, encircling the top of her head. She wore a lilac suit dress with white chiffon ruffles at the neck and cuffs. A black jeweled spider brooch dazzled from the lapel over her left breast. Her skirt ended just above her ankles, befitting a woman of her age, and I guessed her shiny black shoes were made of some exotic leather. She held a silver-handled cane, though she employed it more as an accessory than an aid.

The woman carried herself with an air of royalty, and the porters bowed and attended accordingly.

Jack glowered at Penny when recognition set in, and Penny beamed with admiration. I recognized the woman. The silhouette she cut was engraved in my mind forever since the moment she'd shot Yann Kohler to save my life in France.

Dahlia Lundt had arrived.

"What is that woman doing here?" Jack growled.

Penny didn't answer. She took our arms again and led us back into the hotel, crossing to the café.

Jack refused to back down. "Having Dahlia in Spain complicates everything. We'll waste valuable time protecting her. This was never part of the plan."

We found a table and ordered our meal, which consisted of lentil soup and finger sandwiches.

Penny barely flinched at Jack's vehemence. "This was always part of the plan."

"I wasn't aware." Jack's cheeks flared red.

"Because I didn't tell you." Penny shook out her napkin and slid it across her lap. "Because I was sure you would yell."

Jack's lips puckered and pushed in and out several times. "I am not yelling," he said, *sotto voce*.

Watching their exchange entertained me for a few more seconds, but when a tense grey silence hovered between them, I decided to engage. "I, for one, am glad to see the old woman again. After hearing Penny's tale of demotion, I wondered about Madame Lundt's situation."

Penny shifted in her chair toward me. "She didn't even receive the courtesy of a secretarial position. Mother put her out to pasture as soon as we returned to London."

"Mother?" I hadn't heard Penny use the expression, and I wondered. "That's what you call your superiors?"

"As a term of endearment," she explained. "Assignments often use Mother Goose as codes for identities and instruction."

Jack straightened his spine, obviously indignant at the whole conversation.

I paused while the server placed our soup bowls in front of us. "And when you say, 'put out to pasture,' what exactly do you mean?"

Penny sniffed. "When we returned to London, we were all debriefed." She tapped the table in front of Jack. "The men were sent out on more missions, both big and small, to tie up loose ends as the war came to a close."

The server then brought *un plateau de service* with our sandwiches, and we waited for him to retreat.

Jack started on his soup while Penny continued. "Some of the women, such as myself, were offered temporary training positions to instruct the next round of male recruits in the basics of spycraft. And once the courses were finished, we were allowed to stay on to serve tea and answer the telephones."

"That seems quite a waste of talent, wouldn't you say, Jack?"

He ignored me.

"And then women like Dahlia, gifted with years of priceless experience, were offered small pensions and told to settle in the country," Penny said.

"For their own protection," Jack added. He punctuated his statement by pressing his index finger into the table beside his plate, rattling his silverware.

"Of all the people in the world who need protection, I dare say Madame Lundt is not one of them." I considered the elderly woman every bit as dangerous as Penny. "After all, didn't she assassinate all of her husbands?"

Penny shook her head. "Only the last three. The first one died in the Great War. How she loved him." A wistful expression passed over her face.

Jack took a sandwich and waved the corner at Penny. "If she was part of your plan this whole time, what part does she play?" He took a bite and swallowed quickly. "How will an exiled royal—or whatever she's supposed to be—work into your scheme?"

Both of us focused on Penny. I was eager to hear the plan as well.

"As the widow of a high-ranking German officer, she is looking to sell some of her husband's war treasures in exchange for a new life somewhere unaffected by the devastation of war."

"Plausible," I said. "And did she bring some spoils with her?"

Penny's lip curled. "That was the plan, and I haven't heard otherwise."

My mind raced through the possible scenarios. "So she will take her treasures to one of the shops in the town and sell them there. And we will see who helps her and track who offers her assistance?"

Jack huffed. "And then we track where and how the goods are smuggled out. Train or other, right?"

"You two are sharp as always." She nodded to each of us in turn.

Jack brought up another point. "But today Henri and I are supposed to search the platform storage. Whatever Dahlia has brought with her won't be there yet."

"But we learned there will be a shipment of something going out today. This may prove the train is a regular smuggling route." I cut my eyes toward the bar on the opposite side of the lobby, where the barman had slipped us the message.

Penny nodded. "We don't know what's being shipped. Or whom, if it's a person."

Jack shot her a scathing glance. "Perhaps it was supposed to be the man you murdered last night. That would be something, wouldn't it?"

"Well," I began. "It might be. But if it was, then I do not suppose we'll find anything on the train, will we?"

Penny's expression flagged. "Right, then." She finished her lunch and dabbed her mouth with her napkin. "I'll be locating

Dahlia's room and making contact with her about where to sell her painting."

My mind reeled. "Painting? That's why you were asking about the Schiele?"

"That is why I asked about the Schiele."

Jack leaned in. "The painting from the General's... the one we confiscated after you..."

Penny tightened her lips into a nervous line. "Yes."

"After you did what?" I asked.

She dropped her gaze to her hands. Her voice dropped to a whisper. "I seduced and murdered him in his bed."

Jack leaned even closer. "She used the same method on him as she had with Kohler—with Kohler's decoy."

"Except that I didn't kill Kohler's decoy, remember? Your secretary did that to frame me." She stretched her hand over my arm. "Are you ready?"

Ready? For what? To imagine her seducing another man? Did she seduce him the same way she had seduced me that first night after she arrived? Wearing almost nothing—smelling like jasmine. She might have done anything to me that night. I was glad we were on the same side.

"Ready," I confirmed, unsure if I was ready at all.

Jack punched me in the shoulder. "Let's escort the lady up to her room, and then the two of us can set ourselves to task."

Penny spun around to Jack. "Why don't you go on to the platform and decide where you want to begin. Henri can see me upstairs." She patted his arm. "I think it's for the best. We've already been seen as a couple here. It might seem awkward for me to be with two men, you know? I don't want to be thrown out of the hotel for impropriety."

Jack raised a brow at her and then quirked his mouth at

me. "I'll stake out the whole building." He waggled his finger at us. "Just don't take too long with… whatever."

He strode away toward the platform as Penny and I headed to the elevator. We rode up with the operator in silence, careful not to give anything away. We didn't trust anyone.

I walked Penny to her room as slowly as I could manage—not because I wanted to delay my part of the mission, but because I wanted to spend every quiet second with her. When we got to her door, she took my waistcoat lapels between her long fingers and held me in place.

"I know Jack can be difficult sometimes." She raised her gaze to lock with mine. "And I can be, too."

I cupped her elbows in my hands. "Just a nice challenge."

"There's a great deal about me you don't know."

"Yet."

Penny smiled. "Are you sure you want to know more?"

"You intrigue me." I swiveled my head in either direction to be sure we were alone in the corridor, then leaned closer to her ear. "I want to know everything about you."

"You're not afraid of me?" She tugged my lapels harder, pulling my face closer to hers.

"*Je suis absolument terrifié.*" My lips skimmed the top of her ear.

"Terrified?" she said with a smile in her soft voice. "I think I prefer that in a man."

Her lips pressed against my jaw. "I will find Dahlia, and we'll take care of business in town. Perhaps she will allow me to give her a shopping tour of Canfranc. We should meet this evening at the reception, but you or Jack can leave a message with the front desk if there is any trouble."

"We won't have trouble." I took her face in my hands, letting my fingertips reach into the silky hairline behind her ears. "We'll do our job and see you tonight." My lips hovered over hers as I searched her eyes for sincerity. No fear. No doubt. No deception.

Just as my lips felt the first sensations of hers, a door opened a few yards down the hall. We jumped apart like guilty children at boarding school.

Dahlia Lundt coughed as she closed and locked her hotel room door, and Penny handed me her room key. I opened her door and handed the key back without a word. We both nodded as Dahlia sashayed past us toward the elevator.

"I think I'll walk to the little bakery in town shortly." Penny's tone was clear and just loud enough for Dahlia to hear, I supposed.

"*Merveilleux, ma chère.*" I paused for another second while Dahlia disappeared around the corner. "I want to kiss you," I whispered.

Penny slipped her hand to my jaw, resting her thumb on my bottom lip. "Save your best kiss for me, and I'll have it from you later tonight."

I hurried to the elevator, where I found Dahlia still waiting for the car to arrive. The polished brass doors slid open with a ding, and I bowed and motioned for her to enter before me.

"*Danke, junger Mann,*" she said, accentuating her German.

"*De rien, Madame,*" emphasizing my French.

The operator took us down to the lobby and, with a stiff bow, indicated the café, the post office, the embassy, and the bar with four definitive arm gestures in the cardinal directions.

"Madame, may I escort you somewhere?" I asked Dahlia.

She drew a deep breath and pasted a polite smile on her face. "No need, sir, but thank you. I'm off on a great shopping adventure—my first in Spain." She offered an approving nod. "Perhaps we shall have a chance to meet at tonight's reception. The manager tells me it is quite the thing."

22

I found Jack poking around the side doors of the cargo building at the back of the platform. This was where my not-so-friendly acquaintances had taken me a few nights earlier, and I didn't have the fondest memories of the place. Jack whacked at the base of the building with a stick. I assumed he was searching for something.

"I thought we were trying to be discreet." I kept my tone low.

He pointed back to the trains. "I told one of the porters I'd lost my keys."

"Fifteen yards from the platform?"

"He didn't hang around after that." Jack shrugged.

This was too conspicuous for my liking—two grown men sniffing around a building where suspected smugglers conducted nefarious business. We were going to be caught, and I would not be given a second chance.

"Can we go inside?" My nerves ticked to high alert.

Jack shrugged. "Well, that's the plan, isn't it?" He waved his stick at the door as if I had the key.

His resentment hit me like darts. He didn't want to be here. He didn't want to carry out any mission, let alone one conceived by Penny. She was right. He'd be no real help beyond whatever we forced him to do.

I dropped to one knee and inspected the keyhole to assess the lock. Before I raised my pick to the lock, the knob wiggled and whined. Jack and I scrambled away as the door swung open to the inside.

From our blind in the nearby shrubbery, we observed two porters step out and look around, one fanning himself with his cap. The other unbuttoned the front of his jacket and flapped the front panels.

"I don't remember it getting so warm last summer," the first said.

"It's only because we're working hard." The second man scraped his cap from his head. "Maybe we can manage a little air circulating in there." And they both went back inside.

Jack and I exchanged dubious glances and advanced with caution. Jack had left his stick in the brush and now made a polite *after-you* gesture. Good. His smug British attitude could follow my lead if he had the guts.

With my back against the wall, I inched toward the door and peered inside. Stacks of luggage in every size lined the walls under chalkboard signs labeling the trains on which they arrived or would be departing. Each sign noted the arrival or departure times and the origins or destinations. Very organized. Very helpful.

At the doors nearest the platform, two porters held clipboards and directed others where to take each piece of luggage or crate.

The porters scurried with hand trucks from one side of the small warehouse to the other.

"*Más rápido*," the head porter yelled.

I pulled off my jacket and waistcoat and nodded for Jack to do the same. We transferred anything useful from them into our trouser pockets and left our jackets in a pile back in the brush. We didn't have uniforms for disguises, but at least we might blend in with the many porters who'd already shed their jackets. It might not help us at all, or it might give us an extra minute or two before we were caught.

We edged inside and around to the back, where the largest crates were stacked. From there, we surveyed the whole space.

"We need to see what's inside these crates," Jack whispered, hunching over.

"It looks like most of them are labeled." I squatted to examine the label on the nearest one. LISBON, Senhor Callas, Máquinas Callas. "This one is going to a machine shop in Lisbon."

Jack read the label on the crate in front of him. "Lisbon, to a private home, I'd guess."

I sidestepped to the next crate, and my eyes went wide. "Look at this one," I said. "The size and shape of it."

Jack hunched down beside me. "Six-foot-long, three-foot-wide, two-foot-high. You think there's a body inside?"

"I do." I scanned the sides and ends. "No label, either."

"Hey!" a voice called. "You two."

We raised our eyes above the edge of the crate. The head porter stared back at us. We were about to run or fight. "Yes?" I answered.

"Don't just stand there. Move that crate out of the way. It goes on last, so we need it shifted over there. You two can carry it, no?"

"Of course," Jack said, taking his place at one end. He tilted his head to me. "We can do it."

Adrenaline pumped through my veins as we lifted the crate and pivoted its position against the wall. My back strained from lifting it only a few inches. Four other men scrambled to grab the crates from below it to stow on the train. When they returned, two of them helped us load the crate into the last car of the train. We stacked it over four lower, smaller crates closer to the freight doors.

The other two men hurried out, and Jack and I ducked down and backed into the dark corner of the car. We observed the clip-board-carrying porter check his list and walk back to the storeroom.

I took the notepad from my pocket and began to write furiously, scrawling out names and addresses as fast as I could. The sooner we could determine the smugglers' names and headquarters, the sooner we might stop the whole operation.

"We don't write anything down." Jack tapped the side of his head. "We don't want to leave evidence, so we keep everything up here."

"And have you memorized all the labels on these crates?" I countered.

Jack patted the corner of a crate. "The names and addresses on all these labels will be fronts—ways to divert us from the real players."

Heat seethed in my throat. "This isn't a game, Jack. I'm not looking for players. I'm searching for murderers, thieves, and conspirators."

"But it is a game that they are playing, whether you are or not." He flicked his finger around the freight car. "Pay attention,

Toussaint. Are any of these crates going to the same person or the same address? No."

I glanced down at my notepad. Everything was labeled for Lisbon, but all had different addresses. All different names. My thoughts whirled in confusion. "Then what are we doing here?"

Jack scoffed. "Good question." He edged around another crate. "Have you ever considered that Penny is manipulating you? Us?"

He waited for an answer, but I stayed quiet. I was well aware she was manipulating me. She had been from the beginning, but that didn't mean she was wrong. Jack's brow raised, and he sighed.

"She sold—" Jack began, but was cut short by the car door slamming shut.

Darkness enveloped us, and the latch locked in place. We scrambled through the narrow aisle around the crates and felt around the door for an inner latch, but found none.

"We have to get off this train before it—" But my words drowned in the sudden lurch of the train moving forward.

Minute shafts of light punched through the tiny gaps around the side and front door of the freight car. I squeezed my eyes shut for several seconds in hopes of an easier transition to the pitch black, and when I reopened them, the contents of the carriage now had form, however vague.

"I'll try to reach the connecting door," I muttered. We were not supposed to still be on the train. This wasn't part of the plan. If we didn't get off soon, we'd be stuck on board until we reached Lisbon. By the time I'd maneuvered to the door at the end of the car, my knees were battered, and my body was sweating from every pore.

My slick palms struggled to grab the lever door latch, and it moved without any pressure on my behalf. When the door slid open, bright sunlight flooded in around the silhouette of a man.

"What are you doing in here?" a deep, gruff voice boomed.

Instinct kicked in, and before I could put together any words, I grabbed the man by his jacket and pulled him inside the car. My mind didn't stop to think if he was alone or if he was armed. I simply grabbed, pulled, and threw a punch.

The man punched back, and unfortunately for me, his aim was better than mine. Lightning shot through my jaw into my ear, and bells rang loudly in my rattled brain. The confined space limited our maneuvers to the most basic of jabs. With crates on either side of us, when we veered to avoid a strike, we knocked our heads against the rough wooden boxes, scraping our faces full of splinters. We bounced along as the train picked up speed, adding a new level of difficulty to our fight.

The darkness of the car gave new meaning to the term *blind rage* as our fists flew. I learned his strike pattern and dodged backward between my punches. His fist breezed close by my jaw and crashed into a crate with a loud crack, and I cringed with the knowledge that his hand was most certainly broken.

No time for sympathy, though. I launched my strongest uppercut in his direction. My knuckles scraped up his throat and under his jaw, and I felt the reverberation as his head rocked back. His body went down with a thick thud.

A heavy hand landed on my shoulder, and I whirled around with my fists raised, ready to land a few more blows.

"Hey—it's just me," Jack said, his hands up in surrender. "That was impressive. You don't look the part."

"I've boxed since secondary school." My explanation was unnecessary but automatic. "We need to jump off this train."

"It's too late for that now." Jack pounded on a crate beside us. "Jumping at this speed will kill us. Let's open some crates and see what's being smuggled."

We used the light from the open doorway and found a small prybar hanging on the wall. Pushing our unconscious friend to one side, we used the tool to open the first crate.

Excelsior packing billowed up, and we pushed it aside to reveal the contents. Polished silver candlesticks and a full tea service rested beneath. Nice, expensive, but probably not enough to prove any crime.

"Try again?" I directed Jack to another container while I replaced the packing and cover over the silver.

The next box carried a couple of dozen expensive books and a mahogany box of writing supplies. Another held several rolls of small but fine tapestries. Everything we found was costly but not compelling. Between crates, we found multiple paintings, protected by basic packaging to safeguard the elaborate frames and canvases. The dim lighting limited our ability to identify any of the artwork.

"I wish Penny were here," Jack said. "She knows art. She would tell us the titles and artists, and whether these works were genuine or replicas."

"I wish she were here, too." But I didn't. I wished instead that I was with her, not the other way around. "What do you think about the paintings?" I asked.

"If these are actually masterpieces, we might be looking at priceless works. This could be real evidence of smuggling." Jack gestured to the other open crates. "The rest of these may just be household goods."

"They could still be stolen—looted from the homes of wealthy victims of the Nazi occupation."

"Of course," he replied. "But without identifying marks, we

can't know for sure."

I sighed. My face, hands, and torso throbbed as my adrenaline ebbed away. "Then we continue searching."

Jack took the tool to another crate, but before he wedged it into place, we found the open doorway filled with three men on their way inside.

The first man grabbed his unconscious comrade and dragged him out of the car, and they disappeared.

The other two rolled in like tanks. Jack brandished the prybar and struck the closer man only seconds before the one still in the door unholstered his pistol and fired. The shot missed Jack but sent the iron bar flying past me. It landed somewhere behind me between the crates.

Why had we not brought our handguns? We were searching, and searching didn't require pistols. As an inspector, it wasn't part of my regular gear, but of course, none of this was regular. And I wasn't even on duty; I was on convalescent holiday. My mind argued with itself for several more seconds before I finally focused on the fight at hand.

Jack bent in half and threw himself headfirst into the torso of the man with the pistol, knocking the weapon out of his hand. Jack and his adversary exchanged punches and kicks, and the other man scrabbled over the two of them toward me.

I assumed he didn't have a weapon because I was still alive when he reached me. I threw the first punch, hitting him just below the sternum. He bent forward, and I intended to follow with an uppercut, but discovered he had the same idea. My jaw rattled, and my ears rang. I gathered my senses long enough to hook him in one ear and then the other. I took a straight shot to my nose in the process, sending a stream of crimson down my shirt.

Our fists flew, and the train's rough bounce caromed us off the crates to each side and back into each other. I was so embroiled in our entanglement that I barely noticed Jack and his sparring partner. The tiny car struggled to contain the flailing limbs and curses we spat at each other in multiple languages.

My breath heaved, and my body shuddered as my opponent's fist landed squarely on my chest in my half-healed wound. I fell to the floor, my arms above my head. Electric pain coursed through every inch of me. The floor shook me as if trying to convince me I was still alive, though I wasn't sure it was true.

The knuckles on my right hand throbbed. They'd knocked against something cold and hard. The prybar. I grabbed the thing and swung it forward at the exact moment my opponent brought his leg down over me. Mere inches from my chest, the iron bar connected with his ankle in an echoing crack. His body crumpled down, and I swung again, this time connecting with his skull. He stopped fighting. He stopped moving. He stopped breathing.

With the final traces of strength I had left, I crawled from beneath him and swung the tool again, taking out Jack's rival.

Jack struggled to his feet, and we leaned against the crates, gasping for breath. Our eyes focused on the light in the doorway just long enough to see another man—perhaps the one who carried off our first victim—uncoupling our car from the rest of the train.

23

TUESDAY, JUNE 19, 1945, ON THE TRAIN BETWEEN LISBON, PORTUGAL, AND CANFRANC, SPAIN

A fresh sweat broke over my body, one inch at a time, while the train rushed away from us up an incline. Our car jolted with the sudden loss of power and was carried only by momentum; it slowed as my heart raced.

My mind scrambled through our situation. We still had two train workers in the car with us. Though they were currently unconscious, they'd not remain in that condition for long. Next, we had no idea where we were. I estimated we'd been traveling for at least twenty minutes. If we'd reached ninety kilometres per hour, we'd be as far as thirty kilometres from Canfranc. We might have been going faster.

We had no way to know what kind of terrain we'd been through. While we fought our opponents, we might have been rushing up hillsides or down valleys. We might have made turns through dense forests or crossed elevated bridges. Without familiarity with this country, we had nothing for reference.

We were adrift, as it was. No power and no way to direct our path. If another train came along from either direction, we'd be an obstacle in their path, and trains cannot simply pass one another.

"In a bit of a stew, wouldn't you say?" Jack's posh accent minimized our predicament.

"Rather more perilous than stew." I slapped his shoulder, and he winced. "We need a better vantage point to assess our position."

We stood in the light of the doorway and examined each other. Jack's face showed fresh bruising under a smattering of blood. The shoulder I slapped had a crimson perforation, and I assumed he'd been stabbed. His trousers had several rips and blood stains.

"You look terrible," he said. He raised a brow and shook his head at his appraisal of me. "Were you shot?"

Like Jack, portions of my clothing were soaked in blood. I patted my torso, arms, and thighs, praying he was joking, but my left arm—just above the elbow—suggested he was not. Pain shocked through my body like a bolt of lightning. Folding back my sleeve, I found a slice of skin and flesh missing. I uttered a quiet oath and told myself to worry about it later.

"We need to figure out where we are." I moved past Jack to the small landing outside.

"And do you expect a sign to tell us?"

"That's not what I mean, and you know it." I hooked my right arm around a narrow ladder and leaned out from the car. Ahead on the tracks, the train vanished around a curve. We were currently coasting on a bridge underpinned by Roman arches over a crevice in the mountains. Behind us lay a dense forest that hemmed in the foot of the mountain range from which we came. Unless we'd traversed over several bridges, we were about to be stalled out on the tracks, which was a terrible state, or rolling backward into the valley, which was probably worse.

"Well, we can't jump from here," Jack pointed out the obvious. "Do you think we'll make it to the other side of the bridge?"

I studied the incline and our speed, trying to make calculations. "I'm just not sure." I made the mistake of looking down, and a wave of vertigo swept through me. I clutched tighter to the ladder rail.

"Can you see the bottom here?" Jack asked.

"No. Just the tops of trees, and I can't guess at how tall they may be."

I squeezed my eyes shut until I was back inside the car. Jack pulled the door half-closed and helped me find a seat on a crate.

"You sit for a moment and come up with a plan—you seem to be good at that," Jack said. "I'll search for the prybar and the pistol. Then I'll search our friends here for any other weapons they might have. I don't want them waking up armed."

"Good idea." I leaned forward, my hands braced on my knees, while Jack scurried about the car. Every inch of my body ached and throbbed as my heart rate slowed from Grand Prix speeds.

"Found this, and I think I just see the pistol," Jack coughed as he set the prybar beside me. "Yes, here it is." He tucked the weapon into his waistband and set about searching our two unconscious foes. In a matter of seconds, he'd recovered a large pocketknife. "What do you think?" he asked. "Shall we toss these two?"

I frowned. "I don't know what you're used to, but I certainly don't intend to toss them off a train like so much rubbish. They were only doing their jobs—protecting cargo. We don't even know if they have anything to do with the smuggling."

"They bloody well fought like it." Jack kicked at the foot of the closer man. "So what have you decided? Got a plan for us, yet?"

"Perhaps," I said, scratching across my chin and sending

another flame of pain through my jaw and up the nerves behind my ear. I winced, which pushed another jolt down my spine. It was a domino effect, and I had to put it out of my mind to function. I got back on my feet, limped to the door, and pushed it open.

The car was barely rolling now, and the rest of the train had disappeared. We had almost reached the other side of the bridge, although the drop from the rails could still be deadly, as the mountainside below us ran precipitously down into the valley.

"We're in a bad situation." I slipped the knife into my trouser pocket and picked up the prybar. I motioned for Jack to join me on the narrow gangway. "You can see from here that we can't just hop out. And we absolutely cannot stay here in the car and wait to be hit by another train. We're too close to the forest on this end." I pointed toward where the rest of the train traveled. "And we're on too much of a curve for a train coming from the other direction to stop in time. Either way, this car is going to be struck."

"What happens on impact?" Jack asked.

Flashes from the past crowded my brain, and hot bile crept up my throat. Visions of dismembered comrades and the scent of burnt flesh and chemicals were everywhere. I physically shook my head to clear the memories. "Very bad things. The train that hits us will derail, taking us with it. If we're lucky, we'll be hit from behind and pushed closer to the ground, though I doubt we'd survive. These crates will probably crush us."

"Are you sure about that?"

Heat traveled over my skin and prickled in the cool air. "Have you ever been in a train derailment?" I asked.

Jack laughed, then paused as he realized I posed a serious question. "No. Have you?"

I couldn't form the words, but my face must have told the story.

"So what do you suggest?" Jack rested his hand on the butt of the gun.

"That we get out of here. We can walk the tracks until we can climb down."

Jack shook his head. "We can't leave all this here. This is our evidence."

"When this train car is hit, none of this will be here," I explained, putting as much emphasis as I could into my voice.

"If it gets hit."

"*When*, Jack. This car *will be hit*. The only way it isn't is if the train decides to come back here soon and reconnect. And if they do, we won't be facing two barely armed porters." I shook my head. "They'll be ready to rush us."

"And so?"

"We cannot stay in this car. The best we can do is rouse these two men and drag them out with us." I moved to the nearest body and knelt beside him. "Come on, now," I said, patting his face carefully. A little pain would rouse him, I hoped.

"If the situation is so dire, we should leave them here." Jack scanned the car. "What can we carry with us?" He motioned for the prybar.

"I'm not leaving them here to die." I pushed my arm under the man's shoulders, and his eyelids fluttered open.

The injured man muttered something indistinguishable that I took as a curse. The growl in his voice indicated severe pain and anger.

"Look here," I said. "We have to abandon the train. This car has been abandoned on the tracks. Do you understand?"

His eyes widened, and he allowed me to help him sit upright. He understood.

With a bit of support from me, the man got to his feet, but he couldn't walk on his own. Each time he tried to take a step, he howled. Broken foot or ankle, I suppose.

Jack reluctantly woke the other man, though it took several minutes to rouse his response. "I don't think he's coming to," Jack said. "And I doubt either of us can carry him."

Jack's man suddenly awoke with a low moan. "Go away from me." He kicked both legs, then recoiled like a dying spider. His hands scrambled through his pockets for his knife.

"Looking for this?" I pulled his knife from my pocket, only enough for him to see. "Monsieur, we are in terrible danger and must leave the train."

"My job is to stay with this freight. I'm not getting off the train."

Jack slapped his shoulder. "Sorry, mate, but if you don't come with us, you'll be killed."

"Leave me," the man demanded. "I won't go." He fisted his hands and prepared to strike. Jack leaned out of his arm's reach.

"I don't want to hurt you again, and I don't have enough left in me to carry you out." Jack's voice dropped as he raised his fists and adjusted his stance, but before either man could land a blow, the distant scream of a train whistle shrilled in the air.

There wasn't time for any of this. My heart pounded in my ears. I dragged my foe toward the door. "You're going to have to try to walk." I coughed. My mouth was a desert. I tossed a glance over my shoulder at Jack and his adversary. "We don't have time. If he won't come, leave him. If he has any sense, he'll follow us."

That was all Jack needed to energize his step. We hurried to the gangway and jumped to the rails as another whistle—this time closer—broke the quiet of the mountainside.

At least fifty yards separated us from where the tracks met solid ground. I doubted we'd make it. The only positive I determined was that the oncoming train was coming from behind us, not ahead.

The man draped over my arm pulled heavily, and only after Jack took the other side of him did we make real progress in our race. "Don't look down. Don't look down," I repeated with every step. The rail ties were too close for a normal stride—or too far apart, depending on how you looked at it. Either way, we bumbled over the heavy ties in an awkward gait that resembled a three-legged race, but with too many legs.

The train's howl devolved into the squeal of brakes, and the railway shook beneath our feet. It was close and getting closer.

We picked up our pace. I concentrated on landing every step. The man Jack and I carried became dead weight in our arms. I stole a glance at his face and discovered he was unconscious again. From fear or pain? I didn't have time to ponder the possibilities.

The huff of the train rumbled beneath the screeching. Just a few more yards and we could jump. Ten steps… eight… five…

The cool mountain air was saturated with the crunch of the impact, and the space between us and the train closed in the blink of an eye.

"Jump!" Jack and I screamed simultaneously.

Jack went over the edge first, pulling our sloppy friend with him. I dove after them, feeling a bolt of pain shoot up my heel and calf as a piece of something from the train hit my foot. More pain as I landed eight feet below the tracks, in a heap with Jack and the other man.

24

TUESDAY, JUNE 19, 1945, ON THE TRAIN BETWEEN LISBON, PORTUGAL, AND CANFRANC, SPAIN

*W*e scrabbled behind a broad tree trunk and observed as not only the car we'd been in angled sharply off the track, but also the short train that hit it. It pushed the single car, the engine, and two more freight cars up onto the hillside before the engine exploded. The last three cars went right off the bridge and dragged the rest down the mountainside below us. The cars broke and tumbled, bursting like confetti-filled party balloons.

The car we'd occupied scattered its contents above us, though several crates tumbled past us down the slope. The air soon billowed with black, acrid smoke rolling upward. I pulled my collar over my nose and mouth to breathe. Vivid images of my past—the derailment in France so many years ago—flashed in my mind. The acrid scent of burning flesh, burning coal, burning everything. My body trembled as I was back there, buried under piles of debris. I couldn't breathe then; I struggled to breathe now.

Jack coughed into his fist, trying to tend to our companion, who was still unconscious.

My job now was to help us all back to Canfranc safely. Penny would have no idea that we were on the train, let alone that we barely survived an attack and a derailment. When she discovered we were gone, she'd be searching the hotel, the train station, the platform, and the whole valley.

She'd start asking dangerous questions of dangerous people.

My pulse raced with urgency. "We have to go back."

Jack scoffed, scanning the side of the mountain. "Do you have a plan?"

The train's debris and contents slid down the slope as smoke snaked upward. It was only by God's grace that the forest was still soaked from the recent rain and was unwilling to burn. But that wouldn't last long.

"We'll have to follow the tracks back to town." I gestured to the bridge. It curved in the air at least half a kilometre before the rails touched the ground again.

Our companion, or prisoner, or whoever he was, regained consciousness and began swearing in Spanish. His arms waved with feverish gestures at the train tracks, the smoke, the broken crates. I couldn't let his panic overtake him.

"Stop," I demanded.

He fell silent.

"We can't stay out here like this." I motioned to Jack. "We have to see if anyone else survived the wreck. *Then* we need to scavenge for anything useful. *Then* we have to start back."

"If there were survivors, they'll be doing the same." Jack pulled himself to his feet and braced himself on the nearest tree. "We can't waste time. We should start back now." He turned to face our companion. "We'll send someone back for you."

"Don't leave me out here. I can't even walk," the man pleaded.

I shot Jack a disgusted glance. "We're not leaving you." I strode to his side and offered a hand. "What is your name?"

The man took my hand and pulled himself up to standing on his left leg. "My name is Gregorio."

"Gregorio," I repeated. "I'll do my best to carry you back to Canfranc, but we have to work together. Do you understand what I'm saying?"

He nodded and winced through pain. "You won't try to kill me, and I won't try to kill you."

"*Exactement*," I patted my chest. "I am Henri, and this," I regarded Jack. "This is Jack."

Gregorio nodded to Jack. "Thank you for not leaving me."

Jack shook his head in protest. "For the record, I *would* leave you." He paused, apparently rethinking his statement. "But I, too, promise not to kill you if you don't try to kill me."

I helped Gregorio to stand against a tree. "Jack and I will just be a moment."

Jack was already scanning the area for movement through the smoke. "I think I see someone just below us over there." He gestured through the trees to a heap of splintered wood.

Through the shifting billows of grey and black, an arm lay across the side of a crate. I nodded, and we hurried over the scattered bits of train wreckage and downed tree limbs. We reached the pile of scorched wood and realized at the same time that the arm belonged to the man Penny had poisoned the night before. He'd been ejected from his makeshift coffin, but his body was still intact.

While that surprised me somewhat, it was nothing compared to the revelation we discovered next. Within the coffin crate, beneath the layer of excelsior where the body was, we found a large gold bar.

It took several seconds for my eyes to adjust and my brain to process what I witnessed. Jack picked up the bar and stared with his mouth agape.

"Solid gold," he murmured.

I stepped back and shook my head, as though the action would clear my thoughts. My heel slipped on something. Another gold bar. And all around my feet, I found another dozen smaller pieces of gold. I snatched two and held them up to the sunlight filtering through the trees and smoke. "Ingots. What is this?"

Jack bounced the large bar in his hands. "This is a Good Delivery bar. Over twenty-five pounds of pure gold. About £1700 sterling." He gestured to the ones I held. "Those are probably about a troy ounce each."

I glanced at the broken crate. "The bigger ones are the shipment, and the smaller ones are the payoffs to look the other way?"

"Or payment for the smuggling job." Jack nodded. "No wonder the man weighed so much. He had all this with him. That's how I want to go, Mate."

"Ah, *mon ami*, you know you can't take it with you, eh?"

Jack scoffed. "Well, today we can." He cradled the gold like a rugby ball and gestured for me to pocket my finds. "This is the evidence we're looking for."

"Evidence of what, exactly?" I dropped the small bars into my trouser pockets.

"Smuggling at the very least." Jack shrugged. "The paintings, the gold, and I'm sure we'd find more if we had a proper look about." He scanned the forest floor and pointed out a few more gold bars scattered over the debris field.

"No one would hide gold under a dead body if it were a legal shipment," I surmised. "All the more reason to go back—"

My statement was interrupted by a crack, and a chunk of bark flew from the tree I leaned against. I dropped to the opposite side of the tree as Jack dove behind the crate. Two bullets hit the dead body with a bloodless pft-pft, and Jack scrambled to my side.

"We have to go back to the village," he huffed.

"Leave that gold bar; it's too heavy to carry. The small ones will be proof enough." I poked my head out from behind the tree to see our companion, and another shot ricocheted off the tree trunk. "Too close."

Jack pulled out the pistol he'd taken and checked the rounds. "I have six shots. We can't waste any."

"Then we can't wait around to be found and picked off. We need to start moving." I gestured down the slope. "There are more crates down there. We can check them out as we go. We must reach Canfranc before nightfall."

Jack scoffed. "I'm trained to survive any conditions we might face overnight."

"I understand. But we must assume the train stations will be looking for the cars that didn't arrive with the rest of the train. And the other one that came after it. And we should assume that whoever comes looking will not be friendly to us. They'll likely bury us and act as if we never existed."

Jack and I hurried to our injured friend, with bullets whizzing around us. We found him pressed against the opposite side of the tree.

"You should go on and leave me here," he said. "They won't hurt me."

Jack and I crouched down at Gregorio's feet, counting our

assets and appraising our situation. We exchanged a dire glance, and Jack broke the bad news.

"That's exactly why you're coming with us, mate. Bad luck, I'm afraid, but we may need leverage—if your friends are so persistent."

Gregorio snuffled. "But I'll drag you down. You won't be able to move quickly in the woods if you're carrying me. Leave me behind. It's your best chance."

It was my turn. "Jack's right. At this point, we don't know how many are out there. It could be two or ten. We'll need you. If the situation changes, we can always offer you as an exchange."

Gregorio scowled. "Or shoot me. Or use me for a shield?"

"I promised you I wouldn't kill you. So did Jack." I looked Gregorio in the eye. "My word is my bond."

Gregorio spat on the ground. "Then take me back to Canfranc quickly. My friends won't be so honor-bound."

25

*T*he sunlight filtered through the trees in hard yellow-white shafts, illuminating the rocks and black dirt beneath. The thick spires of beech and heavy canopy of oak branches contained the smoke from the train wreck to its original site. Once we'd moved down the mountain a bit, we could see and breathe more easily.

Jack and I took turns as Gregorio's crutch, and we all wove through trunks and behind rocks for cover from whoever was following us. At first, we could hear their murmurs and mutterings, but even those were swallowed by the forest's quiet.

We descended for another hour before we reached the river that wound through the valley between the mountains. All three of us hurried to the water and scooped it into our hands to lap it like Gideon's mighty men.

Jack finished drinking and broke the silence. "I don't know if we lost them, or if they're simply as exhausted as we are."

I shook my head and rubbed the back of my neck with my wet

hand. "We can't trust that we lost them. Even if we have, it doesn't ensure they won't find us again. We must cross the river and start back up the mountain. If we follow the tracks above, we should find the shortest way back to town."

Gregorio nodded, gulping. "The problem will be crossing. The water flows faster and runs deeper than it looks."

"A felled tree, perhaps?" Jack suggested.

We scanned in both directions for a tree trunk or large branches that might support our weight. Whatever we used for a bridge would need to hold two men at once if we were to carry Gregorio to safety.

To our left, away from the base of the rail bridge, I spied a log, broken from the opposite side of the river, resting halfway into the water. It diverted the stream around the end. I searched our side for another log I might wedge beside it from our side. The first one I came to was too heavy to pick up, let alone drag to the river. The second one, slightly smaller, crumbled in my grip.

"We may have to walk a bit to find a place to cross," I said when I was back with Jack.

Gregorio gestured toward the bridge pillars. "There may be a crossing just beyond the stone base, but that's where the others will expect us to go. If they've gotten ahead of us, we'll be shot on sight."

Jack nodded. "I'll scout ahead there." He sighed. "You rest another minute and drink a little more. One way or another, we'll have to move soon."

Gregorio and I nodded, aware that the others might be close. I held the injured man upright at the water's edge, and we scooped handfuls of cold water to our lips. Sweat poured from every cell of my body, and the icy liquid blazed a trail down my throat to my now-empty stomach, hitting with a gurgle.

"How well do you know this area?" I asked Gregorio.

"Not well. I'm from the southern part of Spain. My father had a vineyard near the Portuguese border." He worked his mouth for a second. "He died, and the land was taken from our family. My brother died at the beginning of the war. My mother and sister—"

"There's not a crossing at the pylons, but there looks like a way across just beyond that." Jack returned, interrupting Gregorio's story.

Gregorio nodded without offense. "We must go, then. We are taking too long already."

As silently as possible, the three of us made our way around the stone bridge supports to a narrow spot in the river, where a previous traveler had placed two logs. Jack walked ahead, bouncing slightly to ensure sturdiness. The makeshift bridge didn't move.

I wrapped my uninjured arm around Gregorio's back, and we were halfway across the logs when I heard a crack and felt a burn just below the outside of my knee. We were under fire again.

"Take cover," I yelled at Jack, pushing Gregorio toward him.

Another shot ripped through my shirt sleeve. I took a long stride after the others, but missed the last step on the log. My ankle twisted, and I slid to one side. A bullet grazed the top of my shoulder as I went down, tumbling into the rushing water below.

I clung to a granite boulder, worn smooth by eons of erosion. Jack pushed Gregorio behind a tree and came back for me.

"Give me your hand," he called between gunshots.

"Just go on. I'll find you later." I pushed myself under the log bridge for cover as Jack disappeared behind some shrubbery. I couldn't stay under the bridge. I'd be found and taken in minutes if I tried. In the early days of the war, I'd employed a technique for escaping an impossible situation like this, and it had worked. But with my injuries, I wasn't sure it would work again.

"You don't have a choice," I muttered to the moss and rocks around me. I spread my arms wide and drew the deepest breath I could manage. Putting my face into the water, I let my feet rise and drifted, facedown, in the frigid river as motionless as a dead man. I had to trust the stream to take me to a place where I might crawl out, beyond the view of my enemies.

Two men with guns paced on the bridge. One fired in my direction, but the other barked something I couldn't understand. They crossed over toward where Jack and Gregorio had hidden.

While drifting, I spied a tree root extending beneath me. I reached out to take hold, but my hand wouldn't close around it. I scrambled in a panic to reach it with my other hand. Though my fingers refused to grip, my shirt sleeve caught fast and began to rip apart. I took the opportunity to bob my head up for a quick breath. If I couldn't manage a secure hold, I would descend into hypothermia and drown.

I fixed an image of Penny in my mind. She needed me. Even if she didn't, I needed her. I had to go back to her. With what we'd done on the train, the smugglers she was after would surely be on guard against her. Against everyone.

Another gulp of air. Another rip in my shirt.

I flexed my fingers once again, desperate to grasp a root, a rock, or anything to leverage my body out of the water before the armed men returned.

Elize's voice drifted through my thoughts. *You must leave Canfranc.* I couldn't do that. At first, I couldn't leave her, but now —if I died out here in the wilderness—Penny would be on her own. Even if Jack made it back, she'd...

My fingers closed around the root. First my right hand, then my left. They held long enough to pull my body upward. Hand over hand, I walked myself up the bank and out onto dry land. I was alive for the moment.

Every bone, muscle, and sinew in my body ached and shivered. I had no strength to crawl into the cover of the forest. I clung to only three things. I must reach Canfranc. I must find Jack. I must move. Now.

Overwhelmed with exhaustion, I closed my eyes for a fleeting moment. That moment must have stretched out, for when I opened my eyes again, I became aware of rustling in the forest near me. I started to call out for Jack, but swallowed my breath when I heard a guttural bark of something in German. They were back.

I rolled one leg over the other to maneuver onto my stomach, then army-crawled beneath a low canopy of branches and shrubs as quietly as possible. I prayed the men didn't notice the drag marks I'd left on my way.

They marched out from the last veil of woods, sweeping their guns from side to side. They turned in slow circles as they inched closer to the riverbank, ready to shoot whatever might be hiding over the edge. Me.

German and Spanish curses dropped from their mouths as they found no trace of me.

I concentrated on slowing my breath. I hadn't survived a war, two train derailments, and a stabbing to die at the foot of a tree in Spain. I studied their faces through the dense branches.

Their mouths drooped at the corners, and their eyes squinted as they scanned their surroundings. Exhaustion hung from their shoulders like a damp woolen cloak. Their feet barely skimmed the ground as they walked, creating their own drag marks everywhere.

More curses.

"Look again," said the one barking orders.

The other man edged back to the riverbank and bent over to look upstream and then downstream. The ground under his foot slipped away, and he began to fall. His arms flailed overhead, and he shot wildly in the air as he jumped back to firmer footing.

The other man rushed to his side to steady him, and for a split second, I might have had a chance to crawl away.

Without thinking, I rose to my hands and knees, rustling the leaves around me. The men turned in my direction, and I froze in place. The pounding in my chest and ears blocked all my senses. Should I run? *Could I run?*

I held my breath as the men stepped closer. A handgun muzzle poked into the first layer of branches, pointing directly at me.

Don't move.

The hand that held it shook. The finger tightened on the trigger.

Click. Click.

He was out of ammunition. A curse in German.

I released my breath, but it was too much, and the other man fired into the shrubs.

Bang! Bang!

Two shots missed by mere inches.

No choice; I had to run. Ignoring the pain that screeched from my shoulders down, I raced into the woods, away from the men.

Again, I heard a click-click-click. But it was followed by German oaths getting louder and closer. In seconds, I was tackled.

I struggled to inhale with the German man's full weight on me. I kicked and punched, but nothing slowed the other man's onslaught. His left forearm wedged across my neck while his right fist slammed into my side over and over.

I tried to push him away. I tried to roll from under him, but he pinned me securely. I had no choice. I reached into my trouser pocket and withdrew the knife while I was still conscious. I depressed the switch on the side, and the blade shot forth. I plunged the knife into his side, from his waist up to his armpit in three swift stabs.

His eyes stared into mine, glazed with shock, then rolled back.

It took every ounce of my remaining strength to push his body off me. I drew one huge breath to regain my presence of mind. I had to move soon. His friend would be on me within seconds.

I got back on my feet, but my ribcage was on fire, and I couldn't breathe without wheezing. I staggered toward a tree to pull myself fully upright. By the time I'd straightened my spine, I'd been spotted. I wiped my blade on my trousers, though by this point, I was covered in the other man's blood.

When my enemy recognized his friend's body, he charged. I readied my stance for impact, but when the attacker was a few yards away, another shot sounded, and the man fell in a heap.

"You're welcome, mate," Jack chirped and tucked his pistol into his waistband.

26

*T*he trek back spanned almost seven hours, included some climbing, walking, and falling, and stole what little dignity we had left. The town glowed golden in the last minutes of sunset, in stark contrast to the bleak sight we presented. We approached cautiously, unsure of how we might be greeted.

Our clothes hung in bloodied and muddied strips from our bodies. We edged around the perimeter of the train station and found our jackets where we'd left them, thank the good Lord.

Jack and I groaned as we slipped our suit coats over our wounded arms. Gregorio stared at us with fear in his eyes.

"Don't worry," I told him. "We'll take you to Elize Belfort. She'll know what's best for you."

Gregorio's expression brightened. "Thank you."

"Don't thank us so soon." Jack squeezed his shoulder. "I'm sure someone will have questions for you."

I glanced up at the back of the hotel, where I guessed Penny's window looked over us. A silhouette walked past the amber light between the heavy curtains. It came back and stopped.

Stepping toward the building, I raised my arm to wave at her, and pain shot through my shoulder. She disappeared from view, and the light blinked off and back on. She returned to the window and pointed down, then hurried away, and the light went out again.

"Penny will meet us at the door." I gestured to Jack and Gregorio to follow me. A bolt of energy recharged my weary muscles, allowing me to hobble more quickly. By the time we got to the back door of the hotel, Penny was waiting, with Elize by her side.

"Thank God you are safe," Penny rushed between Jack and me. "You must have quite an adventure to tell." She kissed Jack's cheek and slipped her arm around my back.

Her cloud of jasmine revived my weary senses. "We are glad we survived. I only hope we make it through the night," I said.

Elize wrapped her arms around Gregorio. "I will see to your injuries, and I'll speak to Klaus. He will take care of you."

Redbeard, the German man who had interrogated me with his fists a few days ago, appeared behind Elize. "What has happened?"

"Klaus, take him to the private infirmary. I will be up in a minute." Elize caught hold of the man's wrist. "Don't hurt him. Gregorio has already suffered. I will talk to him once he's been treated."

Klaus frowned, but took Gregorio away.

Elize turned her severe gaze back on us. "You two." She focused her stare on me. "You have brought trouble to my door. You've caused irreparable damage. That shipment would have changed my life here."

Jack stepped forward. "Don't blame Toussaint. This was all me."

"Then should I put a bullet between *your* eyes?" She growled, only inches from his face.

Penny squeezed my arm, not realizing her hand was over where I'd been grazed.

"Ahh," I groaned.

Penny took half a step back to assess my damages, then glanced at Jack. "You're both a shambles."

"I'm fine," Jack spat out. "But he should have a once-over, considering he started out this trip in poor condition."

Penny shot Elize a ragged stare. "You take care of yours, and I'll take care of mine. They've been through enough today."

Elize squared her shoulders and balled her fists, as she had always done when she was angry or frustrated.

I held up a shaking hand toward her. "Go on and take care of Gregorio. His friends didn't make it—they won't be coming back." I dropped my arms back to my sides. "We almost didn't. The track will need to be repaired. You have a lot to do in a short time."

Elize stomped closer toward me. "Do you have any idea what was on that train?" she whispered. "I'll have a price on my head by dawn."

I nodded. "It's still there. If your men are industrious, you'll recover most of it." I worked my mouth, trying to decide if I dared to say more. I dared. "If I know you, you'll have made sure to put in a bit of extra anyway. For protection, or to give yourself a little something for later."

She pulled back her arm to slap me, but Penny caught her wrist mid-air. "Don't touch him."

"The two of you have marched into a situation you know

nothing about. If you keep making noise, we'll all be killed." Elize pulled free of Penny's grip.

"Dead?" Penny began with a question. "Like the thousands of victims of your cohorts? I've *seen* the camps. I've *seen* the families murdered in the streets. Your friends are nothing more than butchers."

Elize stepped back. "You don't know everything."

"This war has proven one thing to me over and over. One person can make a difference. That's why I do what I do. You think I'm a child battling the ocean, but I'm not." Penny huffed between her words. "And even if I am, when the waves come over me, they don't knock me down. I won't let them. They roll back out to sea, and I'm still standing—with my fists clenched—standing, waiting for the next wave to come."

Her defiant words strengthened my body. My heart slammed against my ribs in solidarity with hers. I'd never seen a woman so determined, and all I wanted was to be at her side.

Elize shook her head. "You can only battle the waves so long before they carry you away." She turned her back on us, then paused and looked over her shoulder. "You'll be swept out to sea with the rest of us." She disappeared after her friends.

Jack raked his fingers through his hair and sighed. "I don't know about you, but I'm going to bed. I've got nothing left in me."

Penny nodded. "Good, you should." She patted his shoulder, and we waited as he walked toward the elevator.

I swallowed hard and nodded to follow him. "Probably a good idea for me, too."

She turned to face me, and a smile crossed her lips, reaching up to her steel grey eyes. "I'll take you up, but I have a feeling," she whispered. Her gaze bore into mine. "Yes, I see it. You have something to tell me." Another beat. "And something to show me?"

My body ached from top to toe. "I do. But you'll have to let me clean up and clear my head before I can tell you everything. My mind's a jumble."

She nodded. "Let me escort you to your room, then. Wash today off and bandage up where you need it."

"I got shot." The words rolled out of my mouth as casually as if I were telling her I'd seen a dog.

Penny led me into the bar area and tucked me in the niche behind the door, adjacent to the counter. "Stay quiet. I'll be right back."

She vanished for a second, returning with the barman, who swore under his breath at the sight of me.

"I know," she answered. "I need to take him to his room without drawing any attention."

He lowered his chin. "I'll show you the service elevator. They've just moved dinner upstairs for tonight's reception. You should have twenty minutes or so before this gets busy again."

We followed him down an empty corridor and into a plain elevator car. No polished brass, no uniformed operator.

"Are you coming with us?" Penny asked.

"I can't." He tapped the lever handle. "Just pull this back until you hear a click. When it gets to the second floor, you'll hear another click—push the handle back to engage the doors. It's easy enough."

"Thank you," Penny and I said at the same time.

Without regarding me, he nodded to Penny. "Was he on the train? What happened?"

She whispered, "I'll let you know everything I find out. In the meantime, keep your eyes and ears open. There are a lot of very angry people around here."

"Always," he said and saluted us as the door closed.

My mind went dull with exhaustion. All I managed was a stupid, "You're marvelous."

Penny smiled again and pulled the lever. "You're sweet, but we don't have time for a mutual admiration society. Dahlia and I already have an operation underway, and I don't want to leave her alone for too long. Not after your recent activities."

I swayed on my heels, but her arm looped around mine, bolstering my spirit and body.

"You're in sorry shape." She pushed the lever back, and the door opened. She peeked out and tugged on my jacket sleeve. "We can make it to your door without too much attention."

I followed her on the short walk down the hall to my room. A split second of panic took me when I didn't find the key in my trousers pocket, but I quickly remembered that it was in the breast pocket of my suit coat. My door opened easily, and Penny made a swift scan inside before pulling me in and closing the door again. She flipped the latch and gestured to the bath.

"Go on and clean up. I'll arrange your kit for this evening while you bathe, and I can stitch up any injuries before you dress." She gave me a once-over glance. "Where were you shot?"

Pointing to my arm, I explained, "Just a graze. And one on my leg, too, I think."

She quirked a smile. "I suppose if you aren't sure, it can't be too bad." She waited as I slipped out of my jacket and waistcoat, then helped to free me from the tatters of my shirt. "Oh," slipped under her breath as she examined my torso.

Her fingers reached out timidly, acting as an extension of her eyes. They grazed over cuts and abrasions and purple bruises blossoming all over my chest and shoulders. "All of this from the train wreck?"

I shook my head. "We were discovered in the car before the derailment. Gregorio and a couple of his friends gave us something to think about. One of them set the car adrift, as you might say. Then another little train came along and rammed our car. That's what caused the whole thing to go off the tracks in the first place."

"Elize said there was an emergency. She didn't give any details." Her palm flattened over my heart and the scar from my surgery.

"She didn't have many details, I'm sure."

Her gaze fixed on mine. "You were in a fight—besides the crash?"

I scoffed. "Several fights. And in the river once." I took a breath, my memories of the day scrambled for attention. Did all this happen only today? "There's so much more to tell you, but…"

"But we don't have time at the moment. You need a bath. We should be at the reception by now. Dahlia needs us." Penny took her hand from my chest.

Dahlia. What in blazes did Penny have arranged for that sweet old woman? Or, probably more accurately, what in blazes did Dahlia have planned for us?

Penny disappeared into my bath, and I could hear her turn on my shower. I searched my waistcoat for my prize and had it ready to show Penny when she returned.

"What do you think we found on the train?" I asked, with a pleased but painful grin on my face. I took her hand in mine and pressed the small gold ingots into her palm.

She stared down for a second, then her wild eyes shifted up to mine. "Where? How?"

"They were hidden beneath the body of the man you assassinated last night. In his coffin crate." My mouth was dry and I had to swallow. "And there was much more than these. Dozens of bigger gold bars—too heavy for us to carry back."

"Do you understand what this means?" she asked.

"Not exactly. But I'm certain you do."

27

TUESDAY, JUNE 19, 1945, CANFRANC, SPAIN

A yawn stretched my lips wide and rippled down my spine. My body ached and longed for sleep, though sleep was its own dream. I still had a job to do. We all did.

I slipped one stiff arm into my dinner jacket, then the other. Wearing clothes without tears, holes, mud, or bloodstains invigorated me with a sense of humanity again, as though I'd returned to civilization. The same sensation as when I'd been stationed at my desk after my war injuries. In a way, everything my body suffered was a war injury.

Adjusting my watch chain and fob, I wondered how much time I had before Penny came to retrieve me for the evening's reception. I stepped from my bedroom into the parlor, and the question became moot. Penny stood at the bar cabinet, swishing a highball of whiskey.

She wore a deep crimson silk gown with drapes of chiffon in the same color from her shoulders to her hips and continuing over her derriere to the floor in a short train. The only kind of train I wanted to think about tonight.

Each time she came near, it inspired the same reaction in me. "You look lovely," I whispered.

Her lips puckered slightly. "Thank you." She took one last drink from the crystal glass, leaving a smudge of red on the rim. She tipped the glass toward me before placing it on the bar. "All they're going to have at the reception is champagne, and I can only take so much, you know."

I chuffed. "I'm French, remember. That is mother's milk to me." I strode to her side and kissed her cheek, careful not to muss her powder. "What are we in for this evening?"

Penny looped her hand into the crook of my arm. "Our job is merely to observe and take mental notes."

"I know we've had this conversation before, but may I ask you not to kill anyone tonight?"

It was Penny's turn to chuff. "How about this? I promise not to kill anyone so long as the rest of the night goes to plan. Will that work for you?"

"I suppose it must," I shrugged. "Our little catastrophe today has left us with limited options."

"Glad to see you're getting the hang of it," she said, with a hint of a giggle.

We shuffled down the hall as stragglers into the reception. The singer was well into her second chorus of "April in Paris," yet another subject upon which I was loath to dwell.

What caught my eye next sent my mind reeling.

The first time I met Madame Dahlia Lundt, she was hobbling down the steps of a train, being helped by Penny and a thin porter. Technically, she was one of the murder suspects in the case that first brought the women into my life.

That elderly woman was nearly a skeleton in an old grey tweed skirt suit. Everything about her, from her hair to her shoes, was faded grey, even her eyes and complexion. The war had ravaged her to a frail frame.

But *this* Dahlia Lundt, the woman at the center of attention in this room, was dancing, smiling, and waving to everyone who met her eye. She was swathed in an ocean blue gown that reflected the light in her eyes. Her silver hair twisted into a graceful chignon, decorated with jeweled hairpins of silver and blue. In the scant six weeks since I'd first seen her, she had grown a dozen years younger.

"I can't believe it," escaped my lips.

"Don't be too mesmerized by Dahlia. We're watching for the people watching her."

"Well, right now that's everybody."

"She's marvelous, isn't she?" Penny turned into my arms as we reached the dance floor.

"Almost as marvelous as the woman in my arms," I said. I inhaled the jasmine scent of her hair. My fingertips pressed into the soft flesh of her back. *Focus.*

We made a circuit around the room and found a table once the song ended. It was near enough to Dahlia's to hear her conversations, but far enough to observe whoever else might be watching, too.

"Is she a cousin of the Romanovs?" someone whispered.

"I hear she has a significant stake in a cattle ranch in Argentina," another said.

"That's where she's going, of course... to meet her German husband who faked his death." This from two men at the table behind us.

The whole room buzzed with murmurs and musings about

our *grande dame*. And the woman basked in the role she played. Her arms stretched out to her admirers as though offering a blessing. Her attendants included the hotel servers as well as the older men who hoped for the next turn with her on the dance floor.

Dahlia's voice carried the whimsy and flamboyance of the late great French actress, Sarah Bernhardt, and her graceful gestures matched. Penny and I were onstage with her, though in a lesser, supporting role.

"She is quite the woman," I whispered to my conspirator.

Penny laughed. "She certainly has every man in the room at her beck and call."

I wrapped my hand around hers. "Are we *un peu jaloux délle?*"

Another soft laugh. "I am not jealous of her," Penny protested. She pursed her lips and held my gaze for several seconds. "I am with the most handsome man in the room. What do I have to be jealous of?"

Her comment, however shallow, sent a warmth through my aching chest, soothing everything with a flutter.

"The hotel attendant who services my room said she has a painting to sell. Czachorski's *Cleopatra*. That's how she intends to pay her way to South America." From the table behind us again.

Penny and I shifted in our seats to observe them covertly. We stared into each other's eyes but listened attentively to the men's conversation.

"Who in Canfranc could afford something like that? The value of the *Cleopatra* would be enough to live on for three life-times." The man wore a green and gold pocket square and had gold-rimmed, round-framed glasses that perched on the high bridge of his nose.

His friend cocked his very round, very bald head. "Look

around us, Garber. This place is filled with money. Practically dripping with it. And those who don't have it are desperate for it."

Garber nodded. "I see. So what might have been a priceless piece of artwork is now slashed to bargain prices."

"Exactly, man." Baldy lowered his voice and leaned closer to Garber. "All one must do is drop a few comments in front of the right people, and you'll soon have a buyer. Or be directed to one by the hotel staff. Seems to be their specialty."

Two women joined the men, and the conversation turned to the quality of the band playing.

"Why don't we dance a little more?" Penny slipped her hand into mine.

"Splendid." I drew her lithe body into mine as we swayed back onto the dance floor. "As you suspected," I whispered into the curve of hair behind her ear. My fingers detected a slight shudder in the muscles of her lower back. "Are you cold?"

"Not at all." Penny half-stepped back, in rhythm with "Night and Day." She gazed into my eyes, her steel grey eyes turning almost blue. "Why do you ask?"

"No reason," I answered, but both of us knew why.

She fixed a crooked smile. "We can't become distracted now; we're working."

My thoughts spun back a bit. "So when you asked the man in the shop about a Schiele, shouldn't you have asked about Dahlia's painting?"

"I was asking about that one, because it was reclaimed and then lost again. I hope to find a lead on who might have *misplaced* it."

"I see," I replied. "Because you already have the *Cleopatra*." I was trying to work out the logistics, unsure of the details.

"Something like that," Penny assured me.

We spun past a table where two men hunched over their drinks, speaking in hushed voices. While we turned again, one raised a finger to a server. The young man nodded and hurried to their table.

I couldn't make out anything they said, but their furrowed brows and frowns indicated serious conspiring. The server bowed at the waist and took a note from one of them. Within another lap on the dance floor, Elize attended to the men with a casual welcome, though she discreetly slipped a note under a bread plate and then breezed to the next table. She displayed the same nonchalance, but left no note.

"Did you see that?" I whispered into Penny's hair.

"Elize making her rounds?" she asked.

"More than that." I turned her to face the table with the conspirators. "These men. They summoned her, and she gave them a note. Very suspicious."

Penny eased closer. "Could it be innocent? Directions to a good café?"

"If it were anyone else, I'd consider it. But it was Elize, and she was not behaving innocently." My heart pounded a steady warning. "I would stake my life on it."

"Well, then," Penny said with a sure nod. "Move me close to the man with the note, and we shall see what it's about. Does he have the note on his person?"

I studied the two men just in time to see one of them pocket the missive. "Yes. Inside breast pocket. You aren't going to kill him, are you?"

She glanced into my eyes and quirked a smile. "Don't be silly. I don't kill everyone."

We danced another round, and when we were very close to the man in question, Penny stepped back, gasped, and slapped my face. "How dare you?" she cried.

She took one more step back, pretended to trip on the train of her gown, and fell into the man's lap.

I clapped a hand to my jaw, staring in awe as she pasted on a visage of shock and dismay, her mouth and eyes wide. She turned to face the man, then hopped to her feet again. "Oh! I'm so sorry." She glared at me. "Look at what you've done." She turned back to the man with her hands on her pink cheeks. "I apologize." She simpered. "However, can I make it up to you?"

"Ehr, umm…" the man sputtered, obviously trying to catch up with the situation.

Penny, always calm, nodded to the man. "Yes, I'd love to have the next dance."

He had no choice but to rise, take Penny into his arms, and take the lead as the band began the slow, sensual "Bésame Mucho."

Jealous as I was, I offered a weak apology to her, for appearance's sake. "*Pardonnez-moi, mademoiselle.* My hand slipped; I did not intend…" And she danced away in his arms.

I stood on the edge of the dance floor for a few more seconds, then decided to take advantage of the situation and see what information I might glean from the source. Ambling to her side, I bowed to Dahlia. "Madame, may I have this dance?"

Dahlia studied me from head to toe and back, and her furtive smile gave me pause. Was I about to be slapped again? Was she going to make a scene? Eat me alive?

"Why, I'd be delighted, young man," she said, and held up her gloved hand for me.

"Wonderful," I said, taking her hand in mine and lifting her into my arms. Until that moment, I hadn't realized how small the woman was. The top of her head didn't reach my shoulder, and her steps were so small that I had to adjust my normal sway to keep from stepping on her toes.

Attempting to maintain her new cover and appear as a stranger, I introduced myself. "My name is Monsieur Toussaint." I hoped she would take over the conversation.

"How lovely to meet you," she said. "I am Madame Romanos-Lundt. Are you enjoying your evening?" She tossed a glance toward Penny. "Perhaps a little too much?"

"*Enchanté*. And *oui*, perhaps too much." We danced closer to the orchestra, where we could speak more freely without being overheard. "You seem to have a wide variety of men to choose from. But a woman like yourself always would, I suspect."

"Penny always did have good taste," she chirped. "You two should meet me later. I intend to take a stroll in front of the hotel. We can meet at the bridge?"

"It is too dangerous for you to walk alone, especially at this time of night." I shook my head and gently squeezed her hand.

"You think I cannot take care of myself?" she asked with a hint of laughter.

"I know better than anyone how well you can take care of yourself." I considered how she had "taken care of" at least two people at our last encounter. "But my first night here, I witnessed a murder up the mountain trail from the bridge. I have been investigating, but as yet, I haven't discovered the identity of the killer or the victim."

"You can't help but investigate. It's who you are." Her words were simply stated, but they hit like another slap to the face. To her, this trait was a flaw.

"But, Madame, I only want to ensure your safety." And before I could still my tongue, I said, "A woman your age…"

Her eyes blazed wide. "How old do you think I am?"

She'd foiled me with one question. How should I answer? Too young, and I was flattering and insincere. Too old, and I was a scoundrel. Even guessing correctly had no advantage. Changing the subject was my only hope. "I mean to say..."

"But you didn't," she snapped. "You *said* a woman my age. That's meaningless unless you have a particular age in mind."

I deflected. "I only know what Penny told me. I never had the chance to interrogate you before. She said that she believed you to be in your seventies." My voice quieted as I finished. "I'd have suspected a little younger." I prayed I hadn't offended too much.

A sly smile spread over her thin lips. "That's perfect, then." Her back straightened a bit beneath my hand, and we made another trip around the dance floor before she added, "Early grey hair has been a good disguise for me. A nice cane and a slow pace, and I can get away with anything, you know."

"You're telling me you're younger than you appear?"

"By design, yes." She gazed up with a glint in her eyes. "Let me tell you a little secret." She nodded toward her chair, and we sat for a moment, sipping our champagne. "I am a woman, therefore I'm always underestimated."

She was correct, of course. I'd been guilty of it many times, but not with Penny or Dahlia. I refuted, "I don't..."

She held up her petite hand. "Tut-tut-tut. Don't bother. A big, strong, clever man like you can't help it." She sipped a little more and placed her hand over her heart.

"Are you all right, madame?" I leaned in with concern.

She scoffed and transformed the huff of a laugh into a shallow cough. "I'm fine," she said. Her voice trailed into another weak cough.

A sudden realization hit me. She was playing me. "This is a

demonstration, eh? The frail old woman?" We exchanged a cool glance. "And how long have you been doing this little... routine?"

A wistful distance settled in her pale blue eyes. "For a very long time now." Her lids fluttered, and she refocused. "Since I began working for Mother. After my first husband passed." She sighed and stared into her glass. "Teddy never got the chance to grow old. So I decided to grow old for both of us."

I raised my glass, and she did the same. "To growing old," I said.

"To growing old."

With a clink, we took a long, slow sip, and then she nodded over my shoulder. I turned to see Penny and her dance partner finding chairs at another table.

Dahlia put her glass down and laid her hand over mine. Her tone darkened. "We have work to do, and tonight isn't half over." She struggled, or rather, pretended to struggle to stand.

I was obliged to steady her. "There you are," I said. Her performance was quite convincing.

She beckoned me to lean down, and she kissed my cheek before whispering in my ear, "I'll see you on the bridge."

I tilted my head toward Penny. "If she agrees."

Dahlia patted my arm and allowed me to lead her toward Penny's dance partner. Under her breath, she said, "You'd follow her into a storm, wouldn't you?"

"I already have." I offered Dahlia into the other man's keeping, and took Penny on my arm, realizing the storm had only just begun.

28

TUESDAY, JUNE 19, 1945, CANFRANC, SPAIN

A blue glow clung to the near-summer night, as if resisting the full pitch of darkness, with thin clouds veiling a half-moon high in the sky. Penny and I walked out the lobby doors into the night as the hotel clock chimed eleven-thirty.

"You know her better than any of us," I reminded her. "What do you think of her plan?"

Penny wrapped herself around my bent arm, hugging it tightly to her warm body. "You two seemed quite intimate on the dance floor. Perhaps you're closer than you think." She laughed. "I suppose we can assess her schemes when she provides more details, but I'll tell you, over the last few weeks, her ideas have impressed me."

We ambled the front walk of the hotel as two tipsy lovers on a midnight stroll. "Don't you think it's dangerous—a woman her age?" I asked, testing Penny's knowledge of her friend.

"I think we've both learned she's not quite as dilapidated as she wants the world to believe."

Good. No secrets. Well, obviously, there were plenty of secrets, but that wasn't one anymore. "And you believe…"

"Can we just walk for a bit and enjoy the night?" Her eyes stared up at me with worry behind them. "Today was terrible for you—for all of us."

I nodded and placed my hand over hers. "Yes." I released a heavy sigh and shed the strain of the day as I pulled the cool air into my lungs. "I wondered, you know, if Jack and I would make it back."

"I was about to beg Elize for a couple of her men to join me in a search for you." She squeezed my arm tighter. "You returned just in time."

"Just in time for me, too." My body aches grew stronger as my mind quieted. "I was ready to collapse when we made it back to the hotel, and somehow you persuaded me back onto that dance floor. What is it about you?"

She kept one hand at my elbow, and inched the other up toward my shoulder. My imagination conjured the memory of her dressed, or rather, undressed, as she was in my suite that first night she'd arrived in Canfranc. She was manipulating me again, wasn't she?

"I suspect you find me irresistible." Her smile was small, but it reached the corners of her eyes.

"Much to the detriment of my health." I tapped the healing stab wound on my chest. "Since I met you, I've been stabbed, shot, and beaten multiple times."

"Only since you met me?" she asked.

"No." I pondered my life since the war had begun. "I suppose I can't blame you for any of it. Today wasn't even the first train wreck I'd been in."

Concern overtook her amused expression. "Listen to me.

We're almost there. I know I've put you in danger, and I wouldn't have done it if I thought for one minute you weren't up to it."

We slowed to a stop a dozen yards or so from the bridge and turned to face each other. I swallowed hard before whispering, "I'm ready for whatever comes next; I just need to know that when it's all over, we'll have a proper farewell. Tell me you won't slip away without at least a kiss goodbye."

Her eyes shimmered in the moonlight, and her lips worked to form words. After a few seconds, she murmured, "Why did you bother investigating? That first morning we met in France, you could have had me sent right to jail. There was more than enough evidence to convict me of murder, but you investigated. Why?"

Without hesitation, I answered. "You were so frightened." I pushed a silken lock of hair behind her ear. "I could see it in your eyes. Oui, the evidence all pointed to you. Everyone else on the train was happy to see the man dead. I was, as well. But you alone were afraid. That intrigued me. What else was I to do but investigate?"

"I thought I was being so tough," she said with a laugh.

"You are a strong woman. That was also obvious from the moment I met you. But one can be strong and afraid at the same time." I cupped her cheek in my hand, and she leaned into it.

A cough from behind us pulled us out of the tenderness. "There you are," Dahlia said. She tapped the hook of her cane on the bridge rail. "We've much to plan; best to start."

"Are you out here all alone?" I asked, though it was plain to see she was.

"Tsk-tsk, Jack just left me." She waited to say more until we were at her side. "The man from the reception tonight says he can help me sell my painting. He knows a man in town with connections."

"What painting, exactly, are you selling? And why?" I was already a pace behind the women.

Dahlia exchanged a glance with Penny. "I thought she'd have explained already."

Penny shook her head a fraction of an inch. "I haven't had a chance."

Dahlia's brows shot high. "So that really was all love-making?" She waggled her finger toward the hotel's walk-way. "My, but I didn't realize I would be the only one on the job tonight." She smirked. "Another advantage to being an old woman. No handsome men to chase me."

Penny and I shared a guilty glance.

"Never mind," Dahlia muttered. "Look at you. You can't help it."

"About the painting?" I asked, hoping to realign the conversation.

"It's Czachorski's *Cleopatra*. Stolen from a private collection by the Nazis. I've let a few know that I need to sell it for a little trav-eling cash for a nice trip to America or—in a pinch—Argentina."

"Your friend has a buyer for the painting?" Penny asked.

Dahlia nodded, turning her head, scanning around us for eavesdroppers. "He says he can sell it and find me a ticket or two to South America."

"Then what is the plan?" I straightened my spine, anticipating orders.

"Jack will accompany me to meet the buyer, and one of us will let you know when and where we'll make the deal. I'd like for you both to be on hand in case anything goes wrong." Dahlia squeezed both our hands. "I doubt they'll know the painting is a forgery right off, but just in case they do, I want you to know what happened to us."

My jaw dropped open. "It's a forgery?"

Dahlia scoffed. "Of course it is. I just told you the Nazis stole the original. And, yes, my late husband was a Nazi, but as far as I know, he didn't steal *that* painting." She paused for a breath. "I don't have an extra original masterpiece sitting about my cottage. Do you?"

I scratched the whiskers on my chin. "No, I do not."

Penny knit her brow and laced her words with urgency. "Dahlia, shouldn't I go with you? I can be your traveling companion again."

"Sweet Penny, you and Henri established your covers before I arrived. It would be dangerous for all of us if we switched partners mid-dance."

The older woman was right. Better to stay to the plan. I just hoped the plan had a few more details than simply standing nearby.

"Do you know who the buyer is? We spoke to several shopkeepers the other day." Penny looped her arms around mine again. "That might make it easier for us to show up unannounced."

"I don't know yet," Dahlia said as Jack appeared from the dark end of the bridge.

He didn't wait for a shift in our conversation. "Here's what I found out tonight." He patted my shoulder with the back of his hand. "It appears we're clear of suspicion. Nobody seems to know who the stowaways were on the train. I even heard some talk that it was an inside job, with the conspiring railworkers turning on each other. Gregorio is pushing that narrative, saying he was being used as a hostage."

"That's good," I said. "But we'll have to be sure our cuts and bruises stay covered until they're healed."

Penny agreed. "I have some face powder and creams that I can use to cover your injuries if need be. But you two will have to walk, move, and behave strong in every way. No moaning or limping."

"Understood," I said, and Jack responded similarly.

"Another thing," Jack continued, nodding to Dahlia. "Your man does have a buyer, but won't say who. I believe he's afraid we'll cut him out and he'll lose his commission on the deal."

"I don't blame him." Dahlia clucked her tongue. "That's exactly what I *would* do if I weren't a poor old widow looking for a little help." Her tone dripped with sarcastic affectation. She snapped her fingers. "Are we set then? We can leave the hotel tomorrow morning after breakfast. Me with my nephew," she took Jack's arm, "and you two lovebirds. We'll go out separately, but stay within sight of you."

Penny and I nodded, and Jack squared his shoulders. "We won't have a special signal if things go wrong. I recommend the shoppers' post for you," Jack said.

Penny explained. "That's where I'll pretend to window shop, and you can make your way down the side or back of the merchant's shop. It works well so long as there are no hidden tunnels or such."

"That only happened once," Jack said. "And we caught him anyway."

Dahlia smiled at the exchange. "We don't have much time. After the derailment this morning, everyone will be on high alert. No room for errors. And take your guns with you—whatever weapons you can carry."

We all nodded in agreement. Jack gestured for Dahlia to walk ahead of him toward the hotel, while I placed my hand on Penny's back and we walked to the other end of the bridge. To anyone watching, it would have been nothing more than a couple showing concern for an elderly woman alone at night, who was waiting for her nephew to escort her back to the hotel. No conspiracies, nothing nefarious.

"We should probably go up once they're out of sight," Penny suggested. "I'm sure you're exhausted."

Once we reached the end of the bridge, I pulled her into my arms, as any lover might do. "I thought before we go back inside, we should wait for another couple to come out. Then it would appear we are simply friendly to anyone taking a midnight stroll."

"Clever," she said. "But what shall we do until then?" Her arms carefully encircled my chest as her voice teased.

"*Chère*, I think we can think of one or two things, eh?" I drew her face into my hands and bent to cover her lips with a long, slow kiss.

She pulled me closer, tighter, and then stepped back slightly. "Let me know if I'm hurting you. I didn't mean to."

"No moaning, complaining, or limping, remember?" I whispered.

She leaned her head into the front of my shoulder, and I stroked her soft hair. "Henri?" she murmured.

"*Oui?*"

"I won't leave you." She swallowed hard. "I know you think I'm using you. I was. I have. But I'm not now. In France, we had a conversation about trust. I wanted to trust you then. I wasn't sure I could. But I trust you now, even if you don't trust me."

"How are you so sure you can trust me?" My heart slammed in my ears. Was this another game? I wanted to believe this was as real for her as for me. I stepped back again and waited for her reply.

"Because you're an honest man. A good man. You've more than proved that to me."

I searched her gaze for any hint of deceit, and found none. "Shall I tell you why I trust you?"

"You trust me? Even when I've lied and manipulated you time after time?"

"I do." I scoffed. "And I might add that I haven't minded some of your manipulation at all. In fact, I quite enjoyed it."

Her gaze fell to my lips. "I think I can guess which parts."

I shook my head. "Yes, I'm sure you could guess. But that is not why I trust you." I waited for her eyes to lock with mine. "It's still there. Behind your beautiful grey eyes, I see a sliver of fear. You're not in complete control. You need me."

"I do need you." Her voice went ragged.

We leaned closer for another kiss, but jumped apart as another couple on the bridge stopped under the lamppost for a kiss. The man appeared a year or so older than I, and perhaps bolder, as he didn't attempt to break their embrace when we approached.

We slowed our steps as we reached them, and the man finally relinquished the woman's lips. She turned to face us, then half-stepped behind the man's shoulder, as if hiding. In that brief action, I recognized that she was much younger than the rest of us —nineteen or twenty, I'd say, if I were a betting man.

They were dressed in evening clothes, like us. His face was familiar, though I couldn't quite place him. He wore a black tuxedo, and she wore a butter-yellow satin gown that grazed the tops of her slippers. The man cocked his head, expecting some sort of exchange with me. I obliged.

Pulling a package of cigarettes from my breast pocket, I asked, "*Pardonnez-moi, monsieur, avez-vous un briquet?* A lighter?"

He nodded and reached into his pockets. "*Einen Moment bitte.*" He pulled out a silver lighter emblazoned with a German national eagle at the top and SS lightning bolts at the bottom. He popped the lid open and flicked the spark wheel a few times, until a flame danced between us.

"*Merci*," I said, as I slipped my cigarette between my lips and inhaled when the tip ignited. "*Bonne nuit.*"

"*Gute Nacht*," he replied.

Penny and I strolled back to the hotel, taking time to scan our surroundings and enjoy the fact that, not only had we both survived today, but we had a plan for tomorrow.

We paused at the entry doors to the lobby. She turned her head to one side. "Do we know that man?" she asked.

"I thought for a moment I recognized his face, but I don't know from when." The fact that she recognized him, too, made me uncomfortable.

She sighed through a shrug. "Take me back to my room and kiss me goodnight. We have a busy day tomorrow." Penny's tone warmed me. Her deep kiss warmed me even more, making my departure from her even more difficult.

I plodded back to my room, feeling the corridor growing longer, my door farther away with every step. Inside, I slowly peeled out of my dinner jacket and trousers, hanging them on the wooden valet stand at the foot of my bed. On my bed pillow lay an envelope embossed with the hotel's name. Within, I found a note from Elize. I recognized the handwriting immediately.

H,

I took care of Gregorio and the whole train situation. This has caused me such trouble. I beg of you to leave tomorrow. If you ever loved me, go back to France, and never utter my name again. Take your friends with you. I cannot protect you forever. I won't protect you again.

-E

. . .

NOTHING AMBIGUOUS ABOUT THE MISSIVE. No other codes, keys, or terms of endearment. She wanted me gone. Such a pity, I would not oblige her.

I paced for a moment after realizing that our plan was merely a skeleton. What would happen after Dahlia sold her painting? Were we to rush in? Take someone into custody? I took a deep breath. Penny would know. I trusted her to tell me when we got there.

I trusted her.

I washed my face and neck and put on my robe. I longed to slip into bed, but something pulled me to the window. I couldn't help but look out. What did I hope to see? Another murder? I didn't know, but I had to look anyway.

The blue glow of the sky had faded to black, and the lampposts were the only visible illumination, besides the lighting on the front of the hotel. I peered out at the bridge. Two figures, no, three, stood under the lamplight. The frail young woman in the yellow dress looked over the railing to the river below.

The man in the suit stood with his back to me, speaking with someone else who also wore a dark suit. I shifted my weight from foot to foot, eager to see who the other was. After several seconds, she stepped into the light. My heart lurched beneath my scarred chest when the brilliant head of blonde hair shone like a beacon. Not Penny, thank God, but Elize.

She took a small package from the German officer and tucked it under her arm. Their meeting ended, and Elize strode back toward the hotel doors, pausing only for a second to look around her, and then up, directly at me.

29

WEDNESDAY, JUNE 20, 1945, CANFRANC, SPAIN

My head throbbed before I opened my eyes. I resisted rousing as long as I could, but the thrum in my ears shouted for aspirin.

I gulped the remedy with tepid water and shaved my jaw, leaving my mustache to grow back to its fullness. I put on my white shirt and charcoal trousers, my navy tie, and black leather belt. I slipped into my charcoal waistcoat and dropped my pocket watch into place. Bending to put on my socks and shoes pained my back and chest so much that I feared a sweat would break before I could reach the door, so I rolled up my shirtsleeves to my elbows.

The plan was in play, and I was only a pawn. I would be watching, ready to react, ready for a chase, ready to… what else?

My revolver. I pulled it from my valise and checked to see that it was fully loaded. Returning it to its holster, I arranged it on my belt and tugged my waistcoat down to partially conceal it. No need to go asking for trouble.

A gentle rapping sound drew my attention. I opened my door to find Penny, wearing a beige, understated day dress, scattered with small pink flowers, and a pale ecru cardigan. Her head swiveled from side to side, aware of her surroundings, always.

She glanced at my holster. "You have your pistol. Good." Her gaze measured me from top to toe. "Any other weapons?"

We skipped pleasantries. "Not on me," I said, closing the door and gesturing to a chair. "I'm almost ready to go. Have a seat if you like."

"No time." She stepped to the side of my window and shifted the heavy curtain to peer out. "Dahlia and Jack have already left. Put on the rest of your weapons so we can go."

"The rest?" I asked, my hands raised.

Her hand flitted in my direction. "Knife and... I don't know; whatever else men carry."

I found my knife in my top drawer and slipped it into my trousers pocket. "What are you carrying?"

Her brow raised as her lips pursed. She lifted her handbag and waggled it toward me. "My Browning, a cyanide sachet, a loaded syringe in the lining, and," she lifted the hem of her dress over the side of one leg to expose a narrow leather sheath. "I have a small dagger in my garter."

"I'm impressed." I paused and quirked a smile. "By all sorts of things."

A broad smile broke over her full lips, pulling at the corners of her eyes. "Let's wait that a bit, shall we?" She blanked her face again. "Don't you have anything else? A vial of chloroform or such?"

"I'm a police inspector, not a spy, *chère*."

"Yes, well, we're working on that, aren't we?" She stepped to my side and took my arm.

I walked her to my door, and we locked up. Within minutes, we were back on the street and heading to a café. "Do we have time for this?" I asked when she sat at an outdoor table.

"Of course." She raised a finger, and a server took our order and hurried back inside. "You need to keep your strength up." She let her eyes drop over my chest. "You look well, though."

"*Merci*," I replied. No need to worry her over my aches and pains when I was sure I'd be collecting a few more today. "You look remarkable this morning."

"That's a shame." She tugged at one of her pearl button earrings. "Whenever I'm conducting surveillance, my goal is to look *un*remarkable."

"Impossible," I said as the server brought us coffee and pastries. I placed my napkin on my lap as he left. "*Tu pourrais essayer, mais tu ne seras jamais banale.*"

A blush fell over her cheeks, which made her even more beautiful.

"Eat. We have much to do."

A moment later, Jack and Dahlia emerged from a shop across the street. Jack carried a leather pouch containing the painting, I assumed, tucked under his arm. He wore a navy suit, with Dahlia on his opposite arm like an accessory. She sported an apricot suit dress with polished gold buttons and a smart straw hat atop her silver coif.

We finished up our breakfast and left our payment under the edge of a saucer. Following the others from a little distance, Penny and I kept an eye out for anyone else showing interest in them. We'd occasionally stop and window shop, using the reflection in the glass fronts to scan our surroundings. Nobody moved erratically on the street around us in either direction.

Jack led Dahlia toward the shop where I had sold my ring, and Penny and I moved closer.

"Henri?" Penny's voice startled me, as we had been walking in silence. She slipped her hand into the crook of my arm. "May I ask you something?"

"You may ask anything you like." I patted her hand and then let my hand rest over hers.

"Are you afraid of me?"

That was perhaps the last question I expected. "Afraid of you?" I pondered the query, searching my emotions, feeling them so close to the surface. "No, I don't think so."

"But you're not sure?" Her tone was soft, in a way that pricked my senses even more.

"I'm not afraid of you—that you'll hurt me, or anything like that. I trust you." And I did.

"Even with my lies? My manipulation?" Her gaze turned to mine, and it hid a little fear. The same as before.

"You have never shown a hint of malice toward me, even when I might have handed you over to the firing squad or guillotine." I considered our first meeting again. "It didn't take me long to realize that you might have assassinated me to save yourself. But I don't think you would now." Another beat. "I think I'm more afraid of myself now."

We continued toward the shop as Jack and Dahlia entered the building. We stopped for a moment to appear to examine the architecture of the church across the street, where, before, I'd followed Elize inside.

"Of yourself?" It was almost a whisper.

I nodded without meeting her eye. "Afraid I'll disappoint you. Afraid I won't perform the way you need me to. Afraid I'm behaving foolishly—letting all this become personal when it may be nothing more than a job for you." And now I was afraid I'd said too much aloud.

She cinched my arm to her body and released a ragged sigh. "You won't disappoint me. I keep expecting you'll hand me off to Elize, after all." She scoffed under her breath. "And I'm putting you through more than anyone deserves."

Penny didn't address my third fear. Perhaps that was for the best.

A few seconds later, Dahlia stepped out of the shop with Jack close at hand. The parcel was nowhere to be seen. Dahlia took off her hat and fanned her face with it before replacing it and looping her arm around Jack's.

"That's the signal that all went well. She sold the painting." Penny gestured to the shop. "I'll keep an eye on the front. You should walk around and see if anyone leaves from or arrives through the back."

We passed Jack and Dahlia without exchange, and Penny and I parted ways. I meandered around the side of the building, watching for anything suspicious. Trying to appear inconspicuous, I drew my pack of cigarettes, lit one, and leaned against the side of the building to enjoy it. Within just a few puffs, the back door opened, and the shopkeeper came out with the parcel peeking out from the top of a large messenger bag.

The moment he recognized me, he took off in a full sprint away from me. I gave chase, but my body still ached and moaned from the beating it had taken the day before. He outpaced me on the street, but I'd almost caught up to him as he climbed the steps to the door on the side of the chapel. The door closed behind him just as I reached the first step.

I took the steps two at a time and slowed as I reached the door. If my experience had taught me anything, it was that a bottlenecked entry point was a distinct disadvantage. I stood to the side of the door and tried the latch. There was no resistance, no lock, so I drew my revolver and prepared for a fight.

Pushing the door inward, I half-stepped through the frame, my revolver leading the way. My eyes adjusted to the darker interior, and I closed myself inside a narrow hallway with doors on either side. I was in the Knights and Knaves puzzle, but without the guards for guidance. Which door leads to the prize, and which leads to death?

Seconds ticked away as I made my choice. The door to the left led to the chapel interior, I was certain. The one to the right led toward the back of the building. Another exit? Offices? Right, then.

Again, I tested the latch, and it gave way easily. Again, my pistol led the way through. But this time, it met with resistance. Another revolver pointed back at me.

"I told you to leave Canfranc," Elize said with a cut-glass tone.

Lord, grant me wisdom; give me patience. "And I told you I couldn't."

She didn't lower her weapon, so I didn't lower mine.

I detected the slightest tremor in her hands, and it radiated out to the muzzle of her gun. Penny told me that part of Elize still loved—maybe not loved, but cared—for me. She was sure of it. I had to trust Penny's instinct here. Perhaps the tremble was an indication of it.

"Henri, what you are doing could jeopardize everything for me." The muzzle dropped an inch. "It already has. I work for very powerful people, and I need them to trust me. How can they when I let you go on like this?"

"I've done my best to act in good faith. Jack and I brought Gregorio back from the train…"

"Oh, yes. Good faith." Elize's voice held the weight of a sob. "You brought me a scapegoat. A sacrifice for the mess you made." She raised a brow and said in an even more clipped tone, *"Eh bien, merci beaucoup pour cela."* Her weapon lowered another inch.

"Sacrifice? What do you mean? We saved him. You said that you took care of Gregorio."

"Oui, the situation demanded blood. Someone had to pay it." Another wave of emotion rode over her words.

"Your boss killed Gregorio?" I asked.

"No. He demanded I kill him. To prove my loyalty. I had to put your guilt on him and execute him on the spot." She let both her arms drop to her side. "He begged me for his life. He had a family."

I ventured a step forward to disarm her, and thought I would take her into my arms, but she raised her weapon again, aimed at my heart. No tremor this time. Her elbow was locked, and her eyes blazed with ferocity.

"I don't want…" I started.

"Make no mistake, Henri." She swallowed hard. "This will come down to you and me. If not now, soon. This is your last chance to leave."

"Just tell me his name. We can free you from his control." My heart slammed in my throat, cutting my words short and dry.

"You still don't understand." The tremor was back. "It's not about me or him, or anything like that." She took a breath, her nostrils flaring with her nerves. "This machine is in position. If one person disappears, another takes his place. Right now, I can do some good."

"By killing people?"

"By killing *the right* people," she said. "You don't mind when your *girlfriend* does it."

What was it about the women I loved? *Loved*? My thoughts shattered, and I lowered my revolver and dropped it into my holster. "I'm not going to shoot you, Elize. Not now. Not ever. You've won."

She held her breath and tightened her lips into a thin line. Her chin quivered. "You're going to leave?"

"No." I backed toward the door. "You'll have to kill me, I'm afraid." I broke eye contact and turned my back as I walked out of the room and into the little hall again.

A gunshot split the silence, a bullet ricocheted off the door-frame behind me, and I raced out the main door and back down the steps. My heart slammed against my ribs as my mind processed what had just happened. Had she missed on purpose and spared my life? I wouldn't wait here to find out.

Penny rounded the corner at the next block and rushed to my side, with something in her hand. Not the parcel, but a folded note.

"You're all right," she said, panting. "I heard a shot." She wrapped her arms around my neck for a second and then released me, instantly resuming our casual demeanor.

"By the skin of my teeth, as you say." I wanted to hold her closer, but it wasn't safe yet. "The shopkeeper escaped. I ran into Elize, and she... she was angry." I took several deep breaths while Penny led me back toward the hotel. "You found something?"

"Yes." She held out the paper for me to see, but quickly dropped it into her handbag. "After you chased the man, this fell from his parcel as he climbed the chapel steps."

"What is it?" I whispered.

"Not quite sure. It's in code, and not one of ours. Maybe one of our friends can tell us something." She paused as we reached the hotel's front walk and pulled me to a stop. "A moment."

I faced her and tried to calm my expression. I needed to show her confidence and bravery, although I had none left inside. "Whatever you need."

An insincere smile tugged at the corner of her mouth and then disappeared. "I need you to—" Her words vaporized, and her eyes shimmered. She blinked until they cleared. "Don't…"

"I won't." I wasn't precisely clear about my assurances, but they came from my innermost being. I scooped her into my tightest embrace and murmured, "I won't, *chère.*"

30

WEDNESDAY, JUNE 20, 1945, CANFRANC, SPAIN

We walked, arm in arm, to the hotel café and found a table in the far corner of the room. The bright midday sun poured through the wall of windows behind us, wrapping us in an extra layer of warmth. Penny held the note so that we would both see it, though I struggled to see its significance.

"Are you sure it's a code?" I studied the numbers and letters scrawled on the slip of paper. "It looks like a receipt to me."

Penny nodded. "Perhaps that's all it is," she said. She settled her index finger on the bottom corner. "But if so, these dates are all wrong."

I focused on the numbers in question. "They're all from last year and the year before. Could it be a simple error?"

She shook her head. "It's June. We're halfway through 1945. Nobody's still writing the dates wrong. Not a shopkeeper who must write it multiple times a day." She bit her bottom lip, and I had to look away so I didn't become distracted.

"Suppose you're right." I sighed. "And why would anyone write three different dates on a receipt anyway?" I looked at the hand-written letters at the top. "Is that a W or a V?"

"C dash WC, I think," Penny whispered. "It might be VC. But is it a cipher? Without a key, it's impossible."

"Could be *Cleopatra* by Wladyslaw Czachorski. Maybe the shopkeeper wasn't sure if it was a V or a W." I shrugged. "But the rest?" A series of another dozen letters and dashes followed. And Penny was right. Without a key, it would just be a guess.

"Your instincts are good." Penny patted my hand and folded the note as a waitress rolled a serving cart to our table.

"Coffee or tea?" the young woman asked.

"I'll have coffee and she'll have tea," I replied, indicating Penny. I recognized the server as one of the singers who'd performed a few nights before. "You sing with the band sometimes?"

She bobbed her chin.

"You're quite good," I said, then thanked her for the coffee.

"Gracias," she said, though her eyes focused on Penny as she poured out the tea. "Would you like brown sugar in your tea?"

Penny's spine straightened at the question. "Brown sugar?"

I'd never heard of anyone adding brown sugar to tea, especially a Brit. I raised a brow to Penny, though she turned to face the server.

"Is it Andalusian?" Penny asked.

The exchange took me aback. I scanned the serving cart and found no brown sugar at all. There was a bowl with white cubes, but nothing more.

"*Sí, señorita,* from the sugar beet." The young woman curtsied as though that was the end of the conversation.

Penny shook her head. "Then no, thank you." She shot a warning glance at me. "I'll have one white sugar and a splash of milk, please."

The server obliged, setting both my coffee and Penny's tea in front of us. "May I bring you anything else? Would you like a luncheon menu?"

I was about to say yes, but Penny interrupted.

"May I speak to the cook, please?" Penny didn't wait for a response, nor did the server offer one, and within seconds, the young woman rolled her cart away.

"What was that about brown sugar from Andalusia and speaking to the cook?" I asked. I suspected either Penny was speaking in code or she'd lost her mind.

Leaning close to my ear, Penny whispered, "She's Resistance. I asked to speak to whoever is in charge."

"How do you know that she isn't?" I asked.

"Because she left." Penny's gaze flashed toward the door as Dahlia and Jack entered the café. They took a table nearer the center of the dining room. Dahlia smiled at me, and Jack tipped his chin toward Penny, manners all around.

"Go and say hello to Dahlia," Penny instructed. "Let her and Jack know we've made contact with an ally."

"How do I do that? What specifically do I say?"

She smiled. "I'm sure you'll think of something."

I stood and spent the next dozen steps mentally rehearsing what I might say. When I reached their table, I wished for a dozen more. Bowing at the waist, I took Dahlia's offered hand and kissed the back. "What a pleasure to see you again, Madame."

She grinned and fluttered her silver lashes. "For me as well, Monsieur."

Jack stood and reluctantly pumped my hand twice, to show anyone watching us that we were new acquaintances and on good terms. "Good to see you, Toussaint. How goes it today?"

Casual. Good. I regarded both of them and drew a breath,

worried I'd say too much. Or worse, too little, and I'll have to elaborate. "Fair—you win some; you lose some. You know how it is." Their faces showed no reaction. "We're just waiting to… speak to the chef… the cook, rather."

Dahlia nodded, and my mind relaxed. "Very good," she said.

Jack's jaw set level, he muttered, "Something wrong with the menu?"

"Not exactly." I reassured myself that he'd have done little better than I in the chase. "It's only that something we hoped for isn't on the menu."

Jack's nostrils flared. "That's unfortunate."

I suppose he understood my message. "Yes, for all of us."

Dahlia waved away the situation with a flick of her wrist. "No matter now. Just let us know what the cook says, won't you?"

Jack sighed and took his seat again, and I returned to mine. Penny offered a satisfied nod, and then, with a slight movement of her finger, she directed my gaze toward the man approaching.

He was broad and square in jaw and shoulders, and wore a blue hotel uniform. After a second, I recognized him as the barman who'd helped us into the elevator last night and given Penny a message a few nights before. How many nights? Two? Three? Twenty? I couldn't focus on that now.

"I am the cook. How can I help the *señorita*?" His voice was deep and smooth.

Penny tilted her head to one side. "*Buenos días*." She raised the note but didn't give it to him. "The waitress said you had brown sugar from beets."

The man straightened his spine. "*Sí*. Yes, from Andalusia. It's excellent."

Confirmation. Good. I was getting accustomed to this.

She slid the folded paper toward him, keeping one fingertip on the edge. "Perfect. Do you think you might use it to make this for me? It's an old family recipe."

He put a finger on it, too. "I will do my best." He waited for her to lift her hand before picking up the missive and examining it. "Is this regarding the… beet situation in the market square this morning?"

"I'm afraid it is." Penny's tone was relaxed, but her lips—I couldn't help but stare at them—tightened as she spoke.

"I don't have all the ingredients," he said as he read it again. "But I can tell you this." He looked around the room and then tapped on the paper. "There is a delivery truck going to Madrid later tonight."

"And it will carry the ingredients from Canfranc?"

"*Sí*," he answered, and handed the page back to her. "I wish I could help more, but after the train yesterday, people are watching closely. We all must be careful."

"Of course," Penny said, tucking the note into her hand-bag. "*Gracias.*"

He tipped forward in a bow and left the dining room, making a slight salute toward Jack as he exited.

Penny shifted in her seat with sparks in her eyes. "Madrid," she breathed out between her teeth. "We need someone on that truck."

"I think you missed the part about being extra careful." I leaned forward and took her hand. It was our cover, after all. "We can't just jump on the back of a truck. Right now, we're in the clear with the whole train debacle."

She wrinkled her nose. "We can't worry about our own safety."

I squeezed her hand gently. "I'm not worried about my safety. I'm worried about yours."

"This is nothing to me."

The server returned with a tray of finger sandwiches and two bowls of soup. "Enjoy," she said and then hurried away.

Penny squeezed back. "Eat something. We can discuss this all after lunch. Perhaps Dahlia already has a plan; there's no sense worrying before we know."

Until the first taste of soup spread over my palate, I would have said I wasn't hungry, but I was halfway through the bowl before I took a breath. The warm broth soothed with herbs from the Provence region, and the roasted chicken reminded me of home.

"It's marvelous," Penny said through a smile. "But you might slow down. It's better for your digestion." She served me a plate with two triangle-cut sandwiches. "Try these. They're quite delightful."

I forced myself to slow down and enjoy the meal. Penny and I didn't speak of the truck or Madrid, or anything for that matter. We simply ate, enjoyed the view of the mountainside beyond the windows, and occasionally exchanged smiles. It wasn't until we'd finished that we realized we were alone in the dining room.

"What now?" I asked my partner.

"We should update the others," Penny said.

"And how do you think Jack will respond?" I pulled out her chair and offered my arm. "And Dahlia? You said you think she'll already have a plan?"

Penny leaned her head on my shoulder for a second as we made our way back to the lobby. "My darling Henri, Dahlia always has a plan. You'll learn this soon enough."

As we passed the main desk, Rocher waved us over. "Monsieur Toussaint, Mademoiselle Tompkins, I have a message for you." He pointed his chin at me and then at Penny. "For each of you."

We paused, with hands ready to receive our notes.

Rocher glanced down at the envelopes. "Ah, yes. One from Monsieur Vogel," he said, offering me one, and then, "And from Madame Belfort." He handed the other to Penny.

She blinked at the note in her hand. "I'm sorry. Did you mix them up?"

He rechecked the names on the envelopes. "No, mademoiselle," he said, bowing. "They are correct."

"*Merci*," I said, and led Penny to a bench facing the entry windows. "Shall we sit and read?"

"Yes, thank you," she said, a perplexed expression clinging to the corners of her mouth.

We sat on the blue velvet settee and opened our missives. After exchanging one more glance with raised brows, we delved in.

HT,

My dear aunt requests the pleasure of your company for an afternoon stroll. Please meet her at the bridge at two o'clock.

-JV

Short. To the point. I pulled my pocket watch out and flipped the cover. Less than ten minutes before two. No time to make additional plans. No time to freshen up. I shifted toward Penny, who was still reading her note.

"Hmm." She folded the letter and dropped her hands to her lap. "What does your pretty girlfriend have in mind, I wonder?"

"What does it say?"

Penny tucked the page into her handbag. "She asked me not to share it with you, yet."

I scoffed. "Yes, but—"

"I'm sorry, Henri, but in this case, I tend to agree with her." She twitched her pursed lips from side to side for a moment. "What about yours?"

"Perhaps I shouldn't share mine, either."

She slipped her hand on my knee and then quickly removed it. "I apologize. Old habits, you know. Of course, you don't have to tell me."

I sighed and handed her my note. "Not because you were about to seduce me."

She giggled. "Are you so easy now?" she said, unfolding it to read.

"You should know better than anyone." I studied her expression as she read.

"So." She pressed her palms on her knees. "Dahlia will take care of you for the next hour or so, and I'll be on my own."

"You could join us," I suggested.

"No. I have errands of my own." Penny stood.

I joined her and took her elbow in my hand. "Be careful, *chère.* Elize is dangerous."

She tiptoed to kiss my cheek. "I know. I'll be careful." She lowered herself and raised her lashes, staring into my eyes. "You should be careful, too." She squeezed my arm before turning and striding toward the elevator.

I stared as she strode away. Kept my eyes on her until the sliding brass doors closed. My heart thumped heavily in my chest; my mind wandered through worst-case scenarios for a few seconds before it snapped back to the present.

"Monsieur, may I be of assistance?" Rocher asked.

"No, *merci.*" I waved him off and started for the door. Dahlia was already at the bridge, chatting with passersby while she waited for me. I expected Jack to be at her side, ready to hand her off, but he was nowhere to be seen. I hurried and greeted her with a kiss on the cheek.

"My dear Henri, I'm so glad you could join me. I was hoping

for a nice walk with you. Jack told me you and Penny had a quite interesting climb on the mountain a few days ago."

I linked my arm with hers. "Indeed, we did." I glanced down at her other hand. "It's a bit of a trek, though. Should we go back for your cane?"

She shooed away the suggestion with a flick of her wrist. "Nonsense. You can be my cane."

And with that, we were off.

31

WEDNESDAY, JUNE 20, 1945, CANFRANC, SPAIN

We took a slow pace; I liked to think it was for Dahlia's sake, but my limbs ached, and my lungs labored to maintain a steady breath. The week had been brutal on my body so far, and it was only half done.

"The first time I walked this path was the day after I witnessed the murder." My words came slowly, with intention to mask any breathiness. I gestured with my free arm toward the trees around us. "I don't remember the tree branches covering so much of the walkway."

"So many things in life are that way," Dahlia said. Her tone wore a philosopher's cloak, and my ears pricked to attention. She continued. "Our first experiences and impressions seem simple enough, but later, we discover the complexities and obstacles were there all along. We don't always appreciate the wisdom our experience gives us."

My recent *experiences* of being stabbed, beaten, and shot now pounded on my lungs, reinforcing her point. "Of course," I added, "I think the reverse is often true, as well. Problems often present themselves as more complicated at first, and then we realize they were quite simple, after all."

Her face lit up like a torch. "Precisely. Now tell me where you believe this murder took place. The event that ignited your investigation of this hotel."

I led us to a curve in the path where we could see the next straight run of the zig-zagging walkway, and indicated two levels above us. "From the view from my hotel room window, I estimated that the murderer struck the victim up there."

Dahlia studied the path as best she was able. "And you said the victim fell? Where do you think he landed?"

"Right up here." I waved my hand at the path ahead, and we hurried to the small clearing. "This is where I found a broken torch lens and blood."

Dahlia bent down in a dainty squat to examine the pathway and the ground around us. She raised a pinch of earth, rubbing it between her fingers and sniffing the dirt. "Blood." She stood and nodded. "But the lens was taken from you?"

"Yes. I believe Elize Belfort picked my pocket, as they say." I didn't make eye contact.

"As they say, indeed." Dahlia waited for me to meet her chilly gaze. "And how did Miss Belfort get close enough for that?"

"Ehr, I made the mistake of trusting her."

"And?" She added with a relentlessly arched brow.

I paused, unsure about how to answer. Was I to apologize? To explain the lesson I had learned as if I were a schoolboy?

She tapped her toe impatiently. There was my answer.

"I shouldn't have trusted her. I allowed her to be too close—both physically and emotionally." I released a heavy sigh and felt a weight drop from my shoulders.

"And what is your solution to that?" she asked.

"I'll keep her at arm's length." I focused on the scene at hand. "Will that be sufficient?"

The corner of Dahlia's lip rose, and she crossed her arms around herself. "That's still to be seen. Keeping your distance—emotionally, as you say—is an absolute must. She betrayed you twice, at least. She'll do it again." She held a long breath and made a show of slowly releasing it. "But you may have to be close to her, physically, and you need to be prepared for that. Ask Penny to teach you how to pick a pocket. She's quite adept." Dahlia looked me up and down. "I expect you'll both enjoy that lesson."

I forced an uncomfortable cough.

She laughed. "I'm sure I would," she murmured. Before I could respond, she turned again to the place in the dirt with the blood. Her gaze traced from there up to where I had indicated. "And tell me again what you witnessed that first night."

"Of course, I was in my room, so I didn't *see* any details." I moved a few more steps forward until I was in line below where I believed the initial struggle began. "A torchlight, perhaps two, just up there."

"Was it one or two?" she asked, her tone impatient. "Come, now. You're an inspector."

I was. My mind flicked through the flash of memories from that night. "Only one to begin. It swayed in the night, bobbing as its carrier walked the path upward."

We started our ascent again.

"Continue," Dahlia insisted.

"When the first reached that point," I gestured upward. "A second light appeared."

"Two? No more than that?"

"Just two." We walked to the next level of the path. "And when they met, they began moving about feverishly." I squeezed my eyes closed, visualizing it again. "At first, I thought it might be lovers. A rendezvous."

Dahlia scoffed. "French," she spat as an explanation of my first impression.

"Yes, well, better that than what did happen." I led her onward. "I realized quickly that it was a struggle. The movements were too jerky. Too frenetic." My arms shook in example. "I cannot explain more than that. I simply knew."

She glanced up to the levels above us and back down to the level below. "How did the struggle play out?"

"As I said, the lights jerked wildly, and then one swept up and crashed down close to the other." I mimicked the action. "It must have been a terrible blow."

"Rather," she replied. "Quite the spectacle." She motioned to another group of people approaching us from below on the path. "And you're the only witness?"

"It was very late. Perhaps midnight?"

"Perhaps? You cannot be more specific?" she scolded.

I dropped my head, and we allowed the other hikers to pass us and move out of earshot. "I wish I could. I was tired from the train, and I'd had a drink and a smoke."

Dahlia quirked a smile and swept an appraising gaze over my wrecked body. "I'd wager you *only wished* you felt that tired now, eh?"

Such a clever woman. "Thinking back, yes." My legs ached as we walked farther. "Once the strike happened, the first torch flailed for a moment and then fell." I indicated the path of the drop. "It looked to me like a straight fall. The blow must have been outward, away from the mountainside, to have sent him that far out and down."

A spark flickered in Dahlia's eyes. "The torch went out that far, yes."

My admiration for the woman swelled through my aching lungs. I embraced the truth that Penny had waved in my face so many times and understood what Dahlia implied. "Yes, I see. The torch may have fallen in one arc, but that doesn't necessarily mean the body did." We stooped in the center of the path at the level just below the original struggle.

"Look at this," she said, directing my gaze to the edge of the hardened walkway.

I stood where she indicated and lowered myself to sit on my heels. On the outer edge, a hunk of earth had been broken from the rest. "Yes, something hit this place. Hard enough to fracture the ground." I wished I'd had gendarmes as sharp as Dahlia in my office.

"Imagine what fractures that kind of fall would inflict on a body," she murmured.

The picture in my mind's eye made me wince in pain. "Even if the strike of the torch didn't kill the man, this certainly would have." I raked my fingers through the low shrubbery dropping off by the walkway. As Dahlia had done before, I pinched it in my fingers and raised the earth to my nose. Copper and decay… and bitterness clawed behind my eyes and in my throat. "More blood."

"Maybe more than blood," she said.

We stepped out of the way for more walkers to pass us, a pair going up and a threesome moving down. Something glinted in the sunlight as the last person shifted past me. When Dahlia and I were alone again, I crouched down to examine the object.

"What is that?" Dahlia asked and inched closer.

I squatted again and reached down to a silver ring caught on a shrub branch. I poked my finger through it and drew the thing up, careful not to touch the sides any more than necessary.

Holding the ring between us, we inspected the silver finish, dented on one side, and found a faint threading on the inside edge. "I think it's the lens brace for the torch—come off in the fall."

"Look at the inner curve," she said.

A dark, red-black stain filled the narrow groove inside the ring. "More blood." I held it closer for Dahlia to examine, and she wrinkled her nose.

"Wrap that in a handkerchief and keep it safe. No pickpockets this time." She edged her toe toward the shrub. "Anything else down there?"

I handed Dahlia the ring and my linen square and let her wrap it. I went back down to one knee and braced myself with my free hand to reach farther down the slope. After a minute of searching, I pulled up two small pieces of broken lens glass, a blood-spattered rock, and a tooth.

Dahlia added them to the handkerchief and tied the corners to make a small bundle. I stood, fighting a flash of dizziness. We finished our walk to the site of the struggle and stopped for a moment.

"From here we can enjoy the view for a moment," Dahlia suggested with the faintest hint of breathlessness in her voice.

I directed her gaze to the set of second-floor windows on the right face of the hotel front. "Those last three double windows are my room, there."

"Yes. Unobstructed line of sight," she said. "Clear night?"

"Yes."

"You understand we can't use any of this evidence against Miss Belfort, don't you?"

I nodded. "I suspect even if we tried, the police here are probably in her pocket." I sighed. "Probably helping her."

"Possibly." Dahlia leveled her chin with mine. "We'll have to confront her directly. You must use whatever sway you have with her to reach the truth."

"I don't have any more sway with her than you. Perhaps less. At least, she hasn't shot at you, yet." I let a laugh pull a shrug from my shoulders. "Anyway, I don't know if this is connected at all with your smugglers. Why is this important to you?"

The old woman drew a thin breath. "Who's to say it's not connected? This place is practically infested with smugglers; I'd wager much more is happening here." She reclaimed my arm, and her chin directed us back to the path downward. "But mostly, it's important to you. Penny has told me, since the first day we met you, that you are a good man. You've proven that true enough. I saved your life back in France, you know. I had my reasons then, too."

"More than just because Kohler was a barbaric Nazi?" I asked.

"More than that."

I felt her hands squeeze my arm, and I slowed our pace to a gentler stroll. "And when we confront Elize?"

"You truly are a delight, aren't you?" Dahlia chirped.

I understood her amusement. "It must be such a pleasure for you." I laughed. "I am new to this game of cloak and dagger, as you call it. In my world, we confront the guilty—the ones we believe are guilty—and they confess. Or sometimes they give us more information and we find someone else."

"Then perhaps it's time for another lesson for you." She paused as a lone hiker zipped by us. Waiting another full minute, she whispered, "We may follow your procedures to begin our talks with your former love. But there is much more to our ways. Maybe not *so much more*, but a little more, for sure."

I raised a brow, and the corners of her mouth dropped ever-so-slightly. "What more can there be?"

Her tone grew more serious. "You understand what an asset is?" she asked.

"Of course, I understand. I'm an asset, not directly employed or deployed by the SOE, but working in conjunction with them for a unified purpose. I have had assets through my police work, too." I paused for a moment, processing my own words. "And you believe we can turn Elize? To be one of our assets?"

"I do," Dahlia said with a confident rise in her chin. "There isn't really another option for us, is there?"

"Turning her won't be easy. She's afraid for her life, of what her superiors will do. Whoever they may be. They have already forced her to kill the man we brought back from the train. There's no way to know how ruthless they are if they have that kind of control over her."

Dahlia cocked her head to one side. "There *is* a way to know."

"Yes, if we turn her." I blew out a short but heavy breath. "I say again, it won't be easy." I repeated the phrase in a whisper, "*Ce ne sera pas facile.*"

We reached the bottom of the walking path, and Dahlia gestured to a bench just ahead. "I'm going to tell you something, because you need to know that this part of the job is never easy." She stopped us, glanced around, and took a seat. She directed me to sit beside her.

"What is it? Are you all right?"

"I am fine, Henri." She used my Christian name, and that alone took me aback. She took a second to fold her hands neatly in her lap, and when she'd done so, she raised a severe gaze to meet mine. "There are two ways to turn an asset. To turn Elize." She paused for a second, waiting for my reaction.

I planted my hands on my knees and gripped them, with just enough understanding of the situation to grasp her implications. "*Oui*, yes."

She continued. "The first is to convince her that she is safer working with us than against us. This may be easier or more difficult, depending upon her allegiance to her superiors."

"Well, she shot at me this morning without much hesitation. She missed, but I couldn't say if that was deliberate or not."

Dahlia drew a deep breath. "That suggests it will be difficult."

I nodded. I did not want to hear what she would say next.

"If we decide to turn her…"

Holding up a hand, I interrupted. "Which we must."

Her brow pinched, and she bobbed a slow nod as she spoke. "We will need her to tell us who she works for and how they operate, and if possible, who their superiors are. We will need to know their plans for the immediate and extended time frames."

"Elize will never give us this information willingly," I said. I hoped I was wrong, but my gut told me I wasn't. "We will have to… exact it… against her will." My heart slammed against my ribs as I said the words. "They will kill her if she betrays them."

Dahlia pressed her lips together so tightly they disappeared. "Then we will have to be just as threatening. We must give her no choice."

"Death at their hands or ours." I didn't bother to make it a question. Acidic bile rose to the back of my throat, and I forced a hard swallow. "With no other options?"

"That is up to her, I'm afraid," Dahlia said.

My heart lurched and ached with the words in my mouth. "Then death it is."

32

WEDNESDAY, JUNE 20, 1945, CANFRANC, SPAIN

*B*ack in my room, I sat fretting over my conversation with Dahlia while I inspected my new evidence. I studied the torch lens ring and the glass shards, making notes and sketches of each piece, and then wrapping them back up in the linen square for safekeeping. I slipped them into the toe of a shoe in the back of the armoire and prayed that Elize's spies didn't find them.

My notebook fit perfectly between the lining and the hard leather shell of my suitcase. Surely no one would pull my belongings apart to find them. But then again, I never would have believed Elize, *my once-dear Lisette*, would try to shoot me.

I dropped into the chair in my parlor and lit a cigarette. I stared as it burned down and pondered whether I was even safe in the hotel or if I should move somewhere else. And Penny? And Dahlia?

They were both so sure that everything was going to plan that they didn't seem to worry about anything. Was worrying my job?

Perhaps that was the division of responsibilities. My thoughts raced with my pulse.

A rap on my door sent me jumping to my feet. My nerves were coming undone. Even if we all stayed here, I needed to walk about. Sitting around was making me itch.

Before I could swing the door wide, Penny grabbed my arm and pulled me into the hallway with her. "We need to go. I just got a call from Jack."

"My jacket," I said, still holding my doorknob.

"You don't need it," she said.

I was exhausted from being dragged around and told what to do, and decided to take my fate into my own hands. I wrapped Penny in a full-body embrace and kissed her hard on her perfect red lips. She stilled in my arms and then melted into a reciprocal kiss, sending an electric pulse down my spine. A wave of tension filtered out of me.

When our lips finally parted, I whispered, "I don't have any weapons on me, and I'm not leaving my room without them."

A dreamy smile misted her eyes. "Go then," she breathed.

I put on my jacket and holster and checked my pistol to be sure it was loaded. I pocketed my knife and turned my watch crown a few times for good measure. I glanced up to discover Penny leaning against my door frame with one hand over her lower ribcage. Her other hand pressed against her flushed cheek.

"I didn't expect that." Her voice held a ragged breath.

"You might just as well get used to that." I closed my door and slipped my arm around her lower back. "I won't be anyone's pawn anymore."

"Well, that didn't take quite as long as I expected. I'm glad."

When we got to the elevator, I blinked. "All this pushing me was for…?"

"Pushing you to take control." She squeezed my arm as we stepped inside. "I like it when you take control."

The poor elevator operator swallowed hard and stared at the ceiling until we reached the lobby.

"You scared the poor boy," I said when we stepped out.

She laughed. "I'm certain he's heard worse. Or better, I don't know."

I spun on her. "We're going out for a drink."

"At four in the afternoon?"

"Call it high tea, or what have you." I scanned the room for watchers. "We're leaving for a few hours, and you're going to tell me everything. From start to finish. Do you understand?"

Penny's smile reached up to her eyes, and she circled both her arms around my elbow. "You have no idea how long I've waited to hear you say this."

We ambled down Canfranc's main street, past the café we'd already visited, past the chapel, and past the shop where Dahlia had sold her painting. We found another small restaurant and took seats on the side terrace.

"Is this quiet enough for you?" I asked.

She cast a sweeping scan of the space around us. "It will do, but we still must be careful what we say aloud."

"All right, then, why don't you begin, and I'll listen. No interrogations, I promise."

Penny straightened her face. "Unless you think I'm holding something back?"

"*Exactement*," I replied.

Before she began, we put in an order for tea for her and coffee for me. A tray of cheeses and pastry arrived with our drinks, and we settled in.

"You know that I arranged for you to come here to convalesce." She puffed a quick breath over her cup and then drew a silent sip.

"Yes. And I know that you understood all about Elize... and me?"

Her cup rattled slightly as she placed it back on its saucer. "When I returned to London after our...first meeting in France, I conducted a little investigation of my own. I was curious about how a fit man in the prime of his life was sitting at a desk in a small village in the north of France, and not fighting on the front lines somewhere less scenic."

"And *qu'as-tu trouvé*? What did you find?"

"That you *had been* on the front lines. That after the loss of your fiancée, you worked with the Resistance to sabotage trains. That one of your missions went wrong, and you were trapped in a train when it derailed, killing almost everyone on board—except you and three others." She paused for another sip. "I discovered who your fiancée was then, and with a few more questions, who she is now."

"Why did you suspect she was still alive?" I asked.

Penny's lip twitched, and her eyes stared into her tea. She lifted her gaze back to mine and drew a deep breath. "The fact that you witnessed her die as you were pulled away. That's what the report said. It was conveniently merciful."

"Merciful?" My eyes stung. "There was nothing merciful about it."

She reached across the table and took my hands. "Don't you see? She wanted you to be free to grieve and then to find someone. She could have just left you with a stack of unanswered letters. Or she might have given you an excuse to be angry and hate her. But she realized that your heart would hold out hope of reconciliation."

Tears burned my eyes, and I blinked them away. "Elize told you this?"

"She didn't need to tell me. This is what I would have done."

I coughed. "So I'm surrounded by compassionate women." I gave her a sarcastic eye-roll. "What more could I ask for?"

"It's what I'd do in her position." She slipped her palm against my jaw. "I'm not in her position—not anymore. She was trying to protect you from a life you didn't know she was leading." Penny rested her thumb on my lower lip. "You know my life now. You know the risks involved."

My lip puckered against her hand. "You're not going to fake your death and leave me mourning you?"

"I won't do that to you." She drew her hand back and wrapped it around her teacup. "But that brings us to my conversation with Elize. She didn't want me to tell you about it, but it isn't fair for you to be left in the dark anymore." Her eyes sparked. "Not if you're taking charge."

"You're going to tell me everything?" I grazed my fingers over the back of her hand.

Penny dipped her chin, and I suspected my touch gave her a flutter. "Elize is in a difficult situation. The men running the smuggling operation in Canfranc have used her for the last two years to move gold and tungsten, Nazis and their plunder, and… more than any of us would want to know."

"She's switched from the Resistance to the enemy? I can hardly believe there's been that much change in her."

"No." Penny stopped me short. "She's still with the Resistance, placed here to work both sides of things. She does what the smugglers ask, and in return, feeds the Resistance with as much information as she can verify."

"But she's still smuggling gold and SS officers?" I had to

know. "Is that really justifiable? A reasonable exchange, that these monsters are allowed to steal away in the night to live a life of luxury in a new country, with a new name, with treasure from the very people they murdered?"

"Of course not." She paused. "Well, yes, in some circumstances that's what happens. But in the very worst cases, she makes sure that they do not… disappear into the sunset."

"And where is the line between evil and not so evil?" My temper flared in my gut. "This one only murdered a few Jewish families, but this one exterminated a whole city's worth."

"It's not so black and white as you think." She regained and held my gaze with steady patience. "She's in a powerful position here. The Nazis have trusted her, and she has gleaned more secrets from them than I would ever hope to find. As long as she has been here, she's fed information back to the Resistance workers all over France, Holland, and England. She's saved hundreds of lives."

"And how many murderers has she allowed to go free?" I squared my shoulders with righteous indignation. "At least you make them pay."

Penny grimaced at my accusation. "I can tell you this: Elize and I are not so different."

I swallowed slowly at her revelation. "She has killed…?"

"And because of that, the people above her in this operation are beginning to question her loyalty to them." She scanned the terrace automatically. "She's in danger because of us. Because I sent you here."

"Why *did* you send me?"

Penny straightened her spine. "For two reasons. First, I'd heard that a lot was happening here, and I—being freshly out of my job of choice—thought perhaps I could make a difference in

Canfranc. I trusted you'd send for me. Second, I thought you needed to know Elize was alive."

"So this was as much about torturing me as you continuing your career as an assassin?" I whispered the last word on instinct.

"No," she said. "But I suppose it was cruel. I didn't mean for all of this…" Her words faded for a moment.

I allowed a long silence to spread between us. "All of this?"

"I didn't want to pursue you—to pursue anything with you until you realized she was alive. I couldn't live with that kind of lie between us." Penny's breath shuddered as though she might cry.

My thoughts spun wildly to process her words. "You wanted to pursue me?" I stared at my hands over hers, then met her gaze. "This isn't just seduction for manipulation?"

Her head shook a fraction of an inch. Her eyes shimmered.

"But you and Jack?" I didn't even want to say the phrase. "I thought you—"

"We were." She didn't allow me further speculation. "I believed he was giving this life up for me. I might have done, too, if he had. But he will stay on with the home office. I've already been assigned a telephone to answer and a tea trolley from which to serve the men. It's not only that. He doesn't love me, no more than I love him. He understands me, and that's comfortable. I believed that was all I should hope for, considering the life I've lived for the last five years."

"You can't settle like that. Not you." The words were out of my mouth before I could stop them. "You think you might let me try to understand you?"

A tear spilled over her cheek. "I wanted to. But I'm not sure that can happen now."

"You think I will hold a grudge against you for all this?" My hand gestured to everything around us.

"Perhaps not for what I've already confessed to; you're too kind. But for what I'm going to tell you—I think you won't be able to forgive." She flicked the tear away as it curved onto her lip. "And I wouldn't blame you."

I wiped her tear-stained cheek with my thumb. I wanted to kiss the salty trail to her lips. "What can you possibly say that would change my heart so, *chère?*"

"Elize asked me to kill her." Her eyes filled to overflowing. "And I agreed to do it."

My mouth went dry. Surely I misheard what she said. "Kill her?" I clarified.

"She wants to disappear—to keep her assets safe. The Resistance contacts—the people she's…"

"I understand what you're saying." I wasn't entirely sure I did, but I had to… I had to what? Put up a brave front? Pretend to be clever? I could do nothing but stare into her face—her perfect and sad and cruel face.

"She wants me to help her stage her murder." Penny's expression revealed no deception; her voice conveyed nothing but honesty and pain. "I'll shoot her in such a way that the people who are suspicious of her will witness it all. I'll use blanks. I have a few, though I've never used them."

"So you won't kill her?" I exhaled in relief. "It will be for show?"

"Yes. But that doesn't mean it won't be dangerous. In situations like this, there's no way to predict how onlookers might react. We don't know precisely how many Nazis and sympathizers are in this hotel."

"Then no." I shook my head. "You'd both be in too much danger."

Penny barely paused. "The whole thing could be a simple

single-shot incident, or it may become a heated shoot-out spectacle. And though I'll use a blank cartridge, nobody else will." She reached out and took my hand. "But even if everything goes perfectly, you'll never see Elize again."

"Where will she go?" The words fell from my lips without a thought.

"No one will know." She blinked her eyes slowly. "She won't tell me, and that is how it should be. I assume she has, or will have, made arrangements with someone to smuggle her out of Canfranc and out of Spain. The wisest move would be to go to America, but there are perhaps a dozen other safe places to hide."

My brain ached with this information. I didn't want to hear any of it. Whatever Elize had done, whatever she was doing, ultimately it was in the name of the Resistance. She had died once for their sake, and now a second time. How would this be fair?

Penny interrupted my ruminations. "I shouldn't even be telling you this. Elize wanted you to be out of it entirely."

"So that she could break my heart a second time?" I moaned. My emotions escaped my throat unchecked.

Penny glanced down at our hands and drew hers back from mine. "That's why I had to tell you. I couldn't let you spend the rest of your life believing a lie. You've already lost too much to lies."

I needed to think about something else. Anything else. "And Jack's message?"

"What?" Penny's face blanked.

"When you first came to find me, you said you'd had a call from Jack. What was it about?" I rubbed my temples. My mind craved a palate cleanser.

"Oh, yes," Penny said. She straightened again, back to business. "He tracked the painting to a collector in Portugal. In Porto.

He's checking whether it will stay in Porto or be shipped elsewhere." She shook her head an inch. "It doesn't sound like much, but it might lead us to a whole new network down there."

I nodded. "Or to a single collector who simply likes the painting." Perhaps I was being petty and cruel. My statement was flat and diminished all her work. At that moment, I wasn't sure I cared.

Her brow rose, and she blinked away whatever emotion might have brewed behind her eyes. "Yes, erhm, that's a chance we always take. Half, *at least* half of our work is chasing ghosts."

"Wait," I said. My thoughts rolled through everything Penny had told me, back to my conversation with Dahlia. "Not even an hour ago, I was on the mountain path with Dahlia." My hand automatically gestured toward the east. "We had a very different conversation."

Penny dipped her chin. "Yes, Dahlia said that you discovered more evidence of the murder you witnessed."

"We talked about turning Elize into an asset."

"I know." She murmured. Her voice softened. "That was what I was supposed to be doing—convincing Elize to work with us. To share her contacts and how this whole operation worked. She gave me some information. She told me she was ready to let it go." Penny chewed on her bottom lip for a second. "Elize told me that she initially wanted you to be the one to kill her, but that she was concerned for your safety. And concerned that you might not be able to do it."

A headache flared behind my right eye. "You agreed with her?"

"It's not that I think you aren't capable, but I've done this type of thing more than you. It will be safer for everyone if I do it."

I didn't want to think about how many times Penny had killed —not in combat, but face to face. My lip twitched, and I rubbed the heel of my palm into my eye, trying to push away the pain. Safer? She was anything but safe.

As if she read my mind, she answered, "It's all war. I wasn't in the trenches, but neither were the men I've killed. Some of them had murdered dozens. Some hundreds, maybe thousands."

My gut panged. Between the realization of Penny's capabilities and the headache, I feared my pastries might make a return. "So I'm supposed to stand by and witness you shoot her?" I clicked my tongue. "Then what? Shrug my shoulders and go back to France?"

"There it is." Penny's expression brightened.

"What do you mean?"

"Weeks ago, when you were first investigating me... all of us... You would click your tongue when you were in thought. At first, it was annoying. But then, I realized you did it whenever you were sorting things out. It became so charming to me, your tongue."

Her mention of my tongue, my tongue-clicking, was a casual comment that somehow turned intimate on her lips, sending a bolt of heat through my body. I wondered if I could ever click my tongue again without it feeling manipulative. "You," I hesitated. "You didn't answer my question."

Penny's lips curved into a soft smile. "I thought you liked that about me." She released a breathy laugh. "Of course, we'll have to work out the details. The when, where, and who the witnesses must be."

A server came and refilled our cups, and we paused the conversation for a moment, giving me a split second of doubt. If Penny wanted to, she could dispose of Elize quietly, and no one would be the wiser. I'd never know, surely. But no, that wasn't my genuine fear. I trusted *this* woman.

When we were alone again, I leaned closer. "And do you trust

Elize? Because I'm not sure that I do. She's been trying to send me out of Canfranc since I arrived."

Penny stirred her tea as though she needed something to do with her hands. "I do not. This might all be a trap for us. Jack suspects that the man on the bridge last night is here to be smuggled away by Elize. Or he may be one of her higher-ups, sent to confirm she is still loyal." Her grey eyes bore deep into mine. "Or both. This whole performance may get us all killed."

33

WEDNESDAY, JUNE 20, 1945, CANFRANC, SPAIN

We finished our tea and took a long circuit around the village market square, scouring each booth and cart for items that were out of place. We studied the vendor's faces for nervous glances. As we walked, we found only casual business exchanges and common gossip among the shoppers, saturating the bazaar with a deep, steady hum.

The afternoon sun penetrated through the cart awnings, casting colored shades of blues, reds, and greens on everything from headscarves and fans to bins of potatoes and beans. The owner of one cart waited as we picked through his collection of brightly glazed pottery—some secondhand, some new.

He tilted his chin upward to catch my attention. "I can also offer other things… if you're looking for something special."

I gestured for Penny to keep browsing and took a step closer to the man. "How special?" I asked.

"I can procure cigarettes and cigars," he whispered. "Finest quality." His eyes cut left and right. "For a fine price, of course."

"Of course," I agreed. I moved to retrieve my wallet. This would be a good opportunity to show that I wasn't concerned with legalities. My mind pondered how easily I leaped to the other side of the law. "And what is this fine price?"

"Twelve pesetas for a pack." The man's statement was flat, with no room for negotiation.

"That's quite a lot." I scratched the back of my neck, hoping to appear unsure. "Perhaps I should give up smoking."

He was undeterred. "This is top-quality tobacco, friend. I have a cousin in Cordoba. But that makes it expensive. Not the cheap army rations, you know?"

"Do you have it here?" My head swiveled back and forth. "Could I buy three packs?"

He nodded and reached down to a crate beneath his cart. "Only three?"

My lip twitched, aching to grin at his highway robbery. "Darling," I said to Penny. "Have you found anything you like?"

"What do you think of these?" She dangled a pair of tomato-red espadrilles toward me.

I smiled broadly. "How much for all?" I asked.

"Sixty *pesetas*." Again, not a question.

"Good. *Bueno*." I counted out the money, aware that I was paying him nearly triple what our purchase was worth. He handed me a small paper bag with the cigarettes, and I slipped them into my pocket. "Gracias."

He tipped his head forward. "If you need more, come back tomorrow."

I crossed my arms, took another step closer, and lowered my voice. I curled one finger over my mustache. "Do you have any other *special* items I might like?" I muffled my words. "My wife and I will be… moving to Lisbon soon, and I'm looking for some nice things for the house."

"Nice things are expensive," he said.

I chuckled. "My wife likes expensive things." I flipped a palm toward Penny.

"Ah, but she is worth it, no?" he asked, perusing Penny's figure.

This time, I thought it might be a question. "*Si*, she is worth every *peseta*."

He patted my shoulder, as if to congratulate me. "Lucky man." He glanced from side to side. Can you come back tomorrow? My… cousin will be in town. He can procure anything."

"I will see you then," I said, offering a hand to shake.

"*Mañana*," he said through a broad grin.

I was the perfect sucker he'd always dreamed of meeting. I wrapped my arm around Penny's shoulder. "Let's go back to the hotel and have you try on those shoes," I said.

We were a dozen steps back down the road when she leaned close to my ear. "You're getting good at this. I think you're starting to enjoy it."

"Which? Buying black market cigarettes or calling you my wife?"

Her eyes sparkled at my response. "Hmm. Thank you for the shoes."

"You know, women generally don't wear stockings with espadrilles." I wiggled my brow. "You can go bare-legged in them."

Penny's face toned to a lovely shade of pink. "What have I done to you?" she asked.

"What would you like to do?"

Her blush deepened. "Now you're simply trying to…"

"Mission accomplished, I'd say." I gestured to the other end of the square. "What now? More shopping, or should we go back

250 | KIM BLACK

soon? I don't know any details of your plan, including the timetable."

She shrugged, then looped her arm with mine. "I'll work out the details with Elize this evening. We need the right witnesses, but no more than that. We don't want to risk a domino effect that could put Resistance workers in more danger."

"You're telling me that I may not find out anything until it's all done?" My words fell flat, considering that I may never see Elize again.

"I know that's not what you wish to hear." She drew a long breath. "But it's for the best. A quiet kill is safer for everyone."

That word. Kill. A punch to my already-sore gut. "You speak as though you're really going to kill her."

"We must treat the whole thing as genuine." She smiled as she spoke, like the conversation was no more important than the weather or what song might play at the reception later. "As far as you're concerned, it must be real."

"If Jack spoke to me like this, I'd have a name or two for him." A frown pulled at the ends of my mustache.

"I know full well what you'd say to him." She beamed up at me. "Don't worry. I know what I'm doing. Elize won't be hurt."

"What about you? Who will protect you?" I shook the frown off, but my gut still knotted. "What if the *right* witness decides there are still too many loose ends?" I huffed. "You'll be alone with your pistol loaded with blanks."

"Pshaw." She puckered her perfect lips. "You know me better than that. At this moment, I have eight weapons on my person." She chuffed. "Oh, nine if you count my new shoes."

"Your shoes?"

"They have long laces. You've seen what I can do with long cords," she said.

"Well, yes, I know what you can do." Just the thought of that night, listening to Penny strangle a man after a furious fight between them, made my stomach ache. I'd drifted in and out of consciousness, making the whole situation surreal. I imagined her struggle lasting hours, though it was little more than ten or twenty minutes. I snugged her closer.

"You know I can take care of myself; you don't need to worry."

"But you worry about me?" I asked.

"I'm not—I've been in this kind of situation dozens of times," she said.

"I've been on the front lines of war. I've worked as a police inspector even after that. I'm not a child, Penny." I knew my words wouldn't change her mind, but I had to say them. "You needn't treat me like one."

"Of course not." Her gaze dropped to the street as we returned to the hotel. "What time is it?" she asked.

I tugged out my pocket watch and glanced at the face through the newly scratched crystal. "It's almost six."

She handed her new shoes to me. "Keep these with you. I'm probably late for my meeting with Elize in the bar." She pecked my cheek. "Pick me up for the reception at eight, all right?" With that, she hurried away, leaving me alone at the elevator.

34

WEDNESDAY, JUNE 20, 1945, CANFRANC, SPAIN

The hall back to my room bustled with people arriving and leaving, chattering as they planned this or that, but I was alone, carrying a pair of women's shoes.

I quickly undressed, laid out my suit, and freshened up, wondering what Penny might wear to the reception. I'd been here almost a week, supposedly to recover from my stabbing injury. Instead, I'd collected half a dozen more scars, an intensified hatred of trains, and a beautiful woman who made me question everything about my life.

With my shaving towel over my shoulder and wearing no more than my pants, I decided to squelch the warning voices and memories echoing in my head.

I poured myself a bourbon and let it burn down my throat while I sat in a chair at the window. The mountainside danced with waning sunlight over the path and trees, tempting me to scan the shadows for villains. The melodies of the band practicing down the hall wafted just beyond my door. Soon I'd be on the dance floor with Penny in my arms. I'd breathe in her honied perfume, press my fingers into the silk of her dress... and skin, and tilt my ear to her every word.

A remembered prayer from months ago popped into my mind, blocking everything else. I'd been sitting at my desk at the end of a particularly tedious day, praying that one day I might make a difference in this world of madness and terror. I prayed that France would regain peace and rebuild the beauty that it had once so intrinsically possessed. I prayed that I would find someone...

"Hah!" The scoff came out louder than I expected, almost startling me. "*Mon Dieu*, you have such a sense of humor."

But with that recognition arrived a moment of resolution. Tonight, things would change. One way or another, my life would take a new course. Determination itched in my blood—coursing beneath my skin. Any other time, I'd have blamed the drink, but not tonight.

Tonight I was ready for my mission.

35

WEDNESDAY, JUNE 20, 1945, CANFRANC, SPAIN

With my joints and muscles loosened by a second glass of bourbon, I dressed in my dinner suit and armed myself with my pistol, knife, and a few extra rounds of ammunition. When I thought of what Penny would be carrying on her person, I felt underdressed.

My pocket watch told me it was time to go, and my heart thumped hard when I drew my door closed with a click.

Tonight.

Ahead, Jack escorted Dahlia into the reception hall. Without remark or salute, I passed them and strode to Penny's room. I'd barely touched my knuckle to the door, and it swung open. She stood solidly, like an angel. Not the haloed, choir-robed cut-out from a Christmas card, but a mighty messenger of God himself. I wouldn't have been surprised to see her holding a sword.

She wore a shimmering gold gown, ruched under and between her breasts, baring her perfectly formed clavicles. Her only jewelry was a pair of diamond-drop earrings, glistening against her shining dark hair. Her pursed lips shone with her signature Victory Red.

"Are you ready?" she asked.

Those three words carried a mountain behind them.

"I am." My response was confident—probably more confident than I felt.

She took my arm with her right hand, her gold shell clutch in her left. "Good. Tonight may be difficult… for all of us."

"Will I be told anything?"

We paused at the reception room door. "You should do as Jack and Dahlia tell you. Don't worry about anything else. It's for the best."

The phrase, *it's for the best*, shot through my ears like a bullet, echoing in my commander's voice when he'd handed me Lisette's ring. Warning sirens blared in my brain.

It was *not* for the best.

But as Penny's protégé, I refused to let on. This was my test, and I would succeed.

I walked her to an empty table, still hoping she'd at least throw me a few crumbs. I couldn't merely be a pawn in this. I wouldn't. The fire in my gut was too great.

The room buzzed with heightened energy tonight, as the hotel manager, Albert Lebeau, roamed from table to table, greeting guests with hugs and handshakes. I scanned the room for Elize, but didn't find her.

Monsieur Lebeau meandered to the stage and took the microphone. After clearing his throat for the room's attention, he welcomed everyone. "I am heartened to see new faces and old friends," he said with a round, cheerful tone.

The room erupted with applause as though he'd announced Armistice.

"I ask you all to dance, to drink, to enjoy the music, and to put away the troubles of the war for a night." He tipped forward in a slight bow and slipped the microphone into its stand with a crackle. He gestured to a curvy redhead, and she took her place in front of the band and then blew a kiss to Lebeau.

The woman waited for her cue after a dramatic introduction and began "Get Happy" with a full sway in her hips. The singer's energy surged through the room, and as she repeated, "get ready, get ready," my adrenaline spiked.

A server offered us champagne, and we obliged with quick nods. We clinked our coupes together, and Penny kissed the rim of her glass. I'd never been jealous of a cup before, but I burned at that moment. Her lashes fluttered, and her gaze locked with mine. I matched her sip and then smiled as I set my drink down.

"What are you grinning at?" she asked, with color rising in her complexion.

"You." Plain truth. "I'm wondering if you will allow me to dance with you."

She let her gaze fall to her bubbly. "Well, you haven't asked yet, have you?" Her eyes cut from side to side. "Next song, if it's not too…"

"Something slow, then?"

"I'd like that." She sipped again, working her eyes around the room.

The song wound down, and as guests applauded, the band began "Stardust." I reached for Penny's hand. "Would you do me the honor of a dance?"

A contented smile settled over her lips. "It would be my pleasure," she whispered when her mouth drew near my ear.

"I assure you, there's plenty of pleasure to share," I murmured in response. My fingertips detected a shudder running down her back. I didn't want the momentum to flag. "If you'll allow."

Her body melted into mine, and she released a deep sigh over my shoulder. For a flash of a second, I considered how disapproving my old schoolmaster would be of our closeness. The idea tugged my whiskered cheeks into a smile.

My thoughts volleyed through a dozen situations we might be in tonight, each one more pleasurable than the last, each one prompted by another sway of her hips or twist in her waist. But then, without preamble, her body stiffened against mine.

I turned with the song until I realized the object of her apprehension. The German from the bridge last night strode in with the very young blonde on his arm.

She oohed and ahhed at the room, jabbing her finger at the band and then the singer and then the trays of champagne. The man whispered something into her ear, and she quickly moved her finger to her mouth, slipping the nail between her teeth like a child.

Penny's hand squeezed mine. "Perhaps we should sit."

I didn't answer, but danced her back to our table. "I suppose we're in it, eh?"

"I suppose we are." She allowed me to hold out her chair as she sat. "Thank you."

Jack slipped past our table, carrying two champagnes to the table where Dahlia sat. She wore a deep sky-blue sheath of crepe with billowing chiffon drapes from her shoulders to her hips. Silver drops hung from each ear, and a double strand of pearls hung over her bosom.

Dahlia waved a gloved hand to me, flipping it over to beckon me to her side.

"I think I've been summoned," I said to Penny.

She caught my hand in hers. "I'll see you later, love."

For a split second, my feet froze in place. I studied Penny's expression—almost languid and pale. Could I see this through?

With her eyes, she directed me to go. Somehow, she assured me that everything would be fine. That it would all be over soon.

Jack gestured to the chair next to Dahlia. "Have a seat, Henri. My aunt wants to speak with you. I need to send a telegram; I won't be a minute."

Dahlia tugged her gloves off her hands and into a pile next to her purse. "This looks to be quite a night," she said, as though that explained everything.

"Did they banish you, too?" I asked.

A half-smile formed on one side of her mouth. "Strictly speaking, I'm not sanctioned to do anything." Her voice stayed low. "No more than you are."

"So what *are* our roles for tonight?" I asked under my breath.

"We sit here and listen to good music and sip good champagne." Dahlia picked up her coupe and tapped it on mine. "And we wait." She wiggled her little finger toward the door where Jack and Penny were following the German into the corridor.

"I don't think I'll be good at this," I said.

Dahlia grimaced, raising her shoulder half an inch. "It could be worse." She tipped her glass up to finish her drink. "I spent one night on my stomach under the branches of a thick pine tree, waiting for my target to appear."

My mind processed her words slowly. "You were a... like Penny?"

"Oh, yes, dear." Her words were flat and matter-of-fact. "I thought Penny had told you."

"Erhm, I guessed a little bit, but I didn't think of it too much." I gulped too much champagne, and the bubbles rushed up the back of my throat.

"Well, that night was certainly the worst of my career so far," she continued.

"The worst?" I decided if we were to stay away from the others, I might as well hear Dahlia's tale.

"The temperature dropped, and it began to rain. I wasn't sure if my man would show up at all." Her tone was quiet, and her lips barely moved.

I sat on the edge of my seat. "And did he ever appear?"

Dahlia sighed at her empty glass. I pushed mine in front of her. She picked it up as if in a toast to me. "Oh, yes. He finally arrived—an hour later."

"And what did you do then?"

She finished another sip. "I shot him through the heart."

My jaw dropped to my chest. "That must have been terrible."

She nodded. "My dress was ruined entirely. I don't want to even mention my hair. I had to hike half a mile back to my place, and by the time I got back, I looked like a drowned rat."

I grabbed two more glasses from a server. This conversation had turned much darker than I expected. We both drained our cups, then stared at each other with discontent in our expressions.

"I suppose you know everything about the plan?" I asked.

"I do." She patted my hand. "But I can't tell you, dear. I'm sorry." She jutted out her bottom lip. "It's much too dangerous."

My thoughts wheeled through her stories and what Penny had told me. My alcohol-fueled state lent itself to ideas I'd never otherwise consider. I leaned closer to her ear. "I understand. I think that's why Penny wanted me to keep an eye on you."

Dahlia pulled her chin in and furrowed her thin

brows. "*You're* not keeping an eye on *me*. *I'm* keeping an eye on *you*."

This might work. I might have had two more drinks than her, but I also had at least seventy pounds on her, possibly a hundred. "Oh, yes, of course. That's what I meant to say."

"Because I've been doing this a long time," she insisted.

"Right." I raised my brow as if I were placating a child. I folded my hands in my lap and sat up straight.

"I could be the one out there," she said, motioning to the mountain. "But Penny thought it would be best if Miss Belfort's people didn't know I was connected to everything else—what, with the painting and all."

I bobbed my head in agreement. "That's best, I'm sure." I stroked my jaw. "Speaking of the painting, I heard Jack was able to track it down. What happens next with that?"

Dahlia hadn't heard me at all. "Of course, Penny's methods are up close. She likes to be sure, she says." She shrugged. "My marks have always been just as dead as hers when it's all over."

The singer started "Someone to Watch Over Me," and I had an idea. I only needed a little more convincing to move her out the door. "If you're keeping an eye on me, what do you do if I decide to go?"

"I'll stop you."

"What are your methods for stopping a man twice your size?" I asked.

She looked me over from head to toe and back. "Well, my methods aren't what they used to be," she admitted. "But don't underestimate me. I'd stop you if I wanted to."

I slouched in her direction. "Dahlia, you minx, you really must tell me about your methods someday. The old ones, I mean."

She wiggled her brow at me.

I took a beat and flashed a facetious grin. "So what if you *didn't* want to stop me?"

She slouched toward me. "Then I'd have to follow you, I suppose."

"And if I were following Penny and Jack?"

"We aren't supposed to." Dahlia sighed. "Remember?"

"Listen to this song," I said, waving a finger into the air. "What if they need us?"

"Someone to watch over…" Her words trailed off. She wrapped her tiny fingers around my wrist. "Do you think they need us?"

"I defer to your experience, Dahlia. I've never been in any situation like what they're in tonight." I let her stew a bit. "After all, you just said your worst night was because of the weather. I'm sure they're fine. The moon is out, no rain. They'll be fine."

Dahlia's grip tightened. "We should go. We can follow at a distance. Just to be sure."

"No, Penny will be mad. Jack will be angry. He said I should keep an eye on… that you should keep an eye on me."

She shook her head. "I know what I'm doing. Just follow me."

36

WEDNESDAY, JUNE 20, 1945, CANFRANC, SPAIN

Ten minutes later, we were downstairs, watching Penny slip out into the night after Elize. Jack was already out of sight. I turned to face Dahlia. "Perhaps I should go alone."

"Don't be a fool." She waved me toward the door. "We go together or we don't go at all."

We took a slower pace across the bridge, trying to appear as if on an evening stroll to clear our heads. The waxing moon provided ample light to the pathway up the hill.

The night air filled my lungs with a chill, and I tugged off my jacket for Dahlia to wear over her thin dress.

"Thank you," she whispered. "But won't you need it?"

"I'm fine." I took her tiny, butter-soft hand in mine. "I don't want you to end up shivering under a tree like before."

"You are a fool, aren't you? A polite fool, but a fool all the same," she said with a chortle. "At least you didn't bring a torch to announce our presence to everyone."

I knew she was right, though part of me wished we had some

light. We slowed further, careful to keep our footfalls as silent as possible. Dahlia made no more noise than a cat, leaving me in awe at her prowess.

She squeezed my hand several times to signal a stop. She didn't speak, and I knew I shouldn't either.

Ahead of us came Elize's voice, muffled. She spoke to the German in low, sharp tones. We moved closer until we could make out words.

"The paperwork is all here. New identification, travel documents, and even a deed to property in your new home under your new name. You won't have trouble traveling."

The man's reply was a gruff, "This is enough? Will there be questions?"

Elize sounded confident. "No more than usual. I'm sure you can find an answer to satisfy anyone along the way."

Papers shuffled, and we moved closer.

"How do I know you won't turn me over to the authorities? Or to your French inspector friend. Now that you know my new name and travel routes—you could do that easily, eh?" His tone was sharp and impatient.

"He's not my friend. He's nothing more than a pest of the worst kind. You know I've been doing this a long time," she said. "I've proven my loyalty."

Another voice. The young companion. "I don't trust her. You have your papers. You should kill her. Just to make sure she keeps her mouth shut."

Elize answered, "That isn't necessary. I assure you." Her tone was tense.

"But my woman has a point," the man said.

His voice sliced through the darkness, and a sudden jolt of recognition rocked me. He was Klaus, or Redbeard, who'd beaten and questioned me the other day. And I'd told him I was Elize's old friend. Without his thick facial hair, he was a different man.

I started forward, but Dahlia's grip kept me in place. She shook her head slightly and raised a finger, urging me to wait.

Klaus continued. "If I shoot you here and now, I won't have to wonder if you will sell my information to anyone. I can leave and start my new life without worry."

"Just as dozens have before you," Elize said. "Dozens that I have helped. And I can help dozens more if you allow me to live."

"If I cared about the others, I wouldn't be here with you now," he replied.

Another voice broke in. "You don't have to worry about her any longer," Penny barked with a perfect German accent. "Your papers are good. I will take care of her, Herr Gooden. That is your new name, correct?"

His voice grew wary. "It is."

Dahlia nudged me, and we walked closer until we could see them all through the trees, staying concealed from view. Elize stood unarmed, but both Penny and Gooden had their guns leveled at her. I carefully drew my revolver, and Dahlia did the same.

Penny waved her pistol at Elize. "Everything she's done has been helpful to the Third Reich, but there have been rumors. We can't leave anyone in the same place too long—always rumors." She nodded toward Gooden. "You can stay and watch if you like, but it's better if you go now so no one will suspect your involvement in Fräulein Belfort's tragic death."

Gooden tucked the documents into his jacket and started to turn, but the young blonde stopped him. "I think we should stay. Just to be sure we're safe."

He stopped mid-turn. "Perhaps you're right."

My heart slammed against my ribs. This was the moment. The plan was coming off perfectly. We just had to stay out of the way.

Penny stepped toward Elize. "I'm sure you understand. We cannot have doubts."

Elize shook her head. "No, please..."

The pistol shot peeled and echoed over the mountainside. This wasn't Penny's Baby Browning, but a full-sized revolver.

Elize dropped to her knees and fell face down. Perfect.

But as she fell, my heart lurched. Penny fell, too. A blossoming crimson spot spread over the side of her gown. The young blonde tossed back her head and turned, revealing a smoking gun in her hand, too.

No!

"Why did you do that?" Gooden asked. He tucked his pistol into his jacket. "One body is trouble enough. Two is... we don't have time for this."

The young woman stomped forward, standing over Elize, aiming her gun mere inches from Elize's head. "I did it to be certain. To make sure there's no one left to talk," she said.

Another shot, and the blonde dropped over Elize's body. Klaus's head swiveled from side to side, and he ran, racing past us and back down the mountain.

None of this was part of the plan.

37

WEDNESDAY, JUNE 20, 1945, CANFRANC, SPAIN

*I*n utter panic, Dahlia and I rushed to Penny's side, while Elize struggled to push the blonde off of her. "What happened?" she asked.

Jack appeared seconds later with a rifle slung over his shoulder. Thank God he'd been there to stop the young woman.

I dropped to my knees beside Penny, scooping her into my arms. "*Je vous salue, Marie,*" I cried to heaven. "Penny, are you alive? *Mon Dieu, please let her live.*"

Penny mumbled, her voice barely a whisper. "I... Henri, I..." and then she faded.

Elize scrambled to examine Penny's side. "It looks like the bullet went right through her, but she's bleeding too much." She took the sash from her dress, and we wrapped and tied it over the wound. Elize leveled a hard stare at Jack and me. "You have to carry her down. Take her to the back of the bar. My friend there will take care of her."

Jack looked around. "What about you?"

"Dahlia and I will clean this mess up. We'll meet you later. Go quickly. She doesn't have time to lose."

I picked up Penny, holding her against me to keep her cooling body warm. "Wake up. Stay with me, Penny. I have you. Hang on."

Jack draped his coat over her. "This will help," he said. He walked ahead at a clipped pace. He motioned for me to step into the brush when a couple of men rushed up. "I heard a shot," he told them. "But I didn't see anyone. It sounded like it came from over there." He pointed in the direction of the other footpath, away from the women. "I've already checked this one out."

The men took his advice and headed up the other side of the mountain, and we hurried down.

When we reached the back of the hotel, the bartender or cook, or whatever he was, stood waiting for us. "Give her to me."

"I have her, just tell me where to put her," I insisted.

He shook his head and led me into a half-empty pantry closet with an island in the middle of it. "Lay her there." He sighed, pulling on a butcher's apron. "We'll make sure the bullet is out and the wound is clean. I have some antiseptic…" He didn't bother finishing; he only unwrapped her makeshift bandages and tore her dress free from her injury.

"How did you know we were coming?" I asked. I took a step back while he worked on her. My mind struggled to sort out what had happened over the last half hour.

"We've had extra eyes on the mountain for days. Expecting something like this." He moved closer to study the hole in Penny's side, then straightened his back. "Not with her, though. She's careful. Must have been a mess up there."

I nodded.

Jack paced in front of the door. "Will she be okay?"

The barman huffed. "I've seen worse." He pulled out a drawer from the island and began selecting his equipment. He gestured to me to stand beside him. "Hold this sponge here. Not too much pressure until I say. I need to stitch a few things up and stop this bleeding."

My face turned hot and then very cold as the blood drained from my cheeks. "Okay."

"Are you able to do this?" he asked. "If you drop, I can't stop with her to take care of you."

"I understand. I'm fine," I lied. "Just don't let her die."

"She's not going to die," he said.

Was he trying to convince me or himself?

The barman began the tedious job of stitching Penny back together.

A knock at the pantry door, and Jack stepped aside. When the door slid open, my whining Spanish friend from that night's pummeling stepped inside. He stood in solemn reverence at the sight of Penny covered in blood.

It took all my self-control to keep the sponge in place over Penny's wound. I'd helped with dozens of injured troops in the field, always steady. But this was different. This was Penny.

I drew a breath to speak, but didn't have the chance.

"Your women are remarkably strong creatures," Whiner said to Jack and me. "Even the old woman."

"What's going on up there?" Jack asked.

"The girl will make a nice substitute for Elize. Blonde, beautiful, and best of all, dead. They're swapping clothes right now. Whoever shot her messed up her face enough to keep the questions to a minimum." He cut his eyes to me and then back to Jack. "As soon as Elize gets back, she and Albert can escape."

"Albert Lebeau, the hotel manager?" I asked.

"I've said too much already." Whiner glanced at the barman. "I just wanted to see if she's going to make it. Elize will want to know."

"She'll make it."

The man nodded and left us.

"All right, now we need to turn her over so I can work on the exit wound."

Jack and I stood side by side and leaned Penny forward in our arms, and then onto her stomach. I turned Penny's head to the side, and she mumbled again, this time in obvious pain.

"I'm here," I sobbed. I knelt beside her and cupped her face in my palm. "I'm here, *chère*."

"Hurts…" she moaned before losing consciousness again.

"How much longer?" I asked. "Can't you give her something? She's in so much pain."

"That's actually a good sign," the barman said with a chuff.

Jack crossed his arms over his chest. "I need to go. To make sure the car is coming. We can't afford a delay."

"Go," the barman and I said in unison, and Jack slipped out.

"Right." The man finished his stitching and wrapped bandages around Penny's stomach. "She needs a few days in bed. Can I trust you to manage her?"

"I won't let her out of my sight," I promised. "I just need to carry her to my room without being seen."

"I can help you with that." The barman left the pantry for a moment, returning with a cart. "We can take her up the service elevator."

"If we're using the service elevator, I can carry her," I said.

"Not safe enough," he replied. "Just because I am Resistance doesn't mean everyone in this place is. We have too many coming and going to be absolutely sure. And even the people I trust, I don't trust, you know?"

"I understand."

We shifted Penny from the island to the cart, arranging her so that her knees were bent and the lower half of her legs hung over the edge. We covered her with a tablecloth and then another, and soon it looked like a cart filled with a late-night dinner for two.

Ten minutes later, we settled Penny into my bed, dressed in one of my undershirts. She made fitful sounds, hovering somewhere between sleep and consciousness.

As the barman piled the cart with the tablecloths and a couple of glasses from my bar cabinet, I offered him my hand. "My name is Henri Toussaint. Thank you for all your help. I'm in your debt."

He took my hand and pumped my arm. "You may call me Manuel. My only request is that you keep her safe." He nodded his chin toward Penny and smiled. "That should keep you busy enough, eh?"

"That is the challenge, is it not?" I laughed and saluted the man as he left the room, pushing out the cart. I'd barely moved a chair to the bedside when I heard a faint rap at the door.

"Yes?" I mumbled through the door.

"Dahlia."

I pulled the older woman inside, quickly locking the door behind her, then swallowing her in a hug. "I am relieved to see you." Her tiny frame was nothing in my arms. "Come and sit with Penny."

She nodded, patting my arm. "What is the prognosis?" She wore a simple day dress and her practical shoes now. She settled into the chair at Penny's side. "Oh, she looks so pale."

"Manuel says she will recover, with one more scar added to her collection." I realized my words revealed more than I intended to say, but I decided that Dahlia would understand. "She has more scars than I expected."

"And many more on the inside." Dahlia sucked in a deep breath and took Penny's hand in hers. "I suppose we all do." She glanced up at me. "She won't heal from those on her own. I know from experience. Being alone only makes the scars run deeper. She needs…"

A low moan from Penny interrupted her.

"There, there," Dahlia whispered. "I'm here, and Henri's here." Penny settled. Dahlia put a palm to her cheek. "She's warm."

"I'll bring a cool cloth," I said, ducking into the bathroom. I glanced into the mirror as I soaked the face cloth in cold water. My shirt was smeared in Penny's blood, and my face smudged with a mix of dirt, blood, and sweat.

"Thank you," Dahlia said, taking the cloth and folding it before placing it over Penny's forehead. The woman regarded my appearance. "I'll sit with her. Go in and wash your face. This night isn't over yet."

I obeyed and scrubbed my face, arms, torso, and neck, watching as all the evidence of the violent night circled the drain and disappeared. My thoughts thumped in time with my heart, aching to the same beat of the water pounding my face and shoulders.

Five minutes later, I was dressed in clean trousers and a plain shirt. My face was clean, my hair combed. I hadn't shaved, but there would be time for that later. I sat in the parlor chair to slip on fresh socks and shoes when a faint *shush* sounded at my door. Not a knock or tap. More like a puff of breath.

I noticed a folded note on the floor, peeking under the threshold.

"Will this night never end?" I muttered. In two paces, I had the note in hand, reading aloud. "The bridge in ten minutes." Nothing else on the page, but I recognized Elize's handwriting.

"Don't worry about Penny. I'll stay here; you go." The edge in Dahlia's voice cut through my thoughts. "Take a gun," she added, handing me a pistol.

I tucked the revolver into my waistband and pulled on my tweed jacket. "I'll be back," I said, and she nodded.

As I strode to the elevators, the grandfather clock in the small lobby struck midnight, each chime matching my step. We'd survived the day. Would we all survive the night?

38

THURSDAY, JUNE 21, 1945, MIDNIGHT,
CANFRANC, SPAIN

*C*ool air whooshed down from the mountain, and fat, icy raindrops dotted the cobblestone walk in front of the hotel. The moon hid behind thick clouds, illuminating only the tattered edges. I flipped the back of my jacket collar up and scanned the black night before me.

The lamppost marking the near end of the bridge struggled to glow in the new rain, flickering with the lightning beyond the mountain ridge.

Beneath the lamp was parked a long black car without distinctive style or markings. I walked toward it, my legs already stiff with cold. The backseat door opened, and out stepped Elize, wrapped in a black coat.

She waved me to join her. "You deserve an explanation," she said. "Come inside."

I slid into the car, and she climbed in beside me. "You don't have to say anything. Penny will tell me whatever I should know." I expected to see someone in the front seat, but we were alone in the car.

"You trust her, don't you?" It wasn't a question.

"I do trust her." I released a long sigh. "And Manuel says that she'll be fine as a matter of fact." The rain grew heavier and louder against the windows. "I am quite sure you were about to ask."

Elize worked the corners of her mouth. "I'm glad. Manuel knows what he's doing."

"Do you?"

"What do you mean?" she asked, though she understood precisely what I meant.

I shifted on the seat to face her. "You're going to run away with your boss—Monsieur Lebeau?"

She looked at her hands. "He isn't only my boss." She slipped my ring off her finger and pressed it into the palm of my hand. "In a few hours, he'll be my husband."

I expected something like that, but it didn't lessen the pain. She wasn't mine anymore, but as I had discovered, she never had been. "So this is farewell."

"You need to know why I have to disappear," she said.

I shook my head. "I understand. You're working with the Resistance, but you've had to cooperate with the enemy to have the access you need to information."

"Yes, but it's not only that. By being here, I've been able to help good people escape the bad. I've helped more than sixty children to safety." She pleaded for me to understand.

I did. I understood more than she suspected. "It's very noble—what you've done here. It's a shame you must leave."

"It is a shame." She mumbled like an embarrassed child. "But too many people know my secret." She added quickly. "I don't blame you, of course."

"You blame Penny."

"Yes. No," she shook her head. "Albert and I have been planning this for months. Since we heard Hitler was dead, we accelerated our schedule. We've risked so much for other people. It's time we took care of ourselves." She paused for a beat, then took my hand. "You should, too, Henri."

My heart pounded. Not for Elize, not even for the Lisette that was. "I'm glad you're not dead." It came out harshly. "What I mean is, I missed you and I was sad. But I wasn't just sorry for myself. I grieved because I thought the world wouldn't know the blessing of you." Then softer. "But it turned out it was only *my* world that wouldn't know it."

"I am sorry," she said.

"Why did you call me to your car tonight? You might have just disappeared. I didn't need an apology, and I didn't need your explanation." I swallowed hard. "I've learned to live without you." I squeezed the ring in my hand before slipping it into my pocket. "You can go."

"Henri," she whispered, but her voice was drowned by the roar of the rain as the front driver door opened and Albert Lebeau got inside.

"We must leave now," he said. "Klaus is following me."

Elize swore under her breath. "He's probably already called his friends." She glanced at me. "You have to go. It's not safe for you."

"It never has been." I opened the door and stepped back into the storm.

I was a dozen strides from the car when Klaus appeared before me as if stepping through a veil of rain. I froze in place.

"You *are* working with her, no?" he asked, his gun aimed at my gut.

"What are you talking about? No. Didn't you see me up there

on the mountain? I ran when you did." I slowly moved my hand to my pistol, ready to draw. Why was the car still idling behind me? Why didn't they drive away? What were they waiting for?

Lightning flashed and thunder pealed as the storm intensified and soaked my jacket through to my skin. The rain was so heavy that I could barely see the car, though it was only a few yards away.

The man took another deliberate step in my direction. "I should not have run; I did not make sure she was dead. And now I saw her out here with another man."

"Where did this other man go? I am looking for *him*, but I can't see anything in this storm." I turned a quick circle, wondering if they had indeed driven away. I couldn't be certain.

Bright light flickered in the black sky, turning the rain to translucent curtains between us.

He shifted forward another step and said something, but his words became nothing as the thunder rolled from mountain to mountain. He waited. "Get out of my way or I'll shoot you."

"I'm on your side," I said, trying to give Elize more time.

"I don't care. At the moment, you're between me and my target. And I have a bullet to spare." He moved forward with determined strides, pushing me back with his forearm.

"Wait." I grabbed his arm. "Let me prove it to you. Let me be the one to kill her, if it is indeed Madame Belfort."

"And what about her husband? Will you kill him, too?"

Husband. The word cut deeper than it should. "I will kill whoever I must to ensure that she is dead." I paused for a moment. "That is why I was sent to Canfranc."

"Then we work together." Klaus raised his pistol and moved toward the car.

Why was the car still there? The lights shone against the rain, and the engine hummed. Why didn't they just drive away?

As we got closer, the back door opened, and Elize stepped out, becoming drenched in mere seconds. I drew my revolver.

"You both need your revenge?" she screamed into the storm. She raised her tiny handgun and shifted it from me to Gooden and back. "You won't have it. I'll shoot."

Gooden leveled his aim at her center. I couldn't let him do it. He'd kill her.

I'd been trained to stop a target with a non-lethal shot. I aimed and shot before he had a chance. It was the only way she'd survive.

Elize fell back against the car, clutching her side. Lebeau reached out, slipping his arm around her, blood seeping between his fingers over her wound. He pulled her into the car, the engine roared, and the car sped away.

The German fired his weapon twice, hitting the front fender of the car with both shots while the car disappeared into the black.

39

THURSDAY, JUNE 21, 1945, CANFRANC, SPAIN

"*Y*ou let her get away," Gooden growled.

"*My* bullet hit her." I waved my revolver toward him. "It's your fault she escaped."

He whirled around at me, his arm still raised in aim. "I'll kill you for this. I should have killed you before—the first night."

"Probably would have been better for both of us." I wondered if Jack or anyone else was with us, watching the scene for what would come next. The worst of the storm finally moved over the mountain, taking the violence with it, leaving only a light shower in its wake. "Now you kill me, eh?"

"That's right. No loose ends. You understand." He steadied his grip on his gun.

I laughed, causing him to pause.

"What is funny to you?"

"No loose ends." I smirked, pushing my dripping hair off my face. "You worked for her. A few days ago, you killed a man on the mountain. Clubbed him with a torch, and they fell." I waited for a response.

He nodded and shrugged. "And?"

"Who was it? A Jewish refugee? A rival?" I studied his face for any reaction, but there was none. "A Nazi officer? It was *Gooden*. You've taken *his* identity, haven't you, Klaus? You're stealing from all the people *he* murdered." His jaw tightened. That was it.

"He was just one more officer of the Third Reich, thinking he deserved more protection than the soldiers under his command. The men carrying out his orders. He thought he was better, because he'd stolen more, hidden away more." He scoffed. "Another…"

I fired. I didn't wait for another word from him. That was all I needed. The shot echoed off the mountain and the clouds, like one last thunder crash, leaving a hollow sound in my soul.

He fell facedown on the walkway next to the bridge. With my foot, I rolled him over to be sure. I wouldn't make the same mistake he had. The man was dead with a hole in his heart—the same as me.

Another push, and he tumbled down the steep bank and vanished into the black swirl of the river.

I picked up his gun and staggered into the lobby, where Manuel directed me to the back pantry. "Come, sit here for a moment to dry." He pulled a metal stool from the corner and handed me a towel. "He's gone?"

"Yes." My voice huffed out between ragged breaths. "Perhaps I should have let him live," I said, though I had no regrets for killing the man. How many had he killed? How many innocents had men like him murdered in cold blood? This was war—it was still war.

Manuel shook his head. "No. Not that man." He cursed the dead man, calling him a name in Spanish I didn't understand.

"He confessed to killing a man on the mountain a few days ago." I scrubbed my hair with the towel and let my waterlogged jacket fall to the floor. "Elize knew all about it." I held out the man's gun. "This was his. You may need it for something."

Manuel slipped the pistol in his pocket and jutted his chin forward. "Your woman—she *was* your woman before?"

"Years ago," I answered. "If she were anyone's."

"*Sí*," he said with a scoff. "She didn't always do what was right, but she did the best she could."

"That might be said of us all, Manuel." I pulled my watch from my trouser pocket, hoping it wasn't damaged. Twelve thirty-eight. "I should go back to my room."

"I'll take your coat to Maria in the laundry. She'll get it dried for you." Manuel yawned. It had been a long day for him as well. "How long will you stay?" he asked.

"Until Penny can travel." I thanked him again. "You'll know when we leave."

He suggested the service elevator again, as my revolver was no longer concealed, and I was still leaving a soggy trail of footprints in the carpet.

My door swung open before I could retrieve my key. Dahlia held up a hand as I stepped inside. "Let me have your gun," she said without preamble.

I handed it to her, butt-first, and she quickly sat at the small table in my parlor and unloaded the barrel, one shell at a time, lining them up in order.

"I shot—"

"I saw," she interrupted. "Everything." She shooed me into the bedroom. "Go clean up and sit with her for a bit. She needs you now."

40

*I*n any other circumstance, I'd revel in the scent of early morning rain in my clothes and on my body, but this morning I only shivered and ached. I emptied my pockets of my knife, watch, and the ring onto the vanity tray in the lavatory.

That damnable ring. It was a ghost I'd carried and treasured for years. Now it haunted me like a specter of doom.

I inspected my body in the small washroom mirror, fogged with condensation. My torso, back, arms, and legs were a quilt of colors. Scrapes, cuts, and scars covered most of me. The rest ached on the inside.

I cast a withering glance at my pajamas. There would be no sleep tonight. I tugged on a plain shirt and trousers, just enough to be presentable for the women on the other side of the door.

"Good, you're dressed," Dahlia said, standing. "I'm going back to my room for a few hours of sleep. I'm not as young as the rest of you." She patted my shoulder. "Keep watch for a bit. I'll see you at breakfast."

I nodded. "Shouldn't I escort you back to your room?"

She shook her head. "I can handle myself. It's just a few doors down."

"At least let me stand guard until you're inside. I'll stay in my doorway," I insisted.

She tugged me to a stooped position and kissed my cheek. "Goodnight, Henri."

"Goodnight, Dahlia." I waved from my threshold, where I could see her and Penny at the same time. I didn't close my door until she was inside her room, and I heard her latch click.

A soft moan came from my bedroom, and I hurried to Penny's side. I found her trying to sit up, her eyes wide.

"Relax," I whispered. "The fight is over for now." I cupped her cheek in my hand. "You are going to be fine, but you have to rest. Let your body heal. Manuel had to put quite a few stitches in you."

She settled, leaning her face into my hand. "It won't be the first time he's had to fix me up."

"Why don't we try to make this the last time, eh?"

Penny smiled, then winced. "I think I'm warming up to that idea." She rocked her head back on my pillow. "Did Elize and Albert make it? Is Dahlia all right?"

"Yes, Dahlia just went back to her room. She's been with you for the last hour." I held her hand firmly. "And Lebeau took Elize. She was shot, but if he gets her to someone half as good as Manuel, she should make it."

She craned her neck forward. "Shot? How?"

Heat flushed my face. "I… shot her. I did it to keep the German from killing her."

Penny squeezed my hand. "You did what you had to do."

"I don't understand why they didn't drive away as soon as they could. They sat in the car and waited. She got out and antagonized him. She could have been killed." My eyes stung more bitterly with every word.

"She *was* killed." Penny released a tight, pained breath. "As far as anyone who might have seen it, as far as anyone who might ask —she was. She is dead now."

I brushed my thumb over her cheek. "It's so easy for you."

Penny relaxed back into the pillow. "Of course it's not easy."

"It was my bullet that struck her." I pushed the words out, but the emotion behind them was as much exhaustion as anything else. "If she dies, it will be me who killed her."

"She won't die." Penny's eyes cut past me and focused on something in the other room for several seconds. "Go look at the bullets on the table."

"What?" I turned my head toward the table where Dahlia had left the emptied revolver.

"Inspect the bullets—the shells." She pushed my hand from hers.

I shrugged and went to the table. The empty pistol lay to the side, with three unspent cartridges lined up beside it. Gleaming little soldiers. Beside them were the three spent shells, empty brass casings still clinging to the scent of gunpowder.

But as I studied them, I detected that the first two casings had faint crimps around the mouth. Blanks. "This was your revolver? The gun Dahlia gave me was yours?"

Penny smiled. "Yes."

"Then what I fired at Elize?"

"A blank."

I shook my head. "There was blood. She was hit."

"A blood squib." Her cheek pinched upward in pain. "She worked it out with Albert. The squibs can be quite convincing."

"So she's all right?" My breath escaped in a long, slow hiss. My composure returned after a few mental cartwheels. "Now close your eyes and don't worry about any of this. You need to rest." I tucked the blankets around Penny and smoothed her hair back from her face.

A gentle smile settled on her perfect lips. "I know you still love her," she whispered. "It's all right if you do."

"Rest." I didn't want to think about who I loved or didn't.

41

SATURDAY, JUNE 23, 1945, CANFRANC, SPAIN

*W*e spent three days resting and tying up loose ends. The storms kept to the French side of the mountains, in more ways than one.

Manuel and Whiner, who I learned was called Alejandro, told me about a makeshift graveyard in the woods, for the bodies of the Nazis—mostly Nazis—who disappeared in Canfranc as they tried to escape their due punishment. The murder victim I'd seen fall the night I'd arrived, the real Herr Gooden, was buried there.

Penny had been right about the difference in the appearance of a clean-shaven man and a man with a full beard. In my mind, I knew it to be true, but until this experience, I hadn't realized how extreme that change could be.

Canfranc proved to be the perfect place to convalesce. Penny soon recovered enough to walk small distances—her own room, the café, and the reception hall in the evening—though she wasn't ready to tread the mountain path or dance.

"I shouldn't be so soft about this," she said when I retrieved her for breakfast. She wore her butter-yellow day dress, scattered with pink and red roses and tiny blue dots. Dressed as she was, there was no sign of bruises or scrapes. She moved timidly, squinting her eyes as she took her seat at the table.

Dahlia and Jack joined us within minutes, and Penny adjusted her face to a more placid expression for them.

I discovered that physical injuries healed more quickly than emotional ones, and that applied to everyone.

"How are you feeling this morning?" Dahlia asked.

"Much better, thanks," Penny replied. She reached under the table and squeezed my hand.

A *please-don't-say-anything* squeeze.

"Jack has word this morning." Dahlia chirped.

Jack leaned over the table toward us. "Lebeau cabled an hour ago, saying they were halfway to America. New York. He has a pilot friend who will take them to a small town where they will be safe." Jack slid a folded note to me. "Manuel asked me to deliver this to you."

I moved to put the missive into my waistcoat pocket, but Penny shook her head. "Go ahead. We won't pry."

Pushing back from the table a few inches, in a display of faux privacy that seemed odd even to me, I unfolded the note. Drawing a deep, preparatory breath, I read silently.

Dear Henri,

I am well and safe with Albert. We will be in America soon and will marry there as soon as we arrive. We will have new names, but I'll not tell you. It may not be safe for you to know. Stay with Penny and take care of her. She loves you more than you understand.

Regards,

Lisette

Unsure of how I was supposed to behave, I pushed the note

into my pocket. "They are well," I confirmed. "Nothing to add to what you said before," I directed toward Jack.

My mind whirred through all the words on the page, though one phrase in particular. *She loves you...*

"What do you think?" Penny asked, her voice shaking me out of my reveries.

"Yes, I do, too." The words spilled out before I could think.

"You do what, exactly?" Jack asked.

Penny smiled and patted my shoulder. "Jack, leave him alone. He's processing a lot of information." She leaned closer in her chair. "Dahlia asked where you wanted to go after this. She and Jack are heading back to London tomorrow."

I cocked my head toward her. "And where will you go?"

"Well," she said with a heavy sigh. "Manuel says I shouldn't travel for another day or two. My stitches are healing, but I need more rest."

"Then I'll stay with you." I crossed my arms over my sore chest, ignoring the pain. "We can recuperate here for another three or four days."

Dahlia smiled, her wrinkles stretching wide across her face. "So, should I expect you back home about the middle of next week?" the older woman asked Penny.

I didn't give her the chance to answer. "No. Penny isn't going back to London just yet."

Penny turned her flickering grey eyes my way. "I'm not?"

"She's not?" Jack sounded.

Dahlia's lips curled more, deepening her creases.

I shrugged. "Of course, if you want to go back to London, that's fine. But..." I bent to her ear. "I thought you and I might spend some time together. I certainly need more training."

Penny sat back in her seat and gawked at my suggestion.

I addressed the others now, too. "She's not going back to serve tea to men who aren't half as capable at the job as she is."

Jack's jaw dropped to rest on the knot of his paisley tie. "You can't keep her from working with us. Her expertise would provide our men with valuable training."

"Rubbish," I spat. "Hire Dahlia for that. She's more experienced."

"But her age," Jack argued.

"Do you have any idea how old she really is?" I shot an apologetic glance at Dahlia, and she beamed back at me. "Look, Jack, I respect you, for the most part. I wish you respected these women as much. The work they've done over the past five years." I paused and gestured to Dahlia. "The past twenty-five years. I'd put them head-to-head against any man in the field."

"They no longer belong in the field," Jack said.

"Well then." I sighed. "That's England's loss, isn't it?"

Jack opened his mouth and snapped it shut. I suppose he didn't feel like arguing.

A server brought us a tiered silver tray of breakfast foods, then filled our cups with tea for the others and coffee for me. Dahlia waited for the young woman to return to the kitchen before speaking.

"Jack, we don't need to know Penny's plans for now. We can go back to London and settle our part in this business. London will only care about your part, anyway. I'll make sure that you receive whatever credit is due." She waited a beat while she sipped her tea. "So long as you don't try to make trouble for Penny or me." Her tone threatened like the broken end of a bottle.

"There won't be trouble for any of us." Jack took a scone from the tray and spread blood-orange marmalade over the end with a vigorous jab. "I can see to that. London will be pleased enough with the names of the gold smugglers and the bars I confiscated. They won't bother with anything else."

"Then England and France are more alike than I thought." I chuffed. Turning toward Penny, I said. "I'll stay with you here for as long as you like. And when you're ready to travel, we can go wherever you like." I scratched the whiskers on my jaw. "I'm not going back to France for now. If you want to return to London, I'll follow you there."

She knit her brows together. "You keep talking about how I don't need anyone to take care of me, but then you say you want to be there for me."

I clicked my tongue, as she liked. "You don't need a handler anymore. I don't want to be that. You need staff. You need someone to train. You need someone who will serve *you* tea."

"Someone to serve me tea?" she asked with a Cheshire cat grin.

"Yes, and I would be happy to carry your bags whenever you decide to go on some far-flung mission." I leaned closer. "Say, to somewhere like… Argentina?" I reached for her hand, noticing she had a smudge of blackberry jam on her knuckles, smeared between her middle and ring fingers. I put the back of her hand to my lips to slowly and thoroughly kiss it away. She became a delicacy for me. "For all those things, I want to be your man."

The skin on her arms prickled into gooseflesh. Her eyes went wide, and her breath puffed hot.

With a trembling voice that razed my heart to its foundation, Penny said, "Henri Toussaint, you are my man."

EPILOGUE

WEDNESDAY, AUGUST 15, 1945, LISBON, PORTUGAL

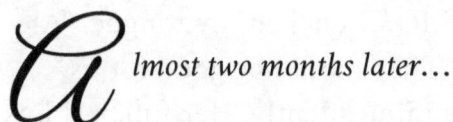*lmost two months later...*

THREE LIGHT TAPS followed by a long rap sounded on the heavy wooden door of the tiny flat we rented over a bakery. When I opened the door, a cloud of yeast, flour, and sugar wafted inside. The lush aroma permeated the studio, recharging my exhausted mind. Books, papers, drawings, maps, and half-filled notebooks cluttered the room, leaving nowhere for guests.

"Two telegrams and a package for you today," said the fair-haired youth who often frequented our landing. He handed me a file box topped with envelopes and a newspaper. "And good news, too." He tapped the paper once I held everything. "Japan has finally surrendered. It's official."

"Thank you. That is good news." I nodded the young man away and closed the door.

"What today?" Penny asked while she twisted her dark hair into a quick chignon and pinned it in place with a pencil. She wore a traditional Portuguese peasant blouse, embroidered with blue flowers, over a very non-traditional pair of wide-leg blue slacks that ended above her ankles. Her red espadrilles added the perfect touch to her ensemble.

"Looks like a telegram from Dahlia and another from Manuel." I placed the box in an empty corner of the table and rolled my shirt sleeves to my elbows.

"Did Luka say that Japan surrendered?" She pulled her knife from her pocket, opened it, and started on the parcel.

"He did." I handed her the telegram from Dahlia while I opened the one from Manuel. I read aloud. "HT, AS moving to Madrid Sept. New contact there. MO." I clicked my tongue. "Alejandro has a new contact in Spain. That should be good for us."

I glanced up as Penny began reading silently. Her full, red lips mouthed the words. I watched but forgot to interpret. I only noticed when they spread into a full smile that crawled over her cheeks and up to the corners of her eyes. "Ah," she breathed.

"Good news from Dahlia, too?"

A giggle escaped her throat, and Penny skipped to my side like a schoolgirl. "What do you think? Dahlia's gotten married."

"What?" Of all that I might have imagined, this news was perhaps the last.

"Yes." She waved the telegram at me. "She ran into an old friend. He's an Air Commodore in the RAF. A widower, a friend of her first husband. She says by the time I read this, she'll be Mrs. Milton Falstaff."

"And this isn't an assignment?" I asked cautiously. "She's not going to…?" I moved my thumb across my throat.

"No, I'm sure she'd have mentioned that." Penny clutched the telegram to her bosom. "I do hope she'll be happy."

I slipped my arm around her waist. "Send her flowers from the two of us. Have Jack send them, if you must." I chuckled. "Hmm, with a man in her life, I'll bet she's shaved twenty years off her age."

"In a way, I'm proud of her. He's her fifth husband. Well, more like her second *real* husband. But I'm proud that she never gave up, even when the rest of the world did."

"You've never given up on her, *chère*."

Penny tilted her head to one side. "I wonder if she'll tell Milton all her secrets." She bumped her hip against mine. "If so, I wonder if he'll be as understanding as you?"

With a few more thoughts on Dahlia's personal life, we set to task on the box.

We unpacked file after file—forged identities, sketches of stolen art, and testimonies of jewelry that had already been stripped and melted down. Each story broke our hearts; every heirloom reduced to memory. I was fortunate still to have my mother's ring in my possession.

We sorted the papers into our usual stacks, South America towering over all the rest. Whenever possible, we matched art with names, though most of it was instinct and guesswork. Manuel's notes gave us hints of buyers and sellers, but the truth lay buried under layers of lies.

By the time we finished, our studio resembled a miniature city of paper, towers of loss and deceit rising from every surface except the narrow beds against the wall.

"I'm hungry," growled Penny, with a long yawn for punctuation.

I stretched my arms to either side and answered with a yawn of my own. "I'll get my hat."

Five minutes later, we strolled the tiled street that led to the nearest market restaurant, Penny's hands clasped together over the crook of my arm.

"Where do you think first?" Penny asked.

"I assumed we were going to Paulo's for fish." I shrugged. "Did you want something else?"

"I'm not talking about where we'll eat." Penny squeezed my arm. "It's been eight weeks now, and I'm feeling better." She poked my shoulder and gave me a sly, side glance. "I know you are, too."

"Where shall our first mission be?" I grinned at her teasing. "That's what you're asking?"

"Yes."

We reached the outdoor dining tables and found our favorite corner for people-watching. "I haven't wanted to make too many plans until you were better."

She waved the server over and ordered one of our regular meals. When he'd left, she drew a deep breath and released it slowly. "Well, now I think we should make some plans. When we were in Canfranc, you suggested maybe Argentina. Do you think that's still a good idea?"

"It's certainly our tallest stack." I corrected, "Two of our tallest stacks." I tapped a finger on the table between us. "I think that will give us the best chance of success."

"I agree." She paused for a beat, then let her lashes flutter as she raised her gaze to mine. "How soon can we leave?"

"You don't love Lisbon?"

She licked her perfect lips, knowing I'd relent to anything she asked of me. "I love Lisbon as much as you," she said. "But every day that passes is another chance for our targets to slip away from us."

I nodded. She was right, as always. "I did have a few more things I wanted to do while we were here," I said.

"Like what?" Penny asked.

I pulled the engagement ring from my pocket. "I was going to take this to the jeweler's."

Penny snatched it from my hand. "No, you mustn't. It was your mother's, and it's too precious. I can't allow you to sell it."

"I didn't think you liked it," I said. "After all, *you* sold it before."

"But I intended to go back and get it. Elize bought it before I could." She blinked slowly, trying pitiable eyes on me.

"You can't manipulate me like you used to," I said. She could, of course, but this was our way now. "But you *do* like it?"

She nodded and handed it back to me. "Please don't sell it. I'd never forgive myself."

I sighed. "Even though I'd given it to Elize?"

"I understand what it symbolizes to you. But can't you give it a second chance? You wore it around your neck for three years. Can't it just be a memento of your mother?"

My heart pounded in my ears. "I'm afraid not. To me, it means abiding, faithful, love now. It represents the woman of my dreams." I dropped to my knees at Penny's feet and slipped the ring onto her finger.

"Is that your way of asking?" she asked, with a shimmer in her eyes.

"I won't ask—you'd only find a way to say no." I swallowed hard. "So I'll tell you what I want instead. I want you to be my wife." My thoughts raced through the thousand scenarios I'd already imagined between us.

Penny allowed a tear to spill down to her lips. "I want to marry you." She pressed her forehead to mine and held my whiskered face in her hands. "I'd marry you right now if Paulo were a priest."

"I don't think he is, but the captain of the ship can perform the wedding if you can wait until Friday."

"Friday?" Her grey-blue eyes sparkled in the golden-pink dusk.

I reached into my waistcoat pocket to retrieve the steamer tickets that Manuel had sent a few days before, with a wish for luck. "The ship sails for Argentina first thing Friday morning." I pressed a hot kiss over her mouth. "If you think you can be ready."

She reciprocated with another kiss, and I noticed a few passersby staring.

"I'll be the one on your arm," Penny said through a ragged breath. "From now on, wherever we go, I'll be the one on your arm."

THE END

EXTRAS TO TRANSPORT YOU TO 1945

Diffuse these essential oils to immerse yourself in 1945.

The Official Playlist for all the
Traveling Companion Novels
Please scan to listen.

ALSO BY KIM BLACK

MORE PAGE-TURNERS FOUND HERE

Keep up with all Kim's titles.
www.kimblackink.com

ALSO BY KIM BLACK

MORE PAGE-TURNERS FOUND HERE

Keep up with all Kim's titles.
www.kimblackink.com

ABOUT THE AUTHOR

Kim Black writes romantic suspense with a vintage twist—stories steeped in espionage, quiet courage, and the complicated language of love. Her novels echo the tension and glamour of a bygone era, where danger often wears a smile and strength hides behind silk gloves.

A Texas Panhandle native, Kim serves on the board of Texas High Plains Writers and believes strong women deserve stories honoring their resilience and heart. When she isn't writing about spies and secrets, she's likely swapping ideas with her husband, a writer, or sharing her chair with their American blue pit bull, Bonnie, affectionately known as *Super Bon-Bon*.